DEATH CLOUD

ANDREW LANE

DEATH CLOUD

Sherlock Holmes
THE LEGEND BEGINS

FARRAR STRAUS GIROUX
New York

macteenbooks.com

Library of Congress Cataloging-in-Publication Data
Lane, Andrew.
    Death cloud / Andrew Lane. — 1st American ed.
        p.   cm. — (Young Sherlock Holmes)
    Summary: In 1868, with his army officer father suddenly posted to
India, and his mother mysteriously "unwell," fourteen-year-old Sherlock
Holmes is sent to stay with his eccentric uncle and aunt in their vast house
in Farnham, where he uncovers his first murder and a diabolical villain.
    Includes bibliographical resources (p.).
    ISBN: 978-0-374-38767-9
    [1. Mystery and detective stories.   2. Murder—Fiction.   3. Great
Britain—History—Victoria, 1837–1901—Fiction.]   I. Title.

PZ7.L231758De 2011
[E]—dc22

                                                              2010021387

*Dedicated to the memory of the writers whose work
I used to devour when I was young: Captain W. E. Johns,
Hugh Walters, Andre Norton, Malcolm Saville, Alan E.
Nourse, and John Christopher; and also to the friendship and
support of those members of the latest generation that I'm
fortunate enough to know: Ben Jeapes, Stephen Cole, Justin
Richards, Gus Smith, and the incomparable Charlie Higson.*

*And with grateful acknowledgment to: Rebecca McNally
and Robert Kirby, for having faith; Jon Lellenberg,
Charles Foley, and Andrea Plunkett, for giving permission;
Gareth Pugh, for telling me all about bees; and
Nigel McCreary, for keeping me sane on the journey.*

PROLOGUE

The first time Matthew Arnatt saw the cloud of death, it was floating out of the first-floor window of a house near where he was living.

He was scurrying along the High Street in the market town of Farnham, looking for any fruit or crusts of bread that a careless passerby might have dropped. His eyes should have been scanning the ground, but he kept looking up at the houses and the shops and at the thronging people all around him. He was only fourteen, and as far as he could remember he'd never been in a town this large before. In this, the prosperous part of Farnham, the older wood-beamed buildings leaned over into the street, with their upper rooms looming like solid clouds above anybody underneath.

The road was cobbled with smooth, fist-sized stones for part of its length, but some distance ahead the cobbles gave way to packed earth from which clouds of dust rose up as the horses and the carts clattered past. Every few yards sat a pile of horse manure: some fresh and steaming, surrounded by flies; some dry and old, like strands of hay or grass that had been clumped together and somehow stuck.

Matthew could smell the steamy, putrid dung, but

he could also smell baking bread and what might have been a pig that had been roasted on a spit above a roaring fire. He could almost see the fat dripping off and sizzling in the flames. Hunger made his stomach clench, and he nearly doubled over with the sudden pain. It had been a few days since he'd had any proper food. He wasn't sure how much longer he could go on.

One of the passersby, a fat man in a brown bowler hat and a dark suit that was showing its age, stopped and extended a hand to Matthew as if to help him. Matthew backed away. He didn't want charity. Charity led to the workhouse or the church for a child with no family, and he didn't want to start out on the path towards either of those destinations. He was doing fine by himself. All he had to do was to find some food. Once he had some food inside him he would be better.

He slipped away down an alley before the man could take his shoulder, then doubled back round a corner into a street that was so narrow that the upper storeys of the houses were almost touching. A person could climb straight from one bedroom to another on the other side of the street, if they had a mind to.

That was when he saw the cloud of death. Not that he knew what it was, then. That would come later. No, all he saw was a dark stain the size of a large dog that seemed to drift from an open window like smoke, but smoke that moved with a mind of its own, pausing for a moment and then flowing sideways to a drainpipe where it turned and slid up towards the roof. Hunger forgotten, Matthew watched openmouthed as the cloud drifted over the sharp edge of the roof tiles and vanished out of sight.

A scream split the silence—a scream from the open window—and Matthew turned and pelted back down the street as quickly as his malnourished legs would carry him. People didn't scream like that when they'd had a surprise. They didn't even scream like that if they'd had a shock. No, in Matthew's experience people only screamed like that if they were in mortal fear of their lives, and whatever had provoked that scream was not something he wanted to see.

ONE

"You there! Come here!"

Sherlock Holmes turned to see who was being called and who was doing the calling. There were hundreds of pupils standing in the bright sunlight outside Deepdene School for Boys that morning, each dressed in immaculate school uniform and each with a leather-strapped wooden chest or an overstuffed pile of luggage sitting in front of him like a loyal dog. Any one of them might have been the target. The masters at Deepdene made a habit of never referring to the pupils by name—it was always "You!" or "Boy!" or "Child!" It made life difficult and kept the boys on their toes, which was probably the reason why they did it. Either that or the masters had given up trying to remember the names of their pupils long ago; Sherlock wasn't sure which explanation was the most likely. Perhaps both.

None of the other pupils were paying attention. They were either gossiping with the family members who had turned up to collect them or they were eagerly watching the school gates for first sight of the carriage that was going to take them home. Reluctantly, Sherlock swung round to see if the malign finger of fate was pointing his way.

It was. The finger in question belonged in this instance to Mr. Tulley, the Latin master. He had just come round the corner of the school, where Sherlock was standing apart from the other boys. His suit, which was usually covered in chalk dust, had been specially cleaned for the end of term and the inevitable meetings with the fathers who were paying for their boys to be educated, and his mortarboard sat straight on his head as if glued there by the headmaster.

"Me, sir?"

"Yes, sir. You, sir," Mr. Tulley snapped. "Get yourself to the headmaster's study *quam celerrime*. Do you remember enough of your Latin to know what that means?"

"It means 'straightaway,' sir."

"Then move yourself."

Sherlock cast a glance at the school gate. "But, sir— I'm waiting for my father to pick me up."

"I'm sure he won't leave without you, boy."

Sherlock made one last, defiant attempt. "My luggage . . ."

Mr. Tulley glanced disparagingly at Sherlock's battered wooden trunk—a hand-me-down from his father's military travels, stained with old dirt and scuffed by the passing years. "I can't see anyone wanting to steal it," he said, "except perhaps for its historical value. I'll get a prefect to watch it for you. Now cut along."

Reluctantly, Sherlock abandoned his belongings—the spare shirts and underclothes, the books of poetry and the notebooks in which he had taken to jotting down ideas, thoughts, speculations, and the occasional tune that came into his head—and walked off towards the columned portico at the front of the school building, pushing through the crowd of pupils, parents, and siblings while still keeping an eye on the gateway, where a scrum of horses and carriages were all trying to get in and out of the narrow gate at the same time.

The main entrance hall was lined with oak panelling and encircled by marble busts of previous headmasters and patrons, each on its own separate plinth. Shafts of sunlight crossed diagonally from the high windows to the black-and-white tiled floor, picked out by swirling motes of chalk dust. It smelt of the carbolic that the maids used to clean the tiles every morning. The press of bodies in the hall made it likely that at least one of the busts would be toppled over before long. Some of them already had large cracks marring their pure marble, suggesting that every term saw at least one of them smashed on the floor and subsequently repaired.

He wove in and out of the people, ignored by every-one, and eventually found himself exiting the throng and entering a corridor that led off the entrance hall. The headmaster's study was a few yards down. He paused on the threshold, drew a breath, dusted down his lapels, and knocked on the door.

"Enter!" boomed a theatrically loud voice.

Sherlock twisted the doorknob and pushed the door

open, trying to quell the spasm of nervousness that shot through his body like lightning. He had only been in the headmaster's study twice before—once with his father, when he first arrived at Deepdene, and once again a year later with a group of other pupils who had been accused of cheating in an examination. The three ringleaders had been caned and expelled; the four or five followers had been caned until their buttocks bled and allowed to stay. Sherlock—whose essays had been the ones copied by the group—had escaped a caning by claiming that he knew nothing about it. In fact, he had known all along, but he had always been something of an outsider at the school, and if letting the other pupils copy his work got him tolerated, if not accepted, then he wasn't going to raise any ethical objections. On the other hand, he wasn't going to tell on the copiers either—that would have got him beaten and, perhaps, held in front of one of the roaring fires that dominated the dormitories until his skin began to blister and his clothes to smoke. School life was like that—a perpetual balancing act between the masters and the other pupils. And he hated it.

The headmaster's study was just the way he remembered it—vast, dim, and smelling of a combination of leather and pipe tobacco. Mr. Tomblinson was sitting behind a desk large enough to play bowls on. He was a portly man in a suit that was slightly too small for him, chosen presumably on the basis that it helped him believe he wasn't quite as large as he obviously was.

"Ah, Holmes, is it? In, lad, in. Close the door behind you."

Sherlock did as he was told, but as he pushed the door shut he caught sight of another figure in the room: a man standing in front of the window with a glass of sherry in his hand. The sunlight refracted in rainbow shards from the cut glass of the schooner.

"Mycroft?" Sherlock said, amazed.

His elder brother turned towards him, and a smile flickered across his face so rapidly that if Sherlock had blinked at the wrong moment then he might have missed it. "Sherlock. You've grown."

"So have you," Sherlock said. Indeed, his brother *had* put on weight. He was nearly as plump as the headmaster, but his suit was tailored to hide it rather than accentuate it. "You came in Father's carriage."

Mycroft raised an eyebrow. "How on earth did you deduce that, young man?"

Sherlock shrugged. "I noticed the parallel creases in your trousers where the upholstery pressed them, and I remember that Father's carriage has a tear in the upholstery that was repaired rather clumsily a few years ago. The impression of that repair is pressed into your trousers, next to the creases." He paused. "Mycroft, where's Father?"

The headmaster *harrumphed* to attract attention back to him. "Your father is—"

"Father won't be coming," Mycroft interrupted smoothly. "His regiment was sent out to India to strengthen the existing military force. There has been some unrest in the North West Frontier region. You know where that is?"

"Yes. We've studied India in geography lessons and in history."

"Good boy."

"I didn't realize the natives there were causing problems again," the headmaster rumbled. "Not been in *The Times*, that's for sure."

"It's not the Indians," Mycroft confided. "When we took the country back from the East India Company, the soldiers out there transferred back under Army control. They've found the new regime to be a lot . . . stricter . . . than the one they were used to. There's been a great deal of bad feeling, and the government has decided to drastically increase the size of the force in India to give them an example of what *real* soldiers are like. It's bad enough to have the Indians rebelling; a mutiny inside the British Army is unthinkable."

"And *will* there be a mutiny?" Sherlock asked, feeling his heart sinking like a stone dropped into a pond. "Will Father be safe?"

Mycroft shrugged his massive shoulders. "I don't know," he said simply. That was one of the things that Sherlock respected about his brother. He always gave a straight response to a straight question. No honeying the pill. "Sadly, I don't know everything. Not yet, anyway."

"But you work for the government," Sherlock pressed. "You must have some idea of what might happen. Can't you send a different regiment? Keep Father here in England?"

"I've only been with the Foreign Office for a few months," Mycroft replied, "and although I am flattered that you think I have the power to alter such important things, I'm afraid I don't. I'm an advisor. Just a clerk, really."

"How long will Father be gone?" Sherlock asked, remembering the large man dressed in a scarlet serge jacket with white belts crossing his chest, who laughed easily and lost his temper rarely. He could feel a pressure in his chest but he held his feelings in check. If there was one lesson he had learned from his time at Deepdene School, it was that you never showed any emotion. If you did, it would be used against you.

"Six weeks for the ship to reach port, six months in the country, I would estimate, and then another six weeks returning. Nine months in all."

"Nearly a year." He bowed his head for a moment, composing himself, then nodded. "Can we go home now?"

"You're not going home," Mycroft said.

Sherlock just stood there, letting the words sink into him, not saying anything.

"He can't stay here," the headmaster muttered. "The place is being cleaned."

Mycroft moved his calm gaze away from Sherlock and

on to the headmaster. "Our mother is . . . unwell," he said. "Her constitution is delicate at the best of times, and this business with our father has distressed her greatly. She needs peace and quiet, and Sherlock needs someone older to look after him."

"But I've got *you*!" Sherlock protested.

Mycroft shook his large head sadly. "I live in London now, and my job requires me to work many hours each day. I would not, I'm afraid, be a fit guardian for a boy, especially an inquisitive one such as you." He turned towards the headmaster, almost as if it was easier to give him the next piece of information than to tell Sherlock. "Although the family house is in Horsham we have relatives in Farnham, not too far from here. An uncle and aunt. Sherlock will be staying with them over the school holidays."

"No!" Sherlock exploded.

"Yes," Mycroft said gently. "It is arranged. Uncle Sherrinford and Aunt Anna have agreed to take you in for the summer."

"But I've never even *met* them!"

"Nevertheless, they are family."

Mycroft bade farewell to the headmaster while Sherlock stood there blankly, trying to take in the enormity of what had just happened. No going home. No seeing his father and his mother. No exploring in the fields and woods around the manor house that had been home to him for fourteen years. No sleeping in his old bed in the room under the eaves of the house where he kept all of his books. No sneaking into the kitchens where Cook would give him a slice of bread and jam if he smiled at her. Instead, weeks of staying with people he didn't know, being on his best behaviour in a town, in a *county* that he didn't know anything about. Alone, until he returned to school.

How was he going to manage?

Sherlock followed Mycroft out of the headmaster's study and along the corridor to the entrance hall. An enclosed brougham carriage sat outside the doors, its wheels muddy and its sides dusty from the journey that Mycroft had already undertaken to the school. The crest of the Holmes family had been painted on the door. Sherlock's trunk had already been loaded on the back. A gaunt driver whom Sherlock did not recognize sat in the dicky box at the front, the reins that linked him to the two horses resting limply in his hands.

"How did he know that was my trunk?"

Mycroft gestured with his hand to indicate that it was nothing special. "I could see it from the window of the headmaster's study. The trunk was the only one sitting unattended. And besides, it was the one Father used to have. The headmaster was kind enough to send a boy out to tell him to load the trunk onto the carriage." He opened the door of the carriage and gestured to Sherlock to enter. Instead, Sherlock glanced around at his school and at his fellow pupils.

"You look as if you think you'll never see them again," Mycroft said.

"It's not that," Sherlock replied. "It's just that I thought I was leaving here for something better. Now I know I'm leaving here for something worse. As bad as this place is, this is as good as it gets."

"It won't be like that. Uncle Sherrinford and Aunt Anna are good people. Sherrinford is Father's brother."

"Then why have I never heard about them?" Sherlock asked. "Why has Father never mentioned having a brother?"

Mycroft winced almost imperceptibly. "I fear that there was a falling-out in the family. Relations were strained for a while. Mother reinitiated contact via letter some months ago. I'm not even sure Father knows."

"And that's where you're sending me?"

Mycroft patted Sherlock on the shoulder. "If there was an alternative I would take it, believe me. Now, do you need to say goodbye to any friends?"

Sherlock looked around. There were boys he knew, but were any of them really friends?

"No," he.said. "Let's go."

The journey to Farnham took several hours. After passing through the town of Dorking, which was the closest group of houses to Deepdene School, the carriage clattered along country lanes, beneath spreading trees, past the occasional thatched cottage or larger house, and alongside fields that were ripe with barley. The sun shone from a cloudless sky, turning the carriage into an oven despite the breeze blowing in. Insects buzzed lazily at the windows. Sherlock watched for a while as the world went past. They stopped for lunch at an inn, where Mycroft bought some ham and cheese and half a loaf of bread. At some stage Sherlock fell asleep. When he woke up, minutes or hours later, the brougham was still moving through the same landscape. For a while he chatted with Mycroft about what was happening at home, about their sister, about Mother's fragile health. Mycroft asked after Sherlock's studies, and Sherlock told him something about the various lessons that he had sat through and more about the teachers who had taught them. He imitated their voices and their mannerisms, and reduced Mycroft to helpless laughter by the cruelty and humour of his impersonations.

After a while there were more houses lining the road and soon they were heading through a large town, the horses' hoofs clattering on cobbles. Leaning out of the carriage window, Sherlock saw what looked like a guildhall— a three-storey building, all white plaster and black beams, with a large clock hanging from a bracket outside the double doors.

"Farnham?" he guessed.

"Guildford," Mycroft answered. "Farnham is not too far away now."

The road out of Guildford led along a ridge from which the land fell away on both sides, fields and woods scattered about like toys, with patches of yellow flowers spreading across them.

"This ridge is called the Hog's Back," Mycroft remarked. "There's a semaphore station along here, on Pewley Hill, part of a chain that stretches from the Admiralty Building in London all the way to Portsmouth Harbour. Have they taught you about semaphores at school?"

Sherlock shook his head.

"Typical," Mycroft murmured. "All the Latin a boy can cram into his skull, but nothing of any practical use." He sighed heavily. "A semaphore is a method for passing messages quickly and over long distance that would take days by horse. Semaphore stations have boards on their roofs that can be seen from a distance, and have six large holes in them that can be opened or closed by shutters. Depending on which holes are open or closed, the board spells out different letters. A man at each semaphore station keeps watch on both the previous one in the chain and the next one with a telescope. If he sees a message being spelled out, he writes it down and then repeats it via his own semaphore board, and so the message travels. This particular chain starts at the Admiralty, then goes via Chelsea and Kingston upon Thames to here, then all the way to Portsmouth Dockyard. There's another chain leading down to Chatham Dockyards, and others to Deal, Sheerness, Great Yarmouth, and Plymouth. They were constructed so that the Admiralty could pass messages quickly to the Navy in the event of a French invasion of the country. Now, tell me, if there are six holes, and each hole can be either open or closed, how many different combinations are there that could signify letters, numbers, or other symbols?"

Fighting the urge to tell his brother that school was over, Sherlock closed his eyes and calculated for a moment. One hole could take two states: open or closed. Two holes could take four states: open-open; open-closed; closed-open; closed-closed. Three holes . . . He quickly worked through the calculation in his mind, and then saw a pattern emerging. "Sixty-four," he said eventually.

"Well done." Mycroft nodded. "I'm glad to see that your mathematics, at least, is up to scratch." He glanced out of the window to his right. "Ah, Aldershot. Interesting place. Fourteen years ago it was named by Queen Victoria as the home of the British Army. Before that it was a small hamlet with a population of less than a thousand. Now it is sixteen thousand and still growing."

Sherlock craned his neck to look over his brother at what lay outside the other window, but from this angle he could only see a scattering of houses and what might have been a railway line running parallel to the road at the bottom of the slope. He settled back into his seat and closed his eyes, trying not to think about what lay ahead.

After a while he felt the brougham heading downhill, and shortly after that they made a series of turns, and the sound of the ground beneath the horses' hoofs changed from stone to hard-packed earth. He screwed his eyes more tightly shut, trying to put off the moment when he would have to accept what was happening.

The carriage stopped on gravel. The sound of birdsong and the wind blowing through trees filled the carriage. Sherlock could hear footsteps crunching towards them.

"Sherlock," Mycroft said gently. "Time for reality."

He opened his eyes.

The brougham had stopped outside the entrance to a large house. Constructed from red brick, it towered above them: three storeys plus what looked like a set of rooms in the attic, judging by the small windows set into the grey tiles. A footman was just about to open Mycroft's door. Sherlock slid across and followed his brother out.

A woman was standing in the deep shadows at the top of three wide stone steps that led up to the portico in front of the main entrance. She was dressed entirely in black. Her face was thin and pinched, her lips pursed and her eyes narrowed, as if someone had substituted vinegar for her cup of tea that morning. "Welcome to Holmes Manor; I am Mrs. Eglantine," she said in a dry, papery voice. "I am the housekeeper here." She glanced at Mycroft. "Mr. Holmes will see you in the library, whenever you are ready." Her gaze slid to Sherlock. "And the footman will transfer your . . . luggage . . . to your room, Master Holmes. Afternoon tea will be served at three o'clock. Please be so good as to stay in your room until then."

"I will not be staying for tea," Mycroft said smoothly. "Sadly, I need to return to London." He turned towards Sherlock, and there was a look in his eyes that was part sympathy, part brotherly love, and part warning. "Take care, Sherlock," he said. "I will certainly be back to return you to school at the end of the holidays, and if I can I will visit in the meantime. Be good, and take the opportunity to explore the local area. I believe that Uncle Sherrinford has an exceptional library. Ask him if you can take advantage of the accumulated wisdom it contains. I will leave my contact details with Mrs. Eglantine—if you need me, send me a telegram or write a letter." He reached out and put a comforting hand on Sherlock's shoulder. "These are good people," he said, quietly enough that Mrs. Eglantine couldn't hear him, "but, like everyone in the Holmes family, they have their eccentricities. Be aware, and take care not to upset them. Write to me when you get a moment. And remember—this is not the rest of your life. This is just for a couple of months. Be brave." He squeezed Sherlock's shoulder.

Sherlock felt a bubble of anger and frustration forcing its way up his throat and choked it back. He didn't want Mycroft to see him react, and he didn't want to start his time at Holmes Manor badly. Whatever he did over the next few minutes would set the tone for the rest of his stay.

He stuck out his hand. Mycroft moved his own hand off Sherlock's shoulder and took it, smiling warmly.

"Goodbye," Sherlock said in as level a tone as he could manage. "Give my love to Mother, and to Charlotte. And if you hear anything of Father, let me know."

Mycroft turned and started up the stairs towards the entrance. Mrs. Eglantine met Sherlock's gaze for a moment, expressionless, then turned and led Mycroft into the house.

Looking back, Sherlock saw the footman struggling to hoist the trunk onto his shoulders. When it was safely balanced he staggered up the stairs, past Sherlock, who followed disconsolately.

The hall was tiled in black and white, lined with mahogany, with an ornate marble staircase flowing down from the upper floors like a frozen waterfall with several paintings of religious scenes, landscapes, and animals on the walls. Mycroft was just passing through a doorway to the left of the staircase into a room that, from the brief glance Sherlock caught, was lined with sets of books bound in green leather. A thin, elderly man in an old-fashioned black suit was rising from a chair that had been upholstered in a shade of leather that perfectly matched the colour of the books behind it. His face was bearded, lined, and pale, his scalp mottled with liver spots.

The door closed on them as they were shaking hands. The footman headed across the tiles to the bottom of the stairs, still balancing the trunk on his shoulders. Sherlock followed.

Mrs. Eglantine was standing at the bottom of the stairs, outside the library. She was staring over the top of Sherlock's head, towards the door.

"Child, be aware that you are *not* welcome here," she hissed as he passed.

TWO

Sitting in the woods outside Farnham, Sherlock could see the ground fall away from him towards a dirt track that snaked away through the underbrush, like a dry river-bed, until it vanished from sight. Over on the other side of the town, on the slope of a hill, a small castle nestled in the trees. There was nobody else around. He had been sitting still for so long that the animals had grown used to him. Every so often there would be a rustling in the long grass as a mouse or a vole moved past, while hawks circled lazily in the blue sky above, waiting for any small animals stupid enough to emerge into an area of clear ground.

The wind rustled the leaves of the trees behind him. He let his mind wander, trying not to think about the past or the future, just living in the moment for as long as he could. The past ached like a bruise, and the imme-diate future was not something that he wanted to arrive in a hurry. The only way to keep going was not to think about it, just drift on the breeze and let the animals move around him.

He had been living at Holmes Manor for three days now, and things had not got any better than his first experience. The worst thing was Mrs. Eglantine. The housekeeper was an ever-present spectre lurking in the deep recesses of the house. Whenever he turned round he seemed to find her there, standing in the shadows, watching him with her crinkled-up eyes. She had barely exchanged three sentences with him since he had arrived. He was, as far as he could tell, expected to turn up for breakfast, lunch, afternoon tea, and dinner, say nothing, eat as quietly as possible, and then vanish until the next meal; and that was going to be the shape of his life until the holidays were over and Mycroft came to release him from his sentence.

Sherrinford and Anna Holmes—his uncle and aunt— were usually present at breakfast and dinner. Sherrinford was a dominating presence: as tall as his brother but much thinner, cheekbones prominent, forehead domed in front and sunken at the sides, bushy white beard descending to his chest but the hair on his head so sparse that it looked to Sherlock as if each individual strand had been painted onto the skin of his scalp and then a coat of varnish applied. Between meals he vanished into his study or to the library where, from what Sherlock could tell from scraps of conversation, he wrote religious pamphlets and sermons for vicars across the country. The only thing of any substance that he had said to Sherlock in the past three days had been when he had fixed Sherlock with an ominous eye over lunch and asked: "What is the state of your soul, boy?" Sherlock had blinked, fork raised to his mouth. Remembering Mr. Tulley, the Latin master at

Deepdene, he said: "*Extra ecclesiam nulla salus*," which he was pretty sure meant: "Outside the Church there is no salvation." It seemed to work: Sherrinford Holmes had nodded, murmured: "Ah, Saint Cyprian of Carthage, of course," and turned back to his plate.

Mrs. Holmes—or Aunt Anna—was a small, birdlike woman who seemed to be in a state of perpetual motion. Even when she was sitting down, her hands constantly fluttered around, never settling for more than a moment anywhere. She talked all the time, but not really *to* anyone, as far as Sherlock could tell. She just seemed to enjoy conducting a continual monologue, and didn't seem to expect anyone to join in or to answer any of her largely rhetorical questions.

The food, at least, was passable—better than the meals at Deepdene School. Mostly it was vegetables—carrots, potatoes, and cauliflower that he guessed had been grown in the grounds of the manor house—but every meal had some kind of meat, and unlike the grey, gristly, and usually unidentifiable stuff that he had been used to at school, this was well flavoured and tasty: ham hocks, chicken thighs, fillets of what he had been told was salmon, and, on one occasion, big flakes carved from a glutinous shoulder of lamb that had been placed in the centre of the table. If he wasn't careful he would put on so much weight that he would start to look like Mycroft.

His room was up in the eaves of the house, not quite in the servants' quarters but not down with the family either. The ceiling sloped from door to window to match the roof above, meaning that he had to stoop while moving around, while the floor was plain wooden boards covered with a rug of dubious vintage. His bed was just as hard as the one at Deepdene School. For the first two nights the silence had kept him awake for hours. He was so used to hearing thirty other boys snoring, talking in their sleep, or sobbing quietly to themselves that he found the sudden absence of noise unnerving, but then he had opened his window in order to get some air and discovered that the night was not silent at all, just filled with a subtler kind of noise. From then on he had been lulled to sleep by the screech of owls, the screaming of foxes, and the sudden flurries of wings as something spooked the chickens at the back of the house.

Despite his brother's advice, he had been unable to get into the library and settle down with a book. Sherrinford Holmes spent most of his time in there, researching his religious pamphlets and sermons, and Sherlock was wary of disturbing him. Instead he had taken to wandering in ever-increasing circles around the house, starting with the grounds at the front and back, the walled garden, the chicken coop, and the vegetable plot, then climbing the stone walls that surrounded the house and moving to the road outside, and finally expanding outward into the ancient woods that nestled up against the rear of the house. He had been used to walking, exploring the forests back home, either alone or with his sister, but the woods here seemed older and more mysterious than the ones he was used to.

"For a townie you really can sit still, can't you?"

"So can you," Sherlock responded to the voice behind him. "You've been watching me for half an hour."

"How did you know?" Sherlock heard a soft *thud*, as if someone had just jumped down from the lower branches of a tree onto the ferns that covered the ground.

"There are birds perching in all the trees except for one—the one you're sitting in. They're obviously frightened of you."

"I won't hurt them, just like I won't hurt you."

Sherlock turned his head slowly. The voice belonged to a boy of about his own age, only smaller and stockier than Sherlock's lanky frame. His hair was long enough to reach his shoulders. "I'm not sure you could," Sherlock said as calmly as possible under the circumstances.

"I can fight dirty," the boy said. "And I got a knife."

"Yes, but I've been watching the boxing matches at school, and I've got a long reach." Sherlock eyed the boy critically. His clothes were dusty, made of rough cloth and patched in places, and his face, hands, and fingernails were dirty.

"School?" the boy said. "They teach boxing at school?"

"They do at my school. They say it toughens us up."

The boy sat himself down beside Sherlock. "It's life that toughens you up," he muttered, then added: "My name's Matty. Matty Arnatt."

"Matty as in Matthew?"

"I suppose so. You live up at the big house down the road, don't you?"

Sherlock nodded. "Just moved in for the summer. With my aunt and uncle. My name's Sherlock—Sherlock Holmes."

Matty glanced critically at Sherlock. "That's not a proper name."

"What, *Sherlock*?" He thought for a moment. "What's wrong with it?"

"Do you know any other Sherlocks?"

Sherlock shrugged. "No."

"What's your dad's name, then?"

Sherlock frowned. "Siger."

"And your uncle? The one you're staying with?"

"Sherrinford."

"Got any brothers?"

"Yes, one."

"What's his name?"

"Mycroft."

Matty shook his head in exasperation. "Sherlock, Siger, Sherrinford, and Mycroft. What a bunch! Why not go for something traditional, like Matthew, Mark, Luke, and John?"

"They're family names," Sherlock explained. "And they are traditional. All the males in our family have names like that." He paused. "My father told me once that one branch of the family originally came to England from

Scandinavia, and that's where those names come from. Or something like that. 'Siger' could be Scandinavian, I suppose, but the others actually sound to me more like place-names in old English. Although where 'Sherlock' comes from is a complete mystery. Maybe there's a Sher Lock or a Sheer Lock on a canal somewhere."

"You know a lot of stuff," Matty said, "but you don't know much about canals. There's no Sher Lock or Sheer Lock that I've ever come across. So what about sisters? Any silly names there?"

Sherlock winced and looked away. "So, do you live around here?"

Matty glanced at him for a moment, then seemed to accept the fact that Sherlock wanted to change the subject. "Yeh," he said, "for the moment. I'm kind of travelling."

Sherlock's interest perked up. "Travelling? You mean you're a Gypsy? Or you're with a circus?"

Matty sniffed derisively. "If anybody calls me a 'Gyptian, I usually punch them. And I don't belong to no circus, either. I'm honest."

Sherlock's brain suddenly flashed on something that Matty had said a few moments earlier. "You mentioned that you didn't know any Sher Lock or Sheer Lock. Do you live on the canals? Does your family have a barge?"

"I've got a narrowboat, but I ain't got a family. It's just me. Me and Albert."

"Grandfather?" Sherlock guessed.

"Horse," Matty corrected. "Albert pulls the boat."

Sherlock waited for a moment to see whether Matty would go on. When he didn't, Sherlock asked: "What about your family? What happened to them?"

"You ask a lot of questions, don't you?"

"It's one way to find things out."

Matty shrugged. "My dad was in the Navy. Went off on a ship and never came back. I don't know if he sank, or stayed in a port somewhere around the world, or returned to England and didn't bother with the final few miles. My mum died a few years back. Consumption, it was."

"I'm sorry."

"They wouldn't let me see her," Matty went on as if he hadn't heard, staring ahead into the distance. "She just wasted away. Got thinner and paler, like she was dying by inches. Coughing up blood every night. I knew they'd be coming to put me in the poorhouse when she died, so I ran away. No way I'd go into the Spike. Most people who go in there don't come out again, or if they do they don't come out right in the body or in the head. I took to the canals rather than walk 'cause I could get further away in a shorter time."

"Where did you get the boat from?" Sherlock asked. "Was it something that belonged to the family?"

"Hardly," Matty said, snorting. "Let's just say I found it and leave it at that."

"So how do you get by? What do you do for food?"

Matty shrugged. "I work in the fields over the summer, picking fruit or cutting wheat. During the winter I do odd jobs: a bit of gardening here, replacing lead tiles on church roofs there. I make do. I'll do anything apart from chimney-sweeping and working down the mines. That's a slow death, that is."

"You make a good point," Sherlock conceded. "How long have you been in Farnham?"

"A couple of weeks. It's a good place," Matty said. "People are reasonably friendly, and they don't bother you too much. It's a solid, respectable town." He hesitated slightly. "Except . . ."

"Except what?"

"Nothing." He shook his head, pulling himself together. "Look, I've been watching you for a while. You ain't got any friends around here, and you're not stupid. You can figure stuff out. Well, I seen something in town, and I can't explain it." He blushed slightly and looked away. "I was hoping you could help."

Sherlock shrugged, intrigued. "I can give it a go. What is it?"

"Best I show you." Matty brushed his hands on his trousers. "You want to go around the town first? I can tell you where the best places are to eat and drink and just watch people going by. Also where the best alleys are to run away down and the dead ends you want to avoid."

"Will you show me your boat as well?"

Matty glanced at Sherlock. "Maybe. If I decide I can trust you."

Together, the two of them headed down the slope towards the road that led into town. The sky above them was blue, and Sherlock could smell smoke from a fire and hear someone in the distance chopping wood with the regularity of a pocket watch ticking away. At one point, as they briefly crossed into a copse of trees, Matty pointed to a bird hovering high above them. "Goshawk," he said succinctly. "Tracking something."

It was a good few miles into town, and it took them nearly an hour to make it. Sherlock could feel the muscles in his legs and lower back stretching as he walked. He would feel stiff and achy tomorrow, but for now the exercise was clearing away the dark depression that had settled over him since he had arrived at Holmes Manor.

As they got closer to the town, and as houses began to appear with more and more regularity along the sides of the road, Sherlock began to detect a musty, unpleasant smell drifting across the countryside.

"What *is* that smell?" he asked.

Matty sniffed. "What smell?"

"*That* smell. Surely you can't miss it? It smells like a carpet that's got wet and not been allowed to dry out properly."

"That'll be the breweries. There's a good few of them scattered around along the river. Barratt's Brewery is the largest. He's expanding 'cause of the troops that are newly billeted at Aldershot. That's the smell of wet barley. Beer's what turned my dad bad. He joined the Navy to get away from it, but there it was the rum that got to him."

They were on the outskirts of the town proper now, and there were more houses and cottages than there were gaps. Many of the houses were constructed from red bricks, with roofs of either thatched reeds tied down and bulging like loaves of bread or dark red tiles. Behind the houses, a gradual slope led up to a grey stone castle that perched above the town. The slope led up further, past the castle, to a distant ridge. Sherlock couldn't help wondering what use a castle was in that position if any attackers could get above it and rain arrows, stones, and fire down on it for as long as they liked.

"They have a market here every day," Matty volunteered. "In the town square. They sell sheep and cows and pies and everything. Good place to check when they're clearing up at the end of the day. They're always in a hurry to get out before the sun goes down, and all kinds of stuff falls off the stalls, or gets thrown away 'cause it's a bit rotten or wormy. You can eat pretty well just on the stuff they leave behind."

"Lovely," Sherlock said drily. At least meals at Holmes Manor were something to look forward to, although the atmosphere over lunch and dinner was not.

The town proper surrounded them now, and the street was filled with so many people that the two boys had to keep stepping off the pavement and into the rutted road to avoid being bumped into. Sherlock spent most of his time looking out for piles of manure, trying to ensure that he didn't end up stepping in one. The general standard of dress had improved, with decent jackets and cravats on the men and dresses on the women predominating over the breeches and jerkins and smocks that had been worn by the people they passed out in the countryside. Dogs were everywhere, either well kept and on leads or mangy and rough—strays looking for food. Cats kept to the shadows, thin and big-eyed. Out in the road horses pulled carriages and carts in both directions, grinding the manure deeper and deeper into the rutted earth.

As they reached an alleyway that ran sideways off the main road, Matty paused.

"What's the matter?" Sherlock asked.

Matty hesitated. "That thing I saw." He shrugged. "It was down there, a few days back. Something I don't understand."

"Do you want to show me?"

Instead of replying, Matty ran off down the alley. Sherlock sprinted to catch up with him.

The alley doglegged into a side street narrow enough that Sherlock could touch the buildings on either side. People were leaning out of upper windows and talking to one another just as easily as if they were leaning over garden fences. Matty was staring up at a particular window. It was empty, and the door below it was shut. The place looked deserted.

"It was up there," he said. "I saw smoke, but it moved. It came out of the window, crawled up the wall, and vanished over the roof."

"Smoke doesn't do that," Sherlock pointed out.

"This smoke did," Matty said firmly.

"Maybe the wind was blowing it."

"Maybe." Matty seemed unconvinced. His brow was furrowed as he recalled what had happened there. "I heard someone screaming inside. I ran off, 'cause I was scared, but I came back later. There was a cart outside, and they was loading a dead body into it. There was a sheet over the body, but it got caught in the door and it got pulled off. I saw the body. I saw its face." He turned to Sherlock, and his face was a mask of fear and uncertainty. "He was covered in boils—big red boils, all over his face and neck and arms—and his face was all twisted, like he'd died in agony. Do you think it was the plague? I've heard about it ravaging the country in the past. Do you think it's come back?"

Sherlock felt a chill run across his shoulders. "I suppose this might be the start of another outbreak, but one death doesn't make a plague. It could have been scarlet fever, or any number of other things."

"And that shadow I saw moving over the roof—what about that? Was that his soul? Or something come to take it?"

"That," Sherlock said firmly, "was just an illusion caused by the angle of the sun and a passing cloud." He took Matty by the shoulder and pulled him away. "Come on—let's go."

He guided Matty away from the house and down the narrow street. Within moments they were back on the main road through Farnham. Matty was pale and quiet.

"Are you all right?" Sherlock asked gently.

Matty nodded. "Sorry," he said, shamefaced. "It just . . . spooked me. I don't like disease, ever since . . ."

"I understand. Look, I don't know what it was that you saw, but I'll give it some thought. My uncle's got a library—the answer might be in there. Or in the local newspaper archives."

They walked across a small bridge and back into town. The street led past a set of wooden gates set into a stone wall. An animal of some kind was lying by the gates, legs outstretched stiffly, not moving. Its fur was dirty and dull. For a moment Sherlock thought it was a dog, but as they got closer he could see the pointed snout, the short legs, and the alternating stripes of black and white—now lighter grey and darker grey—that ran down its head. It was a badger, and Sherlock noticed that its stomach was nearly flat against the road. It had been run over, proba-bly by the wheel of a cart.

Matty slowed down as he approached. "You should be careful going past here," he confided, as if he was perfectly safe and it was Sherlock who had to worry. "I don't know what they do in there, but there's guards inside. They got billy clubs and boathooks. Big blokes too."

Sherlock was about to say something about the likelihood that the men were just providing some protection for the wages of the workers within when the gates swung open. Two men stepped out into the road; their faces were battered, scarred and grim, but their clothes were immaculate in black velvet. They looked left and right, checking the boys out momentarily and dismissing them, then gestured to someone inside.

A carriage pulled by a single black horse nosed out of the courtyard. Its driver was a massive man with hands like spades and a head that was bald and covered in scars. The two men closed the gates, then jumped on the back of the carriage, hanging on as it moved away.

"Let's see if the gent will give us a farthing," Matty whispered. Before Sherlock could stop him, he was running towards the carriage.

Surprised, the horse shied back against the shafts that connected it to the carriage. The driver tried to regain control, slashing at it with his whip, but he just made things worse. The carriage slewed around as the horse tried to prance away from Matty.

Through the carriage window, Sherlock was momentarily shocked to see a pale, almost skeletal face framed with wispy white hair staring at him with unblinking eyes that were small and pink, like the eyes of a white rat. He felt an instant flash of instinctive revulsion, as if he had reached out for a lettuce leaf on his dinner plate and touched a slug instead. He wanted to move, to back away, but that pale, malevolent gaze held him pinioned, unable to budge. And then the burly driver managed to regain control and the horse cantered past the two boys, taking the carriage and its occupant with it.

"Didn't even get a chance," Matty moaned, dusting himself down. "I thought that bloke was going to have a go at me with that whip."

"Who was the man in the carriage?" Sherlock asked, his voice unsteady.

Matty shook his head. "I never even got a look at him. Did he look rich?" he said hopefully.

"He looked like he was three days dead," said Sherlock.

THREE

Clouds of steam from the train's funnel billowed up through the slats of the bridge, scalding the boys' legs. Sherlock ran one way, Matty the other, both of them laughing and damp. The train ploughed majestically underneath them and into Farnham station, slowing as it arrived, and the boys moved back to the centre of the wooden bridge that connected the platforms, watching as it came gradually to a halt with a clanking of chains and a cacophonous hiss as the driver vented the remaining steam.

It was the morning of the following day. The platform had been deserted before the train arrived, but within moments it was magically transformed into a bustling mass of people heading for the exit. Men in black frock coats and top hats emerged from the first-class compartments like insects from cocoons, rubbing shoulders with the paunchy men in tweed jackets and flat caps and the women in decent frocks who had been sitting in second class, and the various muscled and weather-beaten labourers in threadbare shirts and patched trousers who had been squashed together in third. Men in uniform opened a sliding door in one of the carriages and began unloading wooden crates, and bags of what Sherlock supposed were letters. Station porters appeared from whatever offices they normally hid themselves away in and started moving the boxes and bags on trolleys away from the train. Within a few moments the platform was almost clear again, apart from a handful of lingering townsfolk who were chatting together, catching up on the events of the week. A guard, self-important in blue tunic and hat, stepped forward, looked up and down the length of the train, raised his whistle to his lips, and blew a short, sharp blast. The train seemed to shudder and then began to heave itself out of the station, ponderously at first and then with increasing speed. The carriages clanked as their connections pulled taut, one after the other, and they were dragged after the engine.

"Is that the train *to* London or the train *from* London?" Sherlock asked.

Matty looked up and down the line. "To," he said finally. "From here the line goes to Tongham, Ash, Ash Wharf, and then on to Brookwood and Guildford. From there you can get a train straight through to London."

London. Sherlock gazed along the tracks to where the train was just pulling around a bend and out of sight. At the end of its journey it would be within a mile or two of his brother, Mycroft, who would be sitting in his office reading documents, or poring over a map of the world, coloured red where the British Empire had made its mark. For a moment the desire to run after the train and climb on board was almost overwhelming. He missed his brother. He missed his father and his mother and his sister. He even missed Deepdene School for Boys, although not as much.

"What's at Brookwood?" he asked, trying to distract his thoughts more than anything else.

Matty seemed to shiver. "Don't ask," he said.

"No, really." Sherlock's interest was piqued now. "Is it anything worth us going to see?"

Matty shook his head. "There's nothing there that you want to see in daylight," he said with finality, "and you wouldn't want to be there at night, believe me."

"I was thinking that we could get hold of some bicycles," Sherlock pressed. "Get out and about. See some of the villages and the towns around here."

Matty glanced over at him, frowning. "Why would we want to do that?"

"Curiosity?" Sherlock asked. "Don't you ever wonder what things are like before you see them?"

"Towns look like towns and villages look like villages," Matty averred, "and all the people look like each other. That's the way life is. Come on, let's go."

He led Sherlock along the bridge, down the cast-iron stairs, and onto the platform where the passengers had earlier disembarked. From there they walked out into the road.

A cart had drawn up by the side of the road, and three men were loading it up with crates of ice insulated with straw that had come off the train.

One of the men was a weaselly-faced fellow with yellow teeth. He scowled at the boys as they walked past.

"Young Master Sherlock," a cutting voice said from behind them. "I am disappointed to find you consorting with scruffy street urchins. Your brother would be mortified."

Sherlock turned, already blushing despite not knowing who was talking to him, to find the housekeeper, Mrs. Eglantine, standing a few feet away. Two men whom Sherlock recognized from Holmes Manor were loading a series of boxes of groceries onto a cart which was hitched to a large and apparently placid horse. The boxes had almost certainly come off the train.

"Street urchins?" Sherlock looked around. Matty was the only other person there and he was watching Mrs. Eglantine with a cautious eye, looking ready to run if things went bad. "If you think he's a street urchin then you need to get out more, Mrs. Eglantine," Sherlock said boldly, irritated by her attitude.

Her lips twisted. "The master wishes to see you when you return," she said as the two men behind her loaded the last box onto the cart. "Please do not keep him waiting." She turned and stepped up into one of the front seats. "Lunch will be served whether you are present or not," she added, as one of the men swung up to join her at the front and the other climbed on the back. "Your friend is *not* invited."

The horse trotted off, pulling the cart behind it. Mrs. Eglantine didn't turn to look at Sherlock, but kept staring ahead. The man sitting on the back of the cart glanced at the boy and nodded agreeably, touching the front of his cap. He was missing several teeth, and there was a notch in his ear that looked like he'd caught it with a knife, or an axe, or something.

"Who was that?" Matty said, coming up beside Sherlock.

"That was Mrs. Eglantine. She's the housekeeper at the place where I'm staying." He paused. "She doesn't like me."

"I'm guessing that she doesn't like anyone," Matty said.

"I'd better go," Sherlock said. "It'll take me half an hour to get back if I'm fast, and she was serious about food. I'll go hungry until dinner if I miss it." He turned to look at Matty. "Will I see you tomorrow?"

Matty nodded. "Back here, at about ten o'clock?"

It took Sherlock almost forty-five minutes to walk back to Holmes Manor, and he arrived just as the gong was being sounded for lunch. He brushed the worst of the dust from his clothes and entered the dining room. Unusually, Sherrinford Holmes was seated at the head of the table, reading a pamphlet. His wife, Anna, was bustling around, checking the cutlery and talking to herself. Mrs. Eglantine stood behind Uncle Sherrinford. She didn't react as Sherlock entered, but the way she pointedly avoided looking at him told him that she had noticed his arrival.

"Good afternoon, Uncle Sherrinford, Aunt Anna," Sherlock said politely as he sat down.

Sherrinford nodded towards Sherlock without raising his eyes from the pamphlet. Anna managed to incorporate what sounded like a greeting into her continuous monologue.

A maid entered with a tureen of soup and proceeded to spoon it out into bowls, under the supervision of Mrs. Eglantine. Sherlock watched without much interest until Sherrinford put down his pamphlet, leaned forward, and said: "Young man, I have a visitor coming after lunch, and I would be obliged if you could be present. Your brother has exhorted me to ensure that your education is kept up whilst you are away from school, and has also indicated that he wishes you to be kept away from trouble. To that end I have retained the services of a tutor. He will take you on for three hours a day, every day of the week apart from Sunday, when I will expect you to attend church with the rest of the family. His name is Amyus Crowe." He sniffed. "Mr. Crowe is a visitor to this country from the Colonies, I believe, but nonetheless has demonstrated himself to be a man of learning and discrimination. His Latin and Greek are excellent. I expect you to abide by his instructions."

Sherlock felt his face burn with sudden anger. When he'd first arrived at Holmes Manor he'd seen the days stretching out before him, empty and barren, and wondered what he was going to do with his time, but meeting Matty Arnatt had opened up a whole set of possibilities. Now it looked as if they were all going to be closed off again.

"Thank you, Uncle Sherrinford," he murmured. He tried to look pleased, but his face wouldn't follow his instructions. Mrs. Eglantine smiled slightly, without meeting Sherlock's eyes.

A meat pie with thick pastry and gravy followed the soup, and a summer pudding followed the pie. Sherlock ate, but he hardly tasted the food. His thoughts kept revolving around the fact that his holidays were turning into a personal hell, and he couldn't wait to get back to the stability and predictability of school.

After lunch, Sherlock asked to be excused.

"Don't go far," Sherrinford admonished. "Remember my visitor."

Sherlock hung around in the hall while the family went their separate ways—Sherrinford to the library and Aunt Anna to the conservatory. He spent his time looking at the paintings and trying to decide which one was executed in the most amateurish manner. After a while, a maid came up to him. She held a silver tray in her hand, and on the tray was an envelope.

"Master Holmes," she said quietly, "this letter came for you this morning."

Sherlock snatched it from the tray. "For me? Thank you!"

She smiled and moved away. Sherlock looked around, half expecting Mrs. Eglantine to materialize and steal the envelope from his hand, but he was alone in the hall. The envelope was indeed addressed to "Master Sherlock Holmes, Holmes Manor, Farnham." It was postmarked *Whitehall*. Mycroft! It was from Mycroft! Eagerly he ran his fingernail beneath the wax seal and pulled the flap open.

There was a single sheet of paper inside. The address of Mycroft's rooms in London was printed at the top, and underneath, in Mycroft's peculiarly neat script, it read:

> My dear Sherlock,
>   I trust that this letter finds you in good health. You will, no doubt, be feeling abandoned and alone by now, and this will be making you angry. Please understand that I appreciate your feelings, and I only wish there was something I could do to help.

There is! thought Sherlock. *You could let me come and live with you for the holidays!* He dismissed the thought as quickly as it had formed. Mycroft had his own problems: a demanding job, and now acting as de facto head of the family in the absence of their father, looking after their mother, whose physical health was frail, and their sister, who had her own problems. No, Mycroft had done the best thing for both of them. Sometimes, Sherlock thought, the only options open to you were all unfair, and you just had to choose the one that minimized the bad consequences rather than the one that maximized the good ones. It felt like a peculiarly adult thing to think, and he didn't like the implication that this was what adult life was like.

Any letter you send to the address above will reach me within a day, and I promise that I will respond instantly to any request you might make — apart from the obvious one that you should come and live with me here in London.

Ah, ahead of me as usual, Sherlock mused. His brother had always displayed an uncanny ability to predict what Sherlock was about to say. He continued reading:

I have suggested that Uncle Sherrinford employ a tutor in order to further your studies. I have received good reports of a man named Amyus Crowe, and I have mentioned his name to Sherrinford. I believe that you may place your trust in Mr. Crowe. He also, I understand, has a daughter. Through her you may be able to make some friends of your own age in the local area.

That shows how much you know, Sherlock thought. I've already started making my own friends.

In conclusion, I exhort you to remember that this is a purely temporary situation. Things will change, as they always do. Take advantage of the situation you find yourself in. As the Persian poet Omar Khayyam wrote: "Here with a Loaf of Bread beneath the Bough, a Flask of Wine, a Book of Verse — and Thou, Beside me singing in the Wilderness — And Wilderness is Paradise enow . . ."

Reading the words, Sherlock tried to puzzle out their meaning. He was reasonably familiar with the *Rubaiyat of Omar Khayyam*, thanks to a copy that had been donated by its translator, Edward FitzGerald, to the library at Deepdene School. The general thrust of the various quatrains seemed to be that the wheel of fate kept turning and that nobody could stop it, although humanity could take some pleasure along the way. The particular quatrain that Mycroft had quoted implied that Sherlock should seek out his own "loaf of bread"—something simple that would help him get through the days. Did Mycroft have anything specific in mind, or was it just general advice? Sherlock was tempted to write back immediately asking his brother to explain further, but he knew enough about Mycroft to realize that once he had said something, he rarely went into more detail.

Sherlock turned his attention back to the final lines.

One last piece of advice—watch out for Mrs. Eglantine. Despite her position of trust, she is no friend to the Holmes family.

I know that you will not leave this letter lying around untidily, but will store it somewhere safe.

Your loving brother,
Mycroft

Sherlock felt a chill run through him as he read those final lines. For Mycroft to be so direct as to warn him against Mrs. Eglantine was entirely out of character, and raised the question, why *was* he being so outspoken? Was it because he wanted Sherlock to be in no doubt about his opinion of Mrs. Eglantine? His final suggestion—no,

his final *instruction*—not to leave the letter lying around—
was Mycroft's coded way of saying *destroy it*. That was
more in character.

He slipped the letter back into the envelope, but there
was something else in there—another piece of paper.
Sherlock pulled it out and found himself staring at a Post
Office Money Order for five shillings. Five shillings!
He'd been afraid to broach the subject of pocket money
with his aunt and uncle, but it looked as if Mycroft
would provide.

Sherlock found himself pulled in two directions by
the letter. On the one hand he felt reassured and happier
now that Mycroft had got in contact, and now that he
knew that Mycroft approved of Amyus Crowe, but on
the other hand he was now actively worried about something that had previously been just a nagging concern—
Mrs. Eglantine, and her obvious dislike for him.

"Interestin' letter?"

The voice was deep and warm and held an accent that
Sherlock couldn't place. He turned, folding the letter up
and slipping it into his pocket.

The man standing just outside the open front door was
tall and wide-chested. His unruly shock of hair was pure
white and the skin of his neck sagged, but the way
he held his body belied his obvious age. His skin was
leathery and brown, as if he had spent a great deal of
time outdoors in a hotter sun than England could
offer. He wore a beige suit of a cut and material that

Sherlock wasn't familiar with, and held in his hand a wide-brimmed hat.

"From my brother, Mycroft," Sherlock said, uncertain how to proceed. Should he call for a maid, or invite the man in?

"Ah, Mycroft Holmes," the man said. "We have mutual acquaintances, I understand. And as I refuse to believe that you are old enough to be Mr. Sherrinford Holmes, I guess that you must be young Sherlock instead."

"Sherlock Scott Holmes, at your service," Sherlock said, drawing himself up. He looked around. "Ah, would you care to come in, Mr. . . . ?"

"Mr. Amyus Crowe," the man replied. "Formerly of Albuquerque in the territory of New Mexico, part of the United States of America. And you're very kind." He stepped inside. "But you had probably already deduced my identity. I am here at the recommendation of your brother, and he would hardly write to you without mentioning it, now would he?"

"I should find a maid, or—"

Before he could finish the sentence, Mrs. Eglantine stepped out from the shadows beside the main staircase. How long had she been standing there? Had she seen Sherlock reading the letter?

"Mr. Crowe?" she asked. "The master has been expecting you. Please—come this way." She gestured towards the door to the study.

Sherlock shivered despite himself. There was no way

she could have known what was inside his letter short of opening and then resealing it, and he refused to believe that of her, but nevertheless he felt as if he had been caught doing something wrong.

Amyus Crowe entered the hall and left his hat and walking stick on the coatrack. He walked up to Sherlock. "We'll talk later," he said, putting a hand on Sherlock's shoulder. Sherlock was tall for his age, but Amyus Crowe towered over him, making him feel like a ten-year-old. "Hang around, son." He glanced around the hall. "While you're waiting, try to work out how many of these paintings are fakes."

Mrs. Eglantine stiffened. "None of these paintings is fraudulent!" she hissed. "The master would never allow it!"

" 'None of them' *is* an acceptable answer," Crowe said, walking past Sherlock with a wink. He handed Mrs. Eglantine a card. "Grateful if you could announce my presence."

Mrs. Eglantine led Amyus Crowe into the library. Moments later she emerged and moved away without looking at Sherlock. He followed her with his eyes as she vanished into the shadows by the stairs, and wondered whether she had stopped there, turned around, and was watching him.

Sherlock could hear voices from inside the library, but could not make out any words. He wandered along the oak panelling, taking in the details of each of the paintings in turn. None of them were labelled. Art appreciation had not been on the syllabus at Deepdene School, and he found that he could not raise much interest in the various landscapes, seascapes, and hunting scenes. They all appeared to him to be false, with their perfect trees, their wild seas, and their horses with spindly legs.

Albuquerque. America. It all sounded so romantic. Sherlock knew little about the country, save the fact that it had been settled from England over two hundred years before, that it had rebelled against English rule about a hundred years later, and that its people were independent and brash. Oh, and that there had been a civil war a few years ago that had something to do with slavery. But he had liked Amyus Crowe instantly, and if Crowe was at all representative of his countrymen then Sherlock wanted to go to America one day.

It was probably half an hour later that the door to the study opened and Amyus Crowe emerged. He was smiling and shaking Sherrinford Holmes's hand. Behind them, the serried ranks of green leather-bound books blurred together like a grassy landscape.

"Ah, Sherlock," Sherrinford said. "Mr. Crowe, allow me to introduce my nephew, Sherlock."

"We met earlier," Mr. Crowe said, nodding at Sherlock.

"Very well. Thank you for coming. I will have a maid show you out."

"No bother, Mr. Holmes—I'll take a walk through your grounds with young Master Sherlock, if I may."

"Of course, of course." Sherrinford withdrew back into the study like a tortoise into its shell, and Crowe strode over to where Sherlock was standing.

"Well, which one is it?" he asked. "If any."

Sherlock scanned the paintings. Despite careful observation, he still wasn't sure. He pointed to a particularly clumsy painting of a rider on a horse whose legs were so thin they should have snapped under the weight. "That one's not particularly well painted," he hazarded. "The perspective is all distorted and the anatomy is wrong. Is that the fake?"

"The thing about fraudsters," Crowe said, examining the painting, "is that the less talented ones get caught pretty quickly. Often fraudsters are more convincing than the real thing. You're right about the painting being clumsily executed, but it's real." He moved across to a dramatic coastal scene, with waves crashing onto a beach while a ship tossed in the background. "This is the fake."

Sherlock stared at it. "How do you know?"

"Like a number of your uncle's paintings, it's attributed to Claude Joseph Vernet. Your uncle also has a few paintings by Vernet's son, Horace. The elder Vernet was famous for his coastal landscapes. This is a painting of Dover Harbour, but Vernet never visited England. The detail is too realistic: it's obviously painted from life;

therefore, by definition, it's not by Vernet. It's a fake in his style."

"I couldn't have known that," Sherlock protested. "I never learned anything about Vernet, or any painter."

"And what does that tell you?" Crowe asked. He gazed down at Sherlock, his china blue eyes nearly hidden behind crinkled skin.

Sherlock thought for a moment. "I don't know."

"That you can deduce all you like, but it's pointless without knowledge. Your mind is like a spinnin' wheel, rotatin' endlessly and pointlessly until threads are fed in, when it starts producin' yarn. Information is the foundation of all rational thought. Seek it out. Collect it assiduously. Stock the lumber room of your mind with as many facts as you can fit in there. Don't attempt to distinguish between important facts and trivial facts: they're all potentially important."

Sherlock thought for a moment. He'd been prepared to be embarrassed and hurt, but Crowe didn't have a trace of criticism in his voice, and he was making a good point. "I understand," he said, nodding.

"I do believe you do," Crowe replied. "Let's walk and see what we can find."

Crowe retrieved his hat and stick from beside the door, and together they wandered out into the bright summer's sunshine. Crowe struck out across the front lawn and into the trees, talking about the different cloud formations in the sky and how they were related to the weather.

"Have you ever wondered about foxes and rabbits?" he asked after a while.

"Not especially," Sherlock responded, wondering where this change in tack would lead.

"Let's say you had a hundred foxes and a hundred rabbits in a wood, and there was a fence around the wood so that none of them could get out. What would happen?"

Sherlock considered for a moment. "The rabbits would have baby rabbits, the foxes would have baby foxes, and the foxes would eat the rabbits."

"All of them?"

"Most of them. Then the remaining rabbits would be difficult to find, and they'd probably start hiding."

"What would happen then?"

Sherlock shrugged, unsure where this was leading. "The foxes would start dying off from starvation, I suppose."

"And the rabbits?"

"They would keep hidden, eating the grass and breeding, so their numbers would start to increase." A bright light of understanding seemed to explode inside his head. "And then the numbers of foxes would start going up, because they'd be catching more rabbits and eating properly, and breeding. And eventually the number of foxes would be so great that they'd be eating more and more rabbits, and the number of rabbits would start going down again."

"And the process would keep repeatin' itself, like two

waves rising and fallin', one behind the other. Somewhere at the back of all that there's some mathematics called differential calculus, which you should look out for. It's strangely useful. You could apply those same equations to criminals and policemen in a city, if you liked." He laughed suddenly. "The policemen don't usually eat the criminals, but the fundamentals are the same. Isaac Newton and Gottfried Leibniz developed the mathematics independently, but it was recently developed further by Augustin Cauchy and Bernhard Riemann. Riemann died a few months back—great loss to the world, I believe, although I'm not sure the world has realized that yet."

Sherlock privately doubted that mathematics would ever be important, and set it to one side. He was happy to "stock the lumber room of his mind" with stuff about art and music, which he found interesting, but equations he could probably do without.

After a while they reached the drystone wall that marked the edge of the Holmeses' estate. Crowe gestured to the right. "You go that way—collect as many mushrooms and toadstools as you can carry. I'll go the other way. Let's meet back here in half an hour, and I'll show you how you can tell which ones are poisonous and which ones are not. Don't sample any before I tell you, mind. It's a valid analytical technique, to be sure, but it's liable to be a fatal one."

Crowe wandered off to the left, moving bushes and clumps of grass to one side with his walking stick and peering underneath. Sherlock went in the opposite direction, scanning the ground for the telltale white, pulpy knuckles of fungus pushing their way up through the bracken.

Within a few moments he was out of sight of Amyus Crowe. He kept moving, but apart from a series of brown, platelike growths emerging from the side of a tree, which he wasn't sure whether to collect or not, he could find nothing.

A flash of colour through the trees caught his attention: red spots on a white background. He moved closer, thinking it was a clump of toadstools breaking through the ground, but there was something about the shape that bothered him. It looked like . . .

A cloud of smoke began to rise from the object just as Sherlock recognized it for what it was: a man's body, lying twisted on the ground. The smoke wafted away, driven by the breeze, but there was no sign of fire. For a moment Sherlock thought the man was lying there smoking a pipe, his face wrapped for some reason in a red-spotted white handkerchief, but as he got closer he realized that the red blotches were neither markings on a toadstool nor spots on a white handkerchief.

They were bloody boils on the face of a corpse.

FOUR

Amyus Crowe pulled a handkerchief from his pocket and handed it to Sherlock. From another pocket he took a metal flask, flattened and curved to fit the shape of his body. It had a band of leather around it. He unscrewed the top and poured a brownish liquid onto the handkerchief that Sherlock was holding, soaking it. A nose-prickling, eye-watering smell rose up from the sodden material.

"Brandy," Crowe said in reply to Sherlock's dubious expression. "Just in case whatever killed this man is infectious. We don't want to catch whatever it is that took him away from this world." He pulled another handkerchief from a different pocket and soaked it as well.

"Whatever killed him?" Sherlock asked, puzzled. "Surely it was a disease of some kind. Look at his face!"

Crowe's bright blue eyes fixed on Sherlock's face. He gazed at the boy with interest for a few moments, still holding the handkerchief. "Do you believe that illness is just somethin' that happens—that diseases just develop in a body with no help?"

"I suppose so," Sherlock admitted. "I've never really thought about it."

"But you know that diseases can move from one

person to another, if you touch them or are close to them."

"Yes . . ." Sherlock said cautiously, wondering where this was going.

"Then doesn't it make sense that somethin' moves from the ill person to the well person and makes them ill in their turn?"

Sherlock remained silent. He knew that this was going to turn into another lesson, no matter what he said.

"I was in Vienna a few years ago," Crowe said. "I met a man named Ignaz Semmelweis. He was a Hungarian, working with women who were about to give birth. He noticed that the women who were attended by doctors or medical students had more chance of dyin' from puerperal fever than the ones who were attended by midwives. Intelligent man, Semmelweis. Many other doctors would have left it there, but he realized that these physicians had often come to the births directly from autopsies. He made the doctors wash their hands with water and lime before examinin' pregnant women, and the rate of mortality from puerperal fever plummeted in his hospital. Obviously the lime was killing or destroyin' somethin' on the doctors' hands that otherwise would have transferred from the corpses to the women." He held the handkerchief up. "Hence the brandy. Has a similar effect."

"What kind of 'something'?" Sherlock asked.

Crowe smiled. "The Roman writer Marcus Terentius

Varro wrote, 'There are bred certain minute creatures which cannot be seen by the eyes, which float in the air and enter the body through the mouth and nose and there cause serious diseases.' Not the kind of classics you studied at school, I guess. People have been talking about these minute creatures for centuries, but the medical profession just ain't takin' it seriously."

"But couldn't we just leave the body here and tell someone?" Sherlock asked. "Wouldn't that be safer—for us?"

Crowe looked around at the trees and bushes. "Too much chance of a fox or a badger comin' upon it and eatin' its fill. I never met this fellow, but I wouldn't wish that on anyone, alive or dead. No, he'll have to be removed from the woods at some stage for burial, so now's as fine a time as any. We'll be safe as long as we don't touch him, and wear these face masks."

Crowe tied the handkerchief gingerly around his face. The fumes from the brandy made his eyes water. He laughed, the deep lines round his eyes creasing like linen. "I never said it was good brandy," he said. "Mind you don't get a taste for it. Now, run off and fetch a wheelbarrow from the gardens. Bring it back here, sharp."

Leaving Crowe bent over the body and shoving the handkerchief in his pocket for later, Sherlock retraced his steps rapidly through the woods, back towards the house. He navigated his way using the various trees, bushes, and fungi that Amyus Crowe had pointed out along the way, racing through the underbrush and feeling the grasses whipping at his ankles as he ran. The scent of dry bracken and of lavender mingled in his nostrils. He could feel the sweat springing out on his forehead and between his shoulder blades, trickling down his cheeks and his spine.

Bursting out of the woods and into the stretch of open ground that separated them from the house, he paused for a moment to catch his breath and cool down. The afternoon sun blinded him momentarily, as physical as a blow to the head. He bent over, hands on his knees, taking gulps of the warm air. Sounds that had been muffled to silence by the trees—the chopping of wood, the distant grunting of pigs, someone singing—were suddenly clamouring for his attention.

Straightening up, he found himself looking at a figure in the distance, sitting on a horse. They were just beyond the gateway leading out into the road, the other side of the high wall. The horse was stationary, and it looked to Sherlock as if the figure was watching him. He squinted, raising a hand to shield his eyes from the sun, but in the moment that his hand blocked his gaze the horse moved on and the figure was gone.

Putting the figure from his mind, Sherlock found a wheelbarrow near the henhouse and quickly pushed it back through the woods to where the body lay. He found Crowe going through the man's pockets.

"Nothing to say who he is," he said without looking round. His voice was muffled by the handkerchief. "Do you recognize him?"

Sherlock gazed at the swollen face, feeling his stomach rolling uneasily. He tried to see past the boils and the redness to the features beneath. "I don't think so," he said eventually, "but it's difficult to tell."

"Look at the ears," Crowe said. "People's ears are quite distinctive. Some don't have earlobes, some are crinkly, and some are like perfect shells. It's a simple way to tell people apart, especially if they're tryin' to disguise themselves."

Sherlock bit back his immediate response that the man lying dead on the ground was hardly in a position to be disguising his identity, and concentrated instead on his exposed left ear. He noticed it had a distinct nick in the skin, about halfway up, as if it had been caught by a knife in a fight somewhere, or by an axe while he was chopping wood. The thought triggered a memory: he *had* seen this man before. But where?

"I think he works for my uncle," he said at last. "I saw him driving a cart."

"When was that?" Crowe asked.

"Only this morning." Sherlock frowned. "But he looks like he's been ill for days. He was fine when I saw him."

"Instructive," Crowe murmured. "Very well; let's get him into the wheelbarrow and back to the house. Your vinegar-faced housekeeper can send for the local sawbones."

"Sawbones?"

"Doctor," Crowe laughed. "You never heard the word 'sawbones' before?"

Sherlock shook his head.

"They're called that because not so long ago that was about all they could do—amputate fingers or toes, hands or feet, arms or legs if there was an accident." Crowe snorted. "Fortunately, civilization has advanced somewhat since then." He bent down towards the body, then straightened up again and glanced over at Sherlock. "Remember—don't touch his skin," he warned. "Just his clothes. Best not to take chances."

The journey through the woods took them nearly half an hour. Amyus Crowe pushed the wheelbarrow with the dead body balanced awkwardly inside. Sherlock ran ahead of the wheelbarrow, bending down and removing stones and branches that might catch the wheel or cause Crowe to trip. The dead man's hands flopped up and down whenever the wheelbarrow went over a bump, making it seem as if he was trying to struggle up into a sitting position. Sherlock tried not to look.

By the time they saw the house Sherlock's breath was coming in short gasps, and he could feel his muscles burning with fatigue. Someone must have caught sight of them, because Mrs. Eglantine was already striding out towards them.

She met them as they were emerging from the edge of the woods.

"You will *not*," she said stiffly, "bring that *thing* anywhere near the house."

"This *thing*," Crowe rebuked her calmly, "is one of your master's workers. I know he's dead, but I think he deserves a little respect nonetheless."

Mrs. Eglantine folded her arms. "Worker or not," she said, "I will not have him taken anywhere near the house. Look at him. I don't know if it's smallpox or the plague, but the body needs to be burned."

"I agree," Crowe said, "but first I want a doctor to see it. And, of course, his family needs to be told. Be so kind as to send for a doctor from the town. In the meantime, is there somewhere we can store the body?"

Mrs. Eglantine sniffed. "There is a shed over by where the manure is piled," she said. "It's not used for anything. Put him in there." She paused. "We can burn the shed afterwards," she added, then turned and headed back to the house.

"A lovely lady," Crowe murmured.

Sherlock led the way round the house to where the manure was stacked prior to being spread across the vegetable patches and the orchards. The smell was rank and warm despite the brandy-soaked handkerchief, penetrating his nose and mouth and coating his throat with a bilious tang.

The shed was dilapidated, and Sherlock and Crowe had to remove piles of broken wood and rusty farm implements before they could manoeuvre the body inside. Sunlight spearing in through holes in the roof and walls illuminated the body in hand-sized patches, leaving the rest of it mercifully in darkness. It looked to Sherlock like some grotesque life-size doll that had been carelessly thrown away, arms and legs dangling over the edges of the wheelbarrow.

"No point in both of us stayin'," Crowe said, stepping outside and removing his handkerchief. "You head back to the house. Get one of the maids to run a bath for you—a hot one. Scrub yourself down with carbolic soap. Change your clothes, and leave the ones you've got on out for burnin', if you have enough spare. If not, get the maid to take them away for washin'."

After his bath, when his skin was red and raw from scrubbing with the dark red carbolic soap, Sherlock dressed in some spare clothes and left the house. He could still smell the tarry scent that the soap had left on his skin, and his eyes stung. Coming round the corner of the house, wiping the persistent tears from his eyes, he saw Amyus Crowe standing outside the dilapidated shed in conversation with a burly man in a black frock coat. That must be the local doctor. As Sherlock got closer he could hear the doctor's high-pitched, arrogant voice saying: "We need to alert the civic authorities. This is the second body we've found displaying similar symptoms. If this *is* the plague then we need to take precautions right away. Tomorrow's fair will have to be cancelled and all the public houses closed in order to prevent the spread of the disease. Heavens, we may even have to cordon off the roads leading in and out of the town until the danger has passed!"

"Hold your horses," Amyus Crowe said in his slow, deep voice. "We've only got two bodies. Two raindrops don't make a rainstorm."

"But if you wait until the rain is pouring down before you put your umbrella up, you'll get soaked," the doctor rejoined.

Suddenly Sherlock realized that he knew more than they did. The body, the boils, the cloud of smoke—all this was exactly what Matty Arnatt had seen when the man in town had died. What *was* the smoke?

"Let's at least wait until we can get an expert to look at the bodies."

The doctor shook his head in annoyance. "What expert? I can perform an autopsy, but the sight of those swollen buboes is enough for me. We have to assume that we're dealing with bubonic plague and act accordingly."

Crowe raised a reassuring hand. "I'm acquainted with a lecturer in tropical diseases who lives in Guildford. Professor Winchcombe. We could send for him. I'll write a letter."

"Write if you wish," the doctor said, "but while you're doing that I'll be talking to the mayor and the town council, and the Bishop of Winchester as well."

"What's he got to do with it?" Crowe asked.

"Farnham Castle is the official residence of His Grace."

Sherlock moved closer, but Amyus caught sight of him and waved him away. Sherlock felt a flash of irritation. It was he who had found the body, but now Crowe seemed to want to keep him out of it. What did Crowe expect him to do—hang around until the conversation was finished and then just pick up their lesson where it had stopped? He had better things to do with his time. If Crowe wanted to complain, let him write to Mycroft.

Feeling irritation churning inside him, Sherlock turned and walked away into the woods.

Once he was in the trees, the house was lost from sight within moments. The ground gave spongily beneath his feet as he walked. All around there was a slight crackle of vegetation drying out in the afternoon sunshine and the occasional rustle as a bird or a fox moved in the underbrush. The smell of damp leaves rose from the ground, covering the nostril-tingling traces of brandy that he could still smell and the more pungent traces of carbolic. There were no trails, no paths through the bushes to follow, and Sherlock found himself having to step carefully over fallen trees and skirt around hawthorn bushes in order to make any progress.

He had entered the woods at a different point to the one he and Crowe had used earlier, and he wasn't sure where he was. He might just as well have been in the middle of the forest as at its edge, and if he wasn't careful then he might keep walking until he was in the middle. There was no way to check direction, and although he tried to catalogue the shapes of trees that he passed, he found they all ended up looking the same.

Something was drawing him deeper into the woods, something primal that he didn't understand. Some people talked about towns and cities as if they had their own personalities, and Sherlock had experienced something of that in London, on his occasional visits with his father, and to a lesser extent in Farnham with Matty Arnatt, but he could feel a different kind of personality here. Something timeless and dark. Whatever it was, it had seen the death of the farmworker and it didn't care, just as it hadn't cared about any of the hundreds, thousands, millions of animal and human deaths it had witnessed over the millennia.

Shaking off his feelings, he found himself stumbling over the ruts left by the wheelbarrow, and tracked them back to the area of the woods where he had discovered the body. The vegetation that had been crushed beneath the corpse had sprung back now, and there was no trace of where it had been lying. He only knew the exact location by where the wheelbarrow ruts stopped.

Sherlock stared at the ground, not exactly sure what he was looking for. He tried to visualize what the dead man's last few moments had been like. Had he staggered into the clearing, delirious, and dropped to his knees before collapsing full-length on the ground, or had he been walking, unaware that he was ill, before suddenly passing out and lying unconscious while the boils on his face and hands developed? There ought to be some way of telling from his footsteps. If he had been delirious then they would wander about, whereas if he had been walking normally then they would be in a straight line. It might be useful for the doctor to know how quickly the disease had come on, and if nothing else then he might impress Amyus Crowe with his deductive skills.

Sherlock crouched down and examined the ground closely. The man's boots had made a distinct impression in the soil—the heel on one foot was worn down compared with the other, and Sherlock found that he could easily distinguish the man's footprints from his own and from Amyus Crowe's. He traced them back into the trees. They were odd; sometimes the footprints pointed one way and sometimes another, as if the man had been twirling around. Dancing, perhaps? No, that was stupid. Dizzy? That was more likely. Perhaps the illness—whatever it was—had affected his sense of balance.

Sherlock followed the doodle-like path of the footprints away from the clearing to a point where they suddenly straightened out. From there they led away in a line, diverting every now and then around a tree or a fallen trunk, heading away from what he assumed was Holmes Manor. It looked as if whatever had affected him had come on suddenly: one minute he was apparently walking normally, the next staggering in circles as if drunk, and then, shortly afterwards, falling over. And then dying.

Returning to the area where the nature of the footprints changed, Sherlock stood still, looking around in puzzlement. Something about the ground in the vicinity was bothering him. He gazed at the trees, the bushes, and the grass for a few moments, trying to work out what the matter was, and then he realized. The grass was a slightly different colour—more yellow than the grass elsewhere in the woods. Sherlock knelt and touched his finger to the ground. It came away stained and dusty. Something had been scattered there—something that didn't belong.

Sherlock rubbed the tips of his fingers together. They were greasy. Whatever that yellow powder was, it didn't feel like anything else he could think of. He panicked for a moment, heart beating fast, as it occurred to him that the yellow powder might have caused the man's illness, but a few moments' thought persuaded him that diseases didn't come from patches of powder. They were transmitted, person to person. Poison was another possibility, but what poisons caused a man's face and hands to erupt in boils?

Thinking fast, Sherlock took from his pocket the envelope containing the letter he had received that morning from Mycroft. He removed the letter and placed it back in his pocket, then held the envelope by its edges so that it gaped open like a tiny mouth and scooped it along the grass. Some of the yellow dust transferred itself into the envelope. Quickly he closed it again and stowed it in a different pocket. He didn't know if it was important, but Amyus Crowe might recognize the dust.

Wandering through the woods, he eventually found himself emerging onto a road—whether it was the one that led to Holmes Manor or a different one he could not tell. It curved away from him in both directions, making it impossible to work out where he was. He sat down by the side of the road and waited. Eventually, he reasoned, a cart would pass by, and he could ask for a ride.

It was late afternoon. Where did he want to go—the manor house or town? After a few seconds he decided that going back to the manor house would just expose him to an afternoon of boredom. The town sounded more interesting.

The first ten or twelve carts that passed by were all heading in the same direction, and they were all stacked up with boxes, crates, and canvas sacks. The faces of the drivers and their passengers were fearful. Sherlock wasn't sure, but he had a feeling they had heard about the two deaths and were heading out of Farnham, getting as far away from the possible plague as they could. He didn't even bother asking them for a ride: the looks on their faces suggested that they wouldn't be favourable towards him. In the end it was perhaps half an hour later that he heard the rattling of a cart's wheels on the hard dirt surface of the road in the opposite direction to the one the other carts had come from. He stood up and waited for it to round the bend.

"Excuse me," he called to the grey-haired, thin-faced driver. "Which direction are you going?"

The driver nodded his head slightly, indicating the road ahead. He didn't bother looking at Sherlock, although he did at least pull on the reins to slow the single horse down.

"Which way is Holmes Manor?" Sherlock called up.

The man tilted his head and indicated the road behind with a slight jerk.

"Can you take me to town?" he asked.

The man considered for a moment, then jerked his head towards the back of the cart. Taking this to be a "yes," Sherlock climbed in. The cart sped up as he did so, almost causing him to fall off again. Instead, he tumbled forward into a mass of straw.

The driver didn't talk at all during the journey, and Sherlock found he himself had nothing to say. He spent his time thinking alternately about the dead man, the mysterious rider, and the bizarre but engaging figure of Amyus Crowe. For a place that had appeared at first to be a hellhole of boredom, Holmes Manor and its immediate locality were turning out to be anything but.

His thoughts drifted to the story that Matty had told him about the dead body that had been carried out of the house in Farnham, and the strange cloud that Matty said he had seen floating out of the window. Sherlock had dismissed the story at the time—at least, the bit about the cloud—but now he was having second thoughts. If Amyus Crowe was right about diseases being caused by "minute creatures" that could be transferred from person to person, then was that what he and Matty had seen—a cloud of these minute, disease-causing creatures?

It didn't make sense. Nobody had ever mentioned seeing these clouds of creatures before. Surely Sherlock and Matty couldn't have been the only people to come across them? Something else was going on.

It was only when the cart juddered to a halt that he realized they were in Farnham. The driver sat as still as a statue, waiting for Sherlock to clamber off, and then set off again without a backwards glance while Sherlock was still fumbling in his pockets in search of some loose change, expecting to have to pay the man something for his trouble.

Sherlock looked around. He recognized the street: it was the main one that ran through the centre of Farnham. Up ahead was a large, square redbrick building surrounded by arches that Matty had told him was a grain store. He glanced around; the market town was going about its normal business, with people walking along and across the street, stopping at shop windows or at stalls selling pastries, talking with each other or minding their own business. A greater contrast to the dark solitude of the woods would be difficult to find.

It might have been his imagination, but small knots of people appeared to be forming on street corners and outside shops. Their heads seemed to be bowed together, as if they were talking in lowered voices, and they were glancing at every passerby with suspicion in their eyes. Were they talking about the possibility of plague in the village? Were they scanning every passing face for signs of swollen buboes or the red flush of fever?

Sherlock quickly ticked off the list of places where Matty might be found. At this time the market stalls were still an hour or two from closing, so there was little chance that he was lurking around hoping for fruit or vegetables to be thrown away in his direction, and according to the railway timetable that Sherlock had carefully memorized in case he couldn't stand it at Holmes Manor any longer, there weren't any more trains until the evening. Matty might, he supposed, be lurking outside one of the local taverns, hoping for the odd penny thrown by one of the drunken customers.

In the end, Sherlock realized that he didn't have enough evidence to work out *where* Matty might be. As Mycroft had said: "Theorizing without evidence is a capital mistake, Sherlock." Instead, he made his way through the streets until he came to the place that Matty had pointed out to him—the house where the first man had died, and the cloud of death had crawled out of the window, up the wall, and across the roof.

The building seemed abandoned. Doors and windows were tightly shut, and someone appeared to have nailed a sign to the door. Sherlock assumed that it was a warning that someone had died from a fever within. He felt conflicting emotions within himself: part of him wanted to go inside and take a look around, see if there were any traces of the yellow powder in there, but another part, a more primitive part, was scared. Despite the brandy-soaked handkerchief that he still had balled up in his pocket, he didn't want to expose himself to possible contagion.

The door of the house opened a crack, and Sherlock moved back into the shadows of a doorway across the road. Who was in there? Was someone risking cleaning it up, or had someone moved in, or back in, regardless of the risk? For a few moments the door didn't open any further, and Sherlock felt, rather than saw, a figure in the darkness beyond, watching. He pushed himself further back into the shadows, heart pounding although he didn't know why.

Eventually the door opened just enough for a man to slip through. He was dressed in various shades of grey, and he glanced both ways along the street before emerging. He carried a sack in one hand.

And the hand that held the neck of the sack was covered in a fine yellow powder.

Intrigued by the powder and by the man's attitude, which indicated that he didn't want to be noticed leaving the house, Sherlock watched as he followed the road around to where it joined a larger street. The man turned left. Sherlock waited a few moments, then went after him. He didn't know what was going on, but he intended to find out.

There was something strangely familiar about the man. Sherlock had seen him somewhere before. He had a narrow, weasel-like face and prominent teeth that had been stained yellow with tobacco. And then Sherlock remembered—the man had been at Farnham station when he and Matty had been there. He had been loading crates of ice onto a cart.

The man's path took him from one side of Farnham to the other. Sherlock stayed behind him all the way, ducking into doorways or behind other people if he thought the man was going to turn round. Eventually the stranger turned into a side road that Sherlock recognized. It was the one that he and Matty had been in the day before, where they had almost been run down by the carriage containing the strange pink-eyed man.

The man sidled along a high plastered wall, up to the wooden gates from which the carriage had emerged, and knocked—a complicated rhythm that slipped out of Sherlock's mind even as he tried to memorize it. The gates creaked open and the man passed inside. The gates closed again before Sherlock had a chance to see what was inside.

He looked around, frustrated. He really wanted to

get a look over the walls to see what was inside, but he couldn't see how. It was all connected together somehow—the two deaths, the moving clouds, the yellow powder—but he couldn't see the threads that made up that connection. The answers that he wanted could be behind that wall, but they might as well have been in China.

The sun was low and red in the sky. It wouldn't be long before Sherlock needed to be back at Holmes Manor, getting cleaned up ready for dinner. Desperately, he looked around. Behind him, where the wall turned the corner, much of the plaster had crumbled away, battered over the years by passing carts and barrows and further eroded by rain. The rough brick exposed by the missing plaster might just be enough to give Sherlock a foothold, boosting him up onto the wall.

It was worth a try.

Without giving himself time to think, Sherlock slid along to the corner and looked around. Nobody was watching. He reached as high as he could, letting his fingers find a niche between two bricks, then scrabbled with his right foot to find an equivalent purchase. When he thought he was ready, he boosted himself up. The muscles in his legs flared with the sudden activity, but he wasn't going to give up now. He threw his left hand up as high as it would go, and felt it catch the top of the wall. Holding on as tightly as he could, he brought his left foot up and then dragged it down the wall until it caught on something. He shifted his weight from his right foot to his left, hoping that the brickwork wouldn't crumble away. It held, and he simultaneously pulled with his left hand and pushed with his left foot. His body scraped up the wall, and then miraculously he found himself lying flat out on the top of the wall, teetering on the edge of falling inside the yard that was revealed beneath him.

FIVE

From his position lying on top of the wall, Sherlock could see the entire yard spread out before him. There was nobody in sight. A single-storey windowless wooden building—more of a barn than anything else—dominated the ground, and the area around it had been left to dirt and weeds. Multiple wheel ruts linked the huge wooden doors at the front of the building to the gates in the wall. Some of them were barely more than scratches in the earth while others were deep and still filled with water from recent rain. Sherlock decided that carts or wagons were arriving at the barn lightly laden, making the shallow ruts, and leaving containing something heavy, causing them to sink deeper into the soft ground. But what was being stored or made in the barn, and was it somehow linked to the death of the man that Matty had seen, and to the yellow powder?

Sherlock swung a leg over the wall, preparing to lower himself to the ground, but a sudden scuffling made him pull back rapidly. Something dark and fast raced out of the shadows around the building on a blur of legs. Sherlock could see a large, heavily muscled head with tiny ears that were laid back along the skull and a small body covered with bristles. The dog didn't bark at him, but growled instead—a deep, rasping sound like a saw biting into hard wood. Spittle dripped from its exposed teeth. It skidded to a halt just beneath the spot where Sherlock was lying and proceeded to watch him intently, shuffling from side to side on its stumpy little legs, tail held low.

He had to get into that barn. There was a puzzle here, and Sherlock hated unsolved puzzles. But the dog looked hungry and trained for aggression.

He looked back over the other side of the wall, where he had climbed up. Was there another way in? Improbable, and the dog would just follow him round, now it had his scent. Could he make friends with it? Not likely, certainly not without getting down from the wall, and the penalty for failure was too terrible to contemplate. He could find a loose brick or a large stone and drop it on top of the animal, but that seemed unnecessarily brutal. Could he drug it somehow? He supposed he could run back to Farnham Market and buy a chunk of meat with what little money he had, but then what?

He scanned the ground on both sides of the wall, looking for something that might help. In the corner where the wall met the ground, close to the gates, he spotted something like an abandoned fur hat. It was the dead badger that he'd seen earlier. Quickly he half jumped and half fell back down the wall and ran the few steps to where the badger's body lay curled up. He picked it up. The fur was dry and dusty, and the body weighed almost nothing, as if whatever vital spark had fled when it died had actually had a mass. He could smell something rancid and disgusting. With a muttered apology he bent slightly, extended his arm, and pitched the badger over the wall. Its stiff limbs splayed out as it flew, pinwheeling around. It vanished behind the bricks, and Sherlock heard a thump as it hit the ground. Seconds later came the sound he'd been hoping for: the rush of paws on dry earth and snarling as the dog got its teeth into the dead body. Sherlock quickly scrambled up the wall again and glanced over. The dog was holding the badger down with its front paws and was wrestling its body back and forth with its strong jaws, tearing chunks out of it. As he dropped down onto the ground the dog stopped abruptly, glanced suspiciously over at him, and then kept on pulling at the dead creature. Either it had decided Sherlock was its friend for giving it such a great toy to play with, or it was just saving him for later. Sherlock fervently hoped the former explanation was correct.

Quickly, before the dog tore the badger into fragments too small to be of interest, he sprinted across the yard and up to the barn. There was a side door set in one of the walls, and he opened it a crack. Silence and darkness. He pushed the door further open and slipped inside, closing it behind him.

It took a few moments for Sherlock's eyes to adjust to the darkness, but when they had he saw that the space inside the barn was illuminated by skylights. Sunlight shone in through the dirty glass, making diagonal pillars of light that appeared to hold the roof up in an illusory scaffold. The place smelt of old, dry earth and sweat, but underneath those smells was another one—something sweet and flowery. There were piles of boxes and crates in various places around the building, and across on the far side several men were loading them onto a cart. The man he had followed through Farnham was one of them. The canvas sack he'd been carrying had been thrown roughly to the ground nearby. A horse had been attached to the shafts of the cart and was quietly eating hay from a nose bag that had been strapped to its head. A second cart was parked over to one side of the barn, its shafts pointing down and resting on the ground.

A pile of empty wooden crates lay in a rough stack nearby, and Sherlock moved silently over to hide behind them. He watched intently as the men stacked up the cart with what looked like the final load. They were cursing and jostling each other as they picked the boxes up and moved them one by one onto the cart. Judging by the dirt on their clothes and the sweat on their faces, they had been working like that for a while.

The man whom Sherlock had followed through Farnham helped with the last box, then brushed his hands together and wiped them down his waistcoat as if he'd been working there all day. His hands left yellow stains behind as the dust—whatever it was—transferred to the coarse material. One of the other men—a big bruiser with a shaven head, tattoos that covered his arms down to the wrists like sleeves, and a lit oil lamp hanging from a strap on his belt—glanced scornfully at him.

"Enjoy your little excursion?" he asked with mock interest.

"Hey, I was workin' too," the first man replied.

"What's the story with Wint's gaff?"

The new arrival shook his head. "The Baron was right—'e were taking stuff from us on the sly and tryin' to sell it on. There was jackets and trousers all piled up beside 'is bed."

"Anyone see you?"

"Nobody. I was like a rat."

"You got it all?"

The man nodded towards the canvas sack. "I collected it all together and put it in there."

"All right—throw that on the cart as well."

As the newcomer went over to pick up the sack, his burly co-worker called after him: "Did you burn Wint's gaff?"

The newcomer shook his head. "Didn't see the need."

The burly man shrugged. "You can explain that to the Baron when you see him."

"Hey, Clem—we're not gonna use the other one," a man shouted, jerking his head towards the spare cart.

The burly man half turned towards the gang of workers. "Leave it," he said. "Chances were we weren't going to need it anyway, but the Baron don't like to take chances. A cautious man, is the Baron." He turned back to the newcomer and pointed at the powdery yellow stains on the man's waistcoat. "You got some of their stuff on you. Wint's gaff'll be contaminated too. The Baron'll want it burned, just like he does this place. Get rid of any evidence."

The newcomer looked down at his waistcoat. "What *is* this stuff?" he asked.

His co-worker laughed with a sound that was a cross between a snort and a cough. "Best not to know," he said.

The newcomer looked at his hands. He glanced back at the burly man, and his face was suddenly pinched and white. "Hey, Clem, does this mean what happened to Wint'll happen to me?"

Clem shook his head. "Not if you wash it off properly, like the Baron told us." He turned towards the other men, who were standing around talking now that the boxes had been loaded onto the cart. "All right, you lot— time to go. Martin and Joe—you're with the cart. You know where to take it. Stouffer and Flynn—you head off after the Baron." He turned to the newcomer. "Denny, you and me'll sort this place out. Burn it down. Place is so big that there's no knowing what we might have left behind."

The newcomer—Denny—looked around at the barn. "Do we have to?" he asked plaintively. "Just think what we could do wiv this place once the Baron's finished wiv it. Set up a business, maybe, or turn it into the biggest tavern in the area. We could have girls singin', and dancin', an' everything. Seems a shame jus' burnin' it."

Clem's face contracted into a thunderous scowl. "You want to go and explain your little scheme to the Baron, you be my guest. Me, I'm gonna follow the instructions I was given."

Denny seemed to shrink under the other man's heavy gaze. "I was only askin'," he said.

One of the men over by the cart put his hand up to attract Clem's attention. "When do we get paid?" he asked.

"When the gear's been delivered," Clem growled. "Everyone meet up tomorrow, at Molly's tavern. I'll get the cash from the Baron and divide it out then."

"And how do we know you'll be there?" another man asked, half sticking his hand up and then thinking better of it.

Clem stared the man down. "'Cause the Baron's buying our silence, remember—yours and mine. If you don't get paid and decide to tell someone about what we've been doing the Baron'll come looking for me, and that's something I don't want. Everyone gets paid, fair and square, all right?"

The man nodded, mollified. "All right."

Sherlock drew himself further behind the stack of crates as the men dispersed, two of them getting onto the cart and two of them opening the massive wooden doors to let it out, leaving Clem to supervise and Denny to stand around looking lost. The man driving the cart made a clicking noise and flicked the horse's rear end with a stick, and it started to walk off, still eating from the nose bag of hay.

Clem walked towards the large wooden doors, the oil lamp that was clipped to his belt banging against his thigh as he moved. Without turning his head, he jerked his thumb over towards where Sherlock was hiding. "Lock that door," he growled, "then meet me round the front."

Sherlock's heart skipped a beat as Denny started walking towards his hiding place. If he came round the pile of crates he was sure to see Sherlock, and if that happened then Sherlock didn't give much for his own chances of survival. He shifted his position, tensing, ready to run. Could he make it to the side door before Denny could catch him? He wasn't sure, but he was even less sure that there was any alternative.

Denny came level with the boxes, the dirty, sweaty smell of his clothes wafting around him, and Sherlock cast a quick glance towards Clem, trying to work out whether the burly man was close enough to help Denny catch him. Clem was almost at the main doors now. Sherlock quickly ducked round the side of the crates. As Denny passed by, Sherlock slid back round. If Clem turned his head before he went out of the main doors then he would see Sherlock, as plain as anything, but he didn't. Sherlock watched, breath caught in his throat, as Clem vanished into the bright afternoon sunshine outside. Moments later one of the doors began to close, its rough wooden edge dragging in the dirt and its rusty hinges squealing.

Sherlock glanced over the top of the crates. Denny had just checked that the side door Sherlock had entered through was properly closed, and was about to throw the bolts that would make sure nobody could get in. As soon as he left, Sherlock would be able to throw the bolts again, open the door, and make his escape.

Denny picked a padlock up off the floor and slipped it through a loop in the topmost bolt, and then again through a metal ring that had been attached to the door-frame. The padlock shut with a definitive *click*. The key projected from the padlock, and Denny pulled it out and slipped it into his pocket. Then he turned, whistling, and headed across the barn.

Sherlock was aware of his heart pounding and his palms becoming clammy. He glanced over his shoulder briefly at the now-padlocked door. It looked solid. He wasn't going to get out that way; at least, not in a hurry and not without making a lot of noise. He would just have to wait until Denny and Clem had left, hold on for another five minutes, then go out the same way that they had.

Denny got to the main doors just as Clem was pushing the second one shut from the outside. The rectangle of light that showed through from the yard grew narrower and narrower. It shrank to a bar, and then a line, and then nothing. The doors closed with a *thud*.

Sherlock's heart shrank and darkened in the same way as the light had when he heard the unmistakable sound of a heavy wooden bar being slotted into place across the doors. There was no way out!

For a few moments he could just make out the two men talking, but he couldn't hear what they were saying. He straightened up, ready to move across to the main doors to see if he could discern any words, but a sudden sound stopped him in his tracks.

It was the sound of Clem's oil lamp being smashed against the doors.

Glass shattered, and liquid splattered across wood. Silence, for a moment, and then an ominous crackling as the flames from the wick of the lamp took hold of the oil-soaked wood.

Clem and Denny had set fire to the barn.

Panic threatened to overwhelm Sherlock. He wanted to run, but he didn't know where to go, so he ended up just twitching back and forth on the spot. A taste like sour metal flooded his mouth, and his heart was pounding so hard that he could feel the pulse in his throat and his temples. For a minute or so he couldn't think straight, couldn't connect two thoughts together in a sensible way, but gradually he quashed the panic by repeating to himself that there had to be a way out. All he had to do was to work out what it was. He could feel his racing heart gradually slowing down to normal and the twitching in his legs and arms receding.

The sudden smell of smoke began to fill the barn. Tiny flames were beginning to find their way like curious fingers through the joints between the boards of the doors.

Think, he told himself. *Think harder than you've ever done in your life.*

He looked carefully around the barn. Most of the boxes had been taken away by Clem and the rest of the men, and Sherlock still didn't know what had been inside. The crates he had hidden behind were still stacked over by the locked side door, but they were empty.

He ran across to the side of the barn and threw his shoulder against the wooden wall. The wood shook under the impact, but nothing bent or broke. He tried again. Nothing. If he was intending to break it down he was going to need an axe, or a hammer, or something. Not a shoulder.

As Sherlock was desperately looking around the barn for some kind of tool he could use to break the wall down, or prise the boards apart, his gaze suddenly snagged on the spare cart that had been left, abandoned, to one side. It looked functional, and the man, Clem, had indicated that it would have been used if they'd had enough boxes. Could Sherlock somehow use the cart to get out? Could he even *move* it?

There was only one way to tell. Sherlock ran across and grabbed one of the shafts that a horse would have been strapped between to get the cart moving. It came up easily in his hands. He tugged experimentally on it, but the cart didn't move. He tugged again, harder, and the cart shifted fractionally, but the other shaft was still resting on the barn floor and Sherlock's efforts were just pushing it further and further into the dirt and stopping the cart from moving.

Logic. Use logic. If he couldn't pull the cart, perhaps he could push it. Abandoning the shaft, Sherlock threw his weight against the front of the cart, where the driver would sit. It moved! The entire cart rolled a few inches backwards! He thanked whatever deity was watching over him for the mysterious Baron, whoever he was, who had so impressed his workers with his cautiousness that they had not only arranged for a spare cart but kept the axles greased as well. Then he took a few paces back- wards and rushed at the cart, thrusting his shoulder hard against the wood. It was the same shoulder he had thrown against the barn wall, and he felt a spike of red- hot pain flash downward through his arm and up his neck, but the cart rolled a couple of feet backwards be- fore coming to a halt.

Smoke drifted across Sherlock's face, making his eyes sting. He turned, and saw that flames were licking their way up the main doors and onto the lintel. Logically, the barn doors would be weakened by the fire and would be the ideal place to smash the cart through, if he could move it far enough and fast enough, but he would have to turn the cart around in order to aim it at the doors, and besides, the flames scared him. His only realistic chance was to try to smash the cart through the wall at the back of the barn.

Ignoring the sharp pain that radiated through his shoulder, Sherlock braced his hands against the front of the cart and pushed his feet into the soft dirt of the barn floor, knees bent. His body was almost horizontal, and he exerted every scrap of energy he had—more than he had ever used playing rugby football on the fields of Deepdene School for Boys, more than he had ever used fighting in the school boxing ring in the gymnastics hall. For a long moment his body seemed suspended between two immovable objects, and then the cart began to shift. One of its wheels caught on something—a stone, or a clump of dirt—and the cart threatened to roll back to where it had started, but Sherlock dug his feet in and pushed until his muscles screamed. The cart wheel edged over the obstruction, whatever it had been, and then began to roll more and more smoothly backwards. Sherlock shifted his left foot, taking a big step, and then his right. The dirt gave his feet grip, and he threw all his energy into moving the cart, inch by inch. Like a locomotive, it began to pick up speed as it went. Within a few seconds it had gone from a lumbering crawl to a slow walk, then a fast walk, then a trot. Sherlock felt something *ping* in his shoulder as a tendon caught on bone like a violin string plucked by a finger. His arm threatened to flop nervelessly down, but with sheer force of will he kept it locked onto the front of the cart and after a few moments the pins-and-needles sensation subsided. The cart kept on moving. He dared not look up to see how close the far wall was in case shifting position reduced the strength he was bringing to bear and the cart slowed again. All he could do was count footsteps: one, two, three, four, five, six—each one quicker than the one before. Surely he must be at the wall by now? Warmth blossomed on the back of his neck as the fire took hold of the doors. He could see his own shadow cast in front of him by the flames, outlined in red and flickering from side to side.

Suddenly the back end of the cart hit the far wall. The mass of the cart carried it on, the wooden slats splintering around it and the nails that held them together tearing out with painful squeals. Fresh air gusted in past Sherlock's head, blowing the smoke back but causing the fire to spread. The cart's rear wheels snagged on the wood, but Sherlock could see daylight shining around the blocky edges of the cart's body. He scrambled up onto the driver's position, then across the flat bed of the cart, and out into the glorious fresh air and sunshine.

Naïvely, he had expected to see crowds of people and the local fire brigade with hand pumps and buckets, but the yard was deserted. Even the dog had fled, presumably following the ruffians out of the main gates. Although the barn had been perilously close to an inferno on the inside, on the outside the flames were barely distinguishable against the bright sky, and only a thin trail of smoke led upward—barely more than a kitchen fire would make. Eventually someone would notice and investigate, but not for a while.

The main gates were closed, and Sherlock assumed that Clem and his retreating ruffians would have chained and padlocked them. They had displayed similar caution in almost everything else they had done. Ignoring the gates, Sherlock looked around the walls for a suitable place to climb up and get over. The interior was bare brick, and he had no problems in scrambling up.

He paused on the wall and looked back at the barn. The fire was beginning to edge up into the roof space now, and the rafters were burning. He needed to get out of there.

Half climbing and half falling to the ground, Sherlock limped away. He kept going until his lungs felt like they were going to burst and the muscles of his legs were begging him to stop. Slumping to a sitting position beside a low stone wall, he gave in to exhaustion and to the panic that he had been fighting off for what seemed like forever. He sucked in great lungfuls of air and let the shaking that had been building up in him sweep over his chest, his arms, and his legs. After a while he felt strong enough to raise his hands up in front of his face. The skin was scraped and bloody, and there were splinters sticking out of his palms that he hadn't even felt. One by one he pulled them out, leaving his hands dotted with beads of blood.

All that effort, all that danger, and what exactly had he learned? That if the death of the man at the house in Farnham was an accident then it was an accident caused by some kind of criminal activity. The dead man had been stealing something from his confederates, and that something had got him killed. The criminals had packed the rest of that something into boxes and had taken them away by cart to some unspecified location, and then set fire to the barn to cover their activity. And this was all done to the instructions of a mysterious "Baron."

And then Sherlock remembered the first time he had stood outside the gates leading into that yard, when he and Matty had almost been run down by a carriage. The man in the carriage—the man with white skin and pink eyes—was *he* the Baron? And if so, what exactly was he up to?

Sherlock suddenly registered how dark it was getting. The sun had almost set, and he had not only to get back to Holmes Manor but also somehow to clean himself up and change clothes—all before Mrs. Eglantine spotted that something had happened. He'd thought for a moment that his troubles were over for the day, but he realized with a sinking heart that they were only halfway through.

SIX

Sherlock nearly missed breakfast next morning. The adventures of the previous day had left him tired and achy, and his head pounded in time with his heartbeat. He could feel a tightness in his chest and a scratchiness in his throat that were probably due to the smoke he had breathed in. He had missed dinner, but his aunt had made sure that a tray of cold meats and cheese had been left out for him. It had to have been his aunt—Mrs. Eglantine certainly wouldn't have bothered. He had spent the night restlessly balanced between sleep and wakefulness, slipping between dreams and memories until he could no longer tell which were which. He only slid into a deep, dreamless sleep as the sun was coming up, and as a result the gong that was struck by one of the maids to signal breakfast jerked him awake and gave him barely ten minutes to get ready for the day.

Fortunately, another of the maids had left a bowl of water in his room without disturbing him. He splashed his face, brushed his teeth with a chalky powder flavoured with cinnamon that he sprinkled on his bone-handled hog's bristle toothbrush, and quickly dressed. He'd have to make sure that someone washed his clothes soon—he was beginning to run out of clean things to wear.

He checked the time on the grandfather clock in the hall as he rushed down the stairs. Seven o'clock.

He rushed into the dining room, ignoring the dark stare from Mrs. Eglantine, and helped himself to kedgeree from the long table of plates and dishes that took up one side of the room. It was a tasty mixture of rice, egg, and smoked haddock that he'd never come across before arriving at Holmes Manor, but he was developing quite a liking for it. He did his best to avoid eye contact with anyone, shovelling the food into his mouth so fast that he could barely taste it. He was ravenous: the events of the day before had taken a lot of his energy, and he had to replace it. Uncle Sherrinford was reading a religious tract while eating and Aunt Anna was talking to herself, as she always did. As far as Sherlock could tell, every thought that passed through her mind was immediately articulated, whether it was of relevance or not.

"Sherlock," his uncle said, looking up from the pamphlet he was reading, "I understand that you were involved in an unfortunate incident yesterday." There were traces of porridge on his long beard.

For a moment Sherlock was petrified, wondering how his uncle knew about the warehouse and the fire, but then he realized that Sherrinford was talking about the body of the man that he and Amyus Crowe had found in the woods. "Yes, Uncle," he said.

"Man, that is born of a woman, hath but a short time to live," Sherrinford intoned, "and is full of misery. He cometh up, and is cut down, like a flower; he fleeth as it were a shadow, and never continueth in one stay." Fixing Sherlock with a penetrating gaze, he went on: "In the midst of life we are in death: of whom may we seek for succour, but of thee, O Lord, who for our sins art justly displeased?"

Unsure how to respond, Sherlock just nodded as if he understood exactly what his uncle was going on about.

"You have experienced a sheltered life with my brother and his wife," Sherrinford said. "The facts of death may have passed you by, but it is a natural part of God's plan. Do not let it worry you. If you need to talk, then my study door is always open."

Sherlock was touched that Uncle Sherrinford was, in his own way, trying to help. "Thank you," he said. "Did the man we found work here, on the estate?"

"I believe he was a gardener," Sherrinford said. "I cannot say that I knew him, but he and his family will be in our prayers. His dependants will be supported."

"He was new," Aunt Anna said. "He had only just joined us, I believe. Previously he worked making clothing in Farnham for a company owned by an earl or a viscount, or someone from the aristocracy. His references were excellent . . ."

"How did he die?" Sherlock asked, but his aunt kept talking quietly to herself.

"This is not," Mrs. Eglantine said from where she stood over by the table of food, "a fit subject for discussion over breakfast." Sherlock glanced at her, surprised both at the boldness of her words and at the fact that his uncle and aunt didn't admonish her. For a servant, she was very forward. He found himself remembering Mycroft's warning—*she is no friend to the Holmes family*—and he wondered if there was more to Mrs. Eglantine, and her presence in the house, than he had believed.

"The boy is curious," Sherrinford said, fixing Sherlock with a glance from beneath his bushy eyebrows. "I encourage curiosity. It, and our immortal souls, is what distinguishes us from the animals." Turning back to Sherlock, he continued: "The body has been released to the local doctor, and he has sent a telegram to the North Hampshire coroner. It is up to them to pronounce on the cause of death, but I understand that the man's face and hands showed the raised blisters characteristic of smallpox or bubonic plague." He shook his head, frowning. "The last thing we need around here is an outbreak of some fever. The doctor will be hard-pressed to cope if anybody else becomes sick. I understand that some of the market traders are already packing up their stalls and moving elsewhere. Panic can spread faster than disease. Farnham exists because of trade—sheep, grain, wool, and so on. If that trade moves to another town then Farnham's prosperity will just wither and die."

Sherlock glanced down at his plate. He had eaten enough kedgeree to keep him going for a while, and he wanted to go back to Farnham and see whether

Matty was around. "May I be excused, sir?" he asked. His uncle nodded, saying, "Amyus Crowe asked me to tell you that he will be back at lunchtime to continue your studies. Make sure you are here." His aunt might have worked an answer into her continuing monologue—it was difficult to tell. Sherlock stood and headed for the door, but a sudden thought held him back.

"Aunt Anna?" he said. His aunt looked up. "Did you say that the man who died had previously worked for an earl or a viscount?"

"That's right, dear," she said. "In fact, I recall that—"

"Could it have been a baron?"

She paused for a moment, thinking. "I believe you are right," she said. "It *was* a baron. I have the letter somewhere. It was only—"

"Do you remember his name?"

"Maupertuis," said Aunt Anna. "His name was Baron Maupertuis. Such a funny name, I thought. French, obviously. Or possibly Belgian. He didn't write the references himself, of course; they were written by—"

"Thank you," Sherlock said, and left while she was still talking.

He shivered as he walked into the hall. Surely this couldn't be a coincidence? Two men dead, both apparently killed in the same way, one of them associated with a gang of thugs working in a warehouse in Farnham that was owned by a mysterious "Baron" and the other having recently left the employment of a "Baron Maupertuis." There couldn't be two barons associated with this business, could there? The owner of the warehouse, the strange man whom Sherlock and Matty had seen leaving in the carriage, that had to be Baron Maupertuis. And if the man whose dead body Sherlock and Amyus Crowe had discovered in the woods had previously worked for Baron Maupertuis in a clothes-making factory, was that factory based at the warehouse in Farnham? And did that mean that the things that the now-dead Wint had supposedly stolen from the warehouse—the things that Clem and Denny had talked about—were clothes?

It felt to Sherlock as though lots of jigsaw pieces that had been floating around in his mind had suddenly connected together. The picture wasn't clear yet—there were still some pieces missing—but it was all beginning to make a strange sort of sense.

Knowing about the factory, the clothes, the Baron, and the dead men, Sherlock could make some deductions based on the information he had. It wasn't quite guesswork, but he could come up with some likely theories. For instance, two men associated with a clothes factory had died, apparently of smallpox or plague. Did that mean the clothes themselves were somehow contaminated? Sherlock had a feeling, picked up by things he had read in his father's newspapers, that most cloth was manufactured in the mill towns of northern

England, Scotland, and Ireland, but some, he knew, was imported from abroad—China, if it was silk, and usually India for muslin or cotton. Perhaps a batch arriving at a British port from one of these foreign countries had been contaminated by disease, or was infested with insects that might carry the disease, and the workers at the factory had become infected. It was a possible explanation, and Sherlock felt a pressure, an urgency to tell someone. His immediate thought was that he could tell his uncle, but he dismissed that idea straightaway. Sherrinford Holmes might be an adult, but he wasn't very worldly and he would probably dismiss Sherlock's theory instantly. Sherlock's heart fell momentarily. Who else was there?

And then he remembered Mycroft. He could write everything in a letter and send it to his brother. Mycroft worked for the British government. He would know what to do.

He could feel the knot of worry in his chest loosen slightly at the thought of the reliable, dependable Mycroft, but then it occurred to him to wonder what exactly Mycroft was going to do. Abandon his work and rush down to Farnham to take charge of an investigation? Send in the Army? More likely he would just send a telegram to Uncle Sherrinford, which took Sherlock back to square one again.

Sherlock walked out of the house and into the morning light, pausing for a moment to savour the air. He could smell woodsmoke, and new-mown hay, and the faint musty odour of the brewery in Farnham. The sun was just rising above the tops of the trees, catching the leaves and haloing them with gold, casting their long shadows across the lawn towards him like outstretched fingers.

There was another shadow there—a moving one. He traced it back across the lawn to the wall that separated the house and its lands from the road. There, on the other side of the wall, was a figure on a horse. It appeared to be watching him. As he held his hand up to shield his eyes from the glare of the sun, the rider spurred the horse on. It trotted away along the road, vanishing behind a high hedge.

Sherlock walked towards the main gates. The rider and the horse were gone, but if he was lucky there might be a hoofprint, or something that the rider had dropped, that might enable him to identify them.

There was no hoofprint and no dropped item, but Sherlock did find Matty Arnatt sitting by the gates. He had two bicycles with him.

"Where did you get those from?" Sherlock asked.

"Found 'em. Thought you might want to take a ride. It's easier than walking, and we can go to more places."

Sherlock gazed at him for a moment. "Why?"

Matty shrugged. "Got nothing else to do." He paused and looked away. "Thought about casting off, taking the barge down the canal a ways, but that just means starting again in a new town—working out where to get food and stuff. At least here I know people. I know you."

"All right. I could do with some exercise. My muscles are stiff after yesterday."

"What happened yesterday?"

"I'll tell you while we cycle." Sherlock looked down the road that led past the gates. "Did you see someone on a horse ride past here and stop for a while?"

"Yeh. They went past me and stopped down there." He nodded his head towards the point where Sherlock had seen the rider. "Seemed like they were looking at something, then they rode away."

"Did you recognize them?"

"I weren't really paying attention. Does it matter?"

Sherlock shook his head. "Probably not."

They rode together down the road towards Farnham, in the opposite direction to the one that the rider had taken. It had been a while since Sherlock had ridden a bicycle, and he found himself wobbling a lot as he followed Matty, but it only took a few minutes before he got the hang of it and caught up. As they rode, side by side, along shadowed roads where trees bent together to form an arch above their heads and past fields full of bright yellow flowers, he told Matty about what had happened the day before—the man he'd followed away from the house where Matty had seen the strange cloud, the warehouse, the cart stacked with boxes, and the fire. Matty kept asking questions, and Sherlock found that he kept going back and telling bits of the story again, going off at a tangent to explain other things and generally not getting to the point. He wasn't a natural storyteller, and for a moment wished that he had someone who could take the facts in his head and set them out in a way that made sense.

"You were lucky to get out alive," Matty said when Sherlock had finished. "I had a job at a bakery, few months back. Burned down. I were lucky to get out alive."

"What happened?" Sherlock asked.

Matty shook his head. "The baker, he was a fool. He lit a match for 'is pipe, right when we was openin' the sacks of flour."

"What did that have to do with a fire?"

Matty looked at him strangely. "I thought everyone knew that flour, hanging around in the air, is like an explosive. If one grain of flour catches fire then it spreads to the rest within a second, like a spark leaping from one to another." He shook his head. "The whole bakery was blown to rubble. I was lucky: I was behind a table at the time. Even so, it took a month for my hair to grow back proper." Glancing up at Sherlock, he said: "Anyway, what are you goin' to do now?"

"We should tell the local constable," Sherlock said. Even as the words emerged from his mouth they sounded wrong. Two dead bodies, a strange cloud of death, a mysterious yellow powder, and a group of thugs setting fire to a warehouse—it was too much like a child's fantasy game.

Even if half of the story could be verified by facts—two men *had* died, and the blackened, smoking remains of the warehouse would be evident for some time to come—the rest of it was too much like a mass of wild guesses and fantastic assumptions that had been strung together to bridge the gaps.

A look at Matty's face told him that the boy was thinking exactly the same thing. He felt his mouth twist in frustration. He didn't know anybody in the area who could help, and the people he knew who might help weren't in the area. It was a paradox.

And then he remembered the imposing figure of Amyus Crowe, and a feeling of relief swept over him, flushing away the cloud of uncertainty that had gathered around him like cold water scouring dirt and mud from a stone. Crowe seemed like he could talk to young people as if they were adults, and his mind worked logically, using evidence as stepping stones to come to conclusions rather than jumping right to the end of the path. He was the only person who might actually believe them.

"We'll tell Amyus Crowe," he said.

Matty looked dubious. "The big bloke with the funny voice and the white hair?" he asked. "You sure?"

Sherlock nodded decisively. "I'm sure." Then he felt his face fall and his body deflate. "But I don't know where he lives. We'd have to wait until he turns up for lunch at my uncle's house. Or ask my uncle where he is."

Matty shook his head. "He rents a house at the edge

of town," he said. "Used to be a gamekeeper's cottage. We can probably cycle there in half an hour." At Sherlock's surprised expression, he added, "What? I know where everyone lives, pretty much. It's part of knowing where I can likely get food at any time of the day. I need to know how a place like this works—where people live, where they work, where the market is, where the grain is stored, where the constable is likely to be morning, noon, and night, and which orchards are guarded and which ones aren't. It's a matter of survival."

Observation, Sherlock thought, remembering what Amyus Crowe had told him. It all came down to observation in the end. If you had enough facts, you could work almost anything out.

And that was the problem with the two dead bodies and the cloud of death—they just didn't have enough facts.

The two of them cycled through the town, avoiding the main thoroughfares where lots of people milled around. The journey was almost over before it was begun, and yet Sherlock's mind was still simmering with a rich stew of facts, suppositions, and hypotheses when they pulled up at the stone-walled cottage where Amyus Crowe apparently lived.

Movement to one side attracted Sherlock's attention. He glanced across, and noticed a saddled stallion cropping grass in a field. A black stallion with a flash of brown across its neck.

The same stallion he had seen twice now, each time with a mysterious figure sitting astride it, watching him.

He felt a chill run through his arms and chest, causing goose bumps to rise beneath his skin. What was going on?

Matty held back, waiting at the gate as Sherlock walked across the front garden. Sherlock turned to glance at him questioningly. The boy's face was twisted into a scowl. "I'll stay out here," he said.

"What's the matter?"

"I don't know this cove. He might not like me."

"I'll tell him you're all right. That you can be trusted. I'll tell him that you're my friend."

As the word "friend" emerged past his lips, Sherlock felt a sudden flush of surprise. He supposed Matty *was* a friend, but the thought confused him. He'd never really had any friends before—not at school, certainly, and not even back at the family house, the place he thought of as home. The kids there had tended to avoid the house, belonging as it did to the people they thought of as their social superiors, "the landed gentry," and Sherlock had spent most of his time alone. Even Mycroft hadn't been much more than a reassuring presence, sitting in their father's library working his way through the vast collection of books that the family had amassed over several generations. Sometimes Sherlock would leave Mycroft there after breakfast and find him still there at dinnertime, his position unchanged, the only difference in his surroundings being that the pile of unread books was smaller and the pile of finished books had grown.

"All the same," Matty said, "I'll stay outside."

A thought occurred to Sherlock. "Outside," he repeated. "You like being out in the open, don't you? I've not seen you inside since I met you."

Matty's scowl deepened, and he looked away, not meeting Sherlock's gaze. "Don't like walls," he muttered. "Don't like having nowhere to run but through a doorway when I don't know who's on the other side."

Sherlock nodded. "I understand," he said softly. "I don't know how long I'll be. Maybe I'll see you when I come out." He glanced back at the door. "Assuming anyone is at home to begin with." Looking briefly over at the black stallion, which kept on pulling up clumps of grass and chewing them, he knocked firmly on the door.

When he turned his head, Matty had disappeared, along with his bicycle.

The door opened after a few moments. Sherlock was looking slightly upward, expecting Amyus Crowe to be standing inside the doorway, and for a moment he was confused by the empty space. His gaze dropped, and he felt his heart stutter as it came to rest on the face of a girl at the same level as his own. Her clothes were dark, and in the shadows of the hall her face seemed to be floating in midair.

"I—I was looking for Mr. Crowe," he said, feeling himself blush at the unevenness of his voice. He desperately wished that he could sound as confident and as uninterested as Mycroft effortlessly seemed to manage.

"My father is out," the girl said. Her voice had the same twang that Amyus Crowe's had—an American accent?—making the sentence sound more like *mah father is aowt*. Whatever it was, it gave her an exotic appeal. "Can I tell him who called?"

Sherlock found that he couldn't pull his gaze away from her face. She was about the same age as him. Her hair was long and reddish-gold, cascading and curling around her shoulders like a copper waterfall hitting rocks and splashing upward. Her eyes were a shade of violet that Sherlock had only ever seen before on wildflowers, and her skin was brown and freckled, as if she spent a lot of time outdoors.

"I'm Sherlock," he said. "Sherlock Holmes."

"You're the kid he's tutoring."

"I'm not a kid; I'm just as old as you," he said with as much bravado as he could summon up.

She stepped forward into the sunlight, and Sherlock could see that she was wearing tight brown riding breeches, more appropriate for a boy than a girl, and a linen shirt that emphasized the shape of her chest.

"I'll tell Father you were here," she said as if he hadn't spoken. "I think he went over to your uncle's house to look for you. He was expecting to see you today."

"I got distracted," Sherlock found himself explaining. A thought occurred to him, prompted by her riding breeches and the horse in the nearby paddock. "You've been watching me!" he blurted out without thinking, feeling a sudden flush of embarrassment and vulnerability.

"Don't flatter yourself," she said. "I saw you a couple of times while I was out riding, is all."

"Where were you riding to? There's nothing past the manor house except open countryside."

"Then that's where I was riding." She raised an eyebrow. "Do you ride?"

Sherlock shook his head.

"You should learn. It's fun."

Remembering the figure that he'd seen in the distance, he said: "You ride like a man."

"What do you mean?"

"When I've seen women riding they turn sideways on the saddle, with both legs on one side of the horse. Sidesaddle, they call it. You ride like a man, with one leg on each side of the horse."

"That's the way I was taught." She sounded angry. "People here laugh at me for riding that way, but if I rode the way they wanted then I'd fall off if I went any faster than a trot. This country is strange. It's not like home." She pushed past him, the door swinging shut behind her, and strode away from him, towards the paddock. He watched her retreating back.

"What's your name?" Sherlock called.

"Why do you want to know?"

"So I don't have to keep thinking of you as 'Amyus Crowe's daughter.'"

She stopped and spoke without turning. "Virginia," she said. "It's a place in America. A state on the Eastern Seaboard, near Washington, D.C."

"I've heard of it. Is that near Albuquerque?"

She turned, and her expression was somewhere between contempt and amusement. "Nowhere near. Thousands of miles away. Virginia is mostly forests and mountains, but Albuquerque is in the middle of a desert. Although there are mountains there as well."

"But you come from Albuquerque."

She nodded.

"Why did you leave?"

Virginia didn't answer. Instead, she turned away and continued walking on towards the paddock. Sherlock followed, feeling strangely like a puppet being jerked around by its strings, unable to follow his own desires. He glanced around, hoping that Matty wasn't there to witness what was going on, but the boy and his bicycle were absent.

"Don't you want to tell someone where you're going?" he asked as Virginia stepped up into one stirrup, grasped the front of the saddle with her left hand, and pulled herself up into a sitting position on the horse. Her hand caressed its mane.

"There's nobody home," she called. "My father is out, remember."

"What about your mother?" he asked. The way her expression changed into something hard but strangely fragile made him wish he could pull the words right back out of the air.

"My mother is dead," Virginia said flatly. "She died on the ship, coming across the Atlantic to Liverpool. That's why I hate this country, and I hate being in it. If we hadn't come here, she'd still be alive."

With a flick of the reins she turned the horse round and started trotting away. Sherlock watched her go, embarrassed at the pain on her face and angry with himself for causing it.

When he finally turned round to leave he found Amyus Crowe standing patiently at the end of the path, leaning on a walking stick. He was gazing levelly at Sherlock.

"I see you've met my daughter," he said finally, his accent, like Virginia's, making it sound more like *Ah see you've met mah dawter.*

"She didn't seem impressed with me," Sherlock admitted.

"She ain't impressed with nobody. Spends her time riding the countryside dressed like a boy." His mouth twisted into a lopsided grimace. "Can't say I blame her. Getting dragged from Albuquerque to here is enough to put a child into a foul mood, without—" He stopped abruptly, and Sherlock got the impression that he was going to say something else and had just stopped himself in time.

"Did you want to see me about somethin' in particular, or were you just lookin' for the chance to have another lesson?"

"Actually," Sherlock said, "there was something." He quickly sketched for Crowe what had happened in Farnham—the man with the yellow powder, the warehouse, the fire. He found himself trailing off towards the end, aware that he was admitting to what might have been seen as criminal activity if looked at from a certain perspective and uncertain from Crowe's expression what his reaction was going to be.

In the end, Crowe just shook his head and gazed into the distance. "You've had an interestin' time," he said. "But I'm unsure what it all adds up to. There's still two fellows dead, an' a possible outbreak of disease. If you want my opinion, let it be. Let the doctors and the administrators deal with it. There's a useful rule in life along the lines that you shouldn't try to fight all the battles that come your way. Choose the battles that are important, an' let some other fellow fight the rest. An' in this case, it ain't your battle."

Sherlock felt a frustration bubbling up within him, but he kept quiet. He had a strong feeling that this was his battle, if only because nobody else had seen the man in the carriage or thought the yellow powder was important, but maybe Amyus Crowe had a point. Maybe trying to persuade Crowe that something was going on wasn't a battle that Sherlock ought to be fighting. Maybe there was another way around.

"So, what's on the timetable for today?" he asked instead.

"I do believe that we never got to the bottom of edible fungi," Crowe replied. "Let's have a wander, and see what we can find. An' on the way I'll point out some wild plants that can be eaten raw, cooked up, or boiled into a drink that can relieve pain."

"Good," said Sherlock.

He and Amyus Crowe spent the next few hours wandering through the local countryside, eating whatever was safe and within easy reach. Despite himself, Sherlock learned a lot about spending time in the wild, and not only surviving but prospering. Crowe even showed him how to make a comfortable bed by piling bracken up to shoulder height and then climbing on it and using his weight to squash it down to the thickness and softness of a mattress.

Cycling back to Holmes Manor afterwards, Sherlock tried to turn his mind back to the two dead men, the burned-out warehouse, the yellow powder, and the mysterious crawling shadow of death, but he kept having his thoughts interrupted by Virginia's red hair falling around her shoulders and her proud, straight back, by the tightness of her riding breeches, and by the way her body rocked up and down as she rode away from him. He remembered the sample of yellow powder that he had scooped from the ground in the woods and sealed inside the envelope. If the ruffians in the warehouse were right then there was something associated with the deaths of the two men that was contagious, or contaminating, or at least could cause health problems if touched. Assuming it was the yellow powder, he needed to find out what it was, despite Amyus Crowe's thinly disguised warning. He certainly didn't have the knowledge or the equipment to do it himself. He needed a chemist, or an apothecary, or someone similar who could analyse the powder, and he was unlikely to find anyone like that in Farnham. His brother had taken them through Guildford on their way to Farnham, and if that was the nearest big town then that was where Sherlock could find someone trained in natural science who could tell him what the powder was. Amyus Crowe had mentioned an expert there—Professor Winchcombe. Perhaps Sherlock could go and see him.

All he had to do now was get to Guildford.

SEVEN

Sherlock caught up with Matty Arnatt next day at the market. He was beginning to be able to predict Matty's movements. It was late morning, and the market traders had been working since early morning. They would be thinking about food, and possibly taking turns to go and get something to eat—one of them watching over two stalls while the other went to get some bread and some meat, or a pie, and maybe a pint of beer. That meant lunchtime was one of those times when their attention would be spread thinnest, giving Matty the chance to snitch some fruit or vegetables from the corner of a stall without being noticed. Sherlock disapproved of theft, but he also disapproved of people starving and of kids being rounded up and sent to a workhouse, so he supposed it was a balance of ethical dilemmas, and to be honest he didn't begrudge Matty the odd worm-eaten apple. It wasn't going to bring down the Empire.

The market was spread over a small field with buildings on three sides. There were stalls selling piles of onions and parsnips, potatoes and beets, and other vegetables in a variety of colours that Sherlock didn't even recognize. Other stalls had knuckles of ham suspended from hooks with flies buzzing around them, and fish laid out on straw. There were people selling various materials and clothes as well—druggets and bombazines, barragons and shalloons, tub greens and serges. A makeshift pen to one side held a herd of sheep along with a couple of pigs that were lying down, sleeping despite the hubbub. The mixture of smells was almost overwhelming, with only a faint hint of decay in the air. By sundown, Sherlock guessed, the whole place would stink of rotting vegetables and fish, but by then most of the shoppers would have gone and only the poorer locals would remain, hoping the market traders would start to reduce their prices to get rid of their stock.

There seemed to be a subdued air to the market. It wasn't as lively as Sherlock remembered. Rather than the hustle and bustle that a small town market ought to generate, with people treating it as much as a social event as an opportunity to buy things, the shoppers appeared to be set on heading towards whatever they needed, buying it with the minimum of bartering and then heading out again.

"Was Crowe in?" Matty asked as Sherlock approached. He was sitting on an upturned wooden crate, watching the market traders intently for a moment's inattention.

"Not at first, but I met his daughter."

"Yeh, I've seen her around."

"You could have told me about her," Sherlock complained. "She caught me by surprise. I wasn't expecting her to be there. I must have looked like an idiot."

Matty glanced momentarily at Sherlock, eyeing him up and down. "Yeh, pretty much," he said.

Sherlock felt self-conscious and changed the subject. "I've had a thought—"

He stopped as Matty suddenly darted off into the crowd, slipping between shoppers like an eel between rocks. Within moments the boy was back again, brushing dirt off a pork pie. "It fell off the edge of a stall," he said proudly. "I've been waiting for that to happen. Too much stuff piled too high—something was bound to fall off eventually." He took a huge bite, then handed it to Sherlock. "Here, try it."

Sherlock nibbled a bit off the edge of the crust. It was salty, buttery, and thick. He took another bite, managing to scoop up some of the pinkish meat and transparent jelly inside. The meat was tasty, studded with bits of fruit—prunes, perhaps? Whatever it was, the combination was incredible.

He handed the pie back. "I already had some apple and cheese," he explained. "You finish this."

"You said you had a thought."

"I need to get to Guildford."

"Take a good few hours on the bike," Matty said, still scanning the crowd.

Sherlock thought back to his trip from Deepdene School for Boys to Farnham, passing through Guildford and then Aldershot on the way. He didn't particularly relish the thought of cycling all the way to Guildford and then all the way back again, and he wasn't sure he could do it in a day—and find an expert to talk to about poisons and diseases as well.

He sighed. "Forget it," he said. "It was a stupid idea."

"Not necessarily," Matty replied. "There are other ways of getting to Guildford."

"I can't ride, and I haven't got a horse."

"What about the train?"

"I'd rather do it without leaving a trail—without anyone knowing. Mrs. Eglantine seems to be friendly with the stationmaster—I don't want her knowing what I do all the time."

She is no friend of the Holmes family. The words from Mycroft's letter suddenly floated across his mind, causing him to shiver.

"There's another way," Matty said cautiously.

"What's that?"

"The Wey."

"What way?"

"No, the *Wey*. The River Wey. Runs from here to Guildford."

Sherlock considered the thought for a moment. "We'd need a boat." And then, before Matty could say anything, he exclaimed, "And you've got one—a narrowboat, at least!"

"And a horse to pull it."

"How long would it take?"

Matty considered for a moment. "Prob'ly as long as

cycling, but it's a lot less effort. I don't think we can do it today. You could meet me at sunrise tomorrow, and we could spend the day on the water, but that wouldn't give you much time in Guildford."

"What about if we start before dawn?" Sherlock asked.

Matty glanced curiously at him. "Won't your aunt and uncle worry?"

Sherlock's mind was whirring away like a grandfather clock about to strike. "I can go back for dinner, then tell them I'm going to bed. I can sneak out of the house later, when it's dark and everyone's gone to sleep—I'm sure of it. Nobody ever checks on me. And I can leave a note in the dining room saying that I've got up before breakfast and gone out with Amyus Crowe. They won't find it until the morning. It'll work!"

"The river loops close to your uncle's house," Matty said. "I can draw you a map and meet you there around four o'clock. We can be in Guildford for morning, and back before sunset."

Quickly, Matty scratched a map on a scrap of wood that he pulled from the crate he was sitting on, using a sharp stone from the ground. Sherlock suspected that the boy couldn't read or write, but his map was perfect and nearly to scale. Sherlock could visualize exactly where they would meet.

"I need you to do something," Sherlock said.

"What?"

"Ask around. See if you can find out about the man

who died—the man whose house you were standing outside. Find out what he did."

"What do you mean?"

"What he did for a job. Where he earned his money. I've got a feeling that might be important."

Matty nodded. "I'll do what I can," he said, "but nobody usually tells kids anything."

After that, everything went smoothly. Sherlock rode back to Holmes Manor and arrived just as the family was sitting down for lunch. He tried to think through his plan, testing each step for resilience against unexpected events and checking the details for flaws, but he found that his thoughts kept shifting around to Virginia Crowe. He couldn't get the shape of her face, and her cascading hair, from his mind.

Amyus Crowe arrived after lunch, and spent several hours outside, on the veranda, testing Sherlock's thinking processes with mind games and puzzles. One in particular stuck in Sherlock's mind.

"Let's imagine there's three fellows who decide to split the cost of a hotel room," Crowe said. "The room costs thirty shillings a night includin' dinner an' breakfast— obviously a prestigious place. So the fellows pay the manager ten shillings each. Okay so far?"

Sherlock nodded.

"Good. Next mornin' the manager realizes he's made a grievous error. There's a special rate on the room 'cause of buildin' work in the hotel. So he sends a bellboy to the fellows' room with five shillings to give back. The fellows are so pleased they decide to keep a shilling each an' tip the bellboy two shillings. So, each of the men ended up payin' nine shillings instead of ten, an' the bellboy made two shillings. Right?"

Sherlock nodded again, but his mind was rushing to keep up. "Hang on—if each man ended up paying only nine shillings, that's twenty-seven shillings in total. Add that to the two shillings the bellboy got, and you get twenty-nine shillings. There's a shilling missing."

"That's right," Crowe said. "You tell me where it went."

Sherlock spent the next twenty minutes working it out, first in his mind and then on paper. Eventually he admitted defeat. "I don't know," he said. "The manager gave back five shillings, so he didn't keep it; the bellboy got two shillings, so he didn't get it, and the men each got one shilling back, so they didn't get it."

"The problem's in the description," Crowe explained. "Yep, three times nine shillings does equal twenty-seven shillings, but the tip is already included in that. It makes no sense to add the tip to that to make twenty-nine shillings. If you restructure the problem, you realize that the men paid twenty-five shillings for the room and two shillings for the tip, then got a shilling back each, making thirty shillings. And the upshot is . . . ?"

Sherlock nodded. "Don't let someone else phrase the problem for you, because they might be misleading you.

Take the facts they provide, then rephrase the problem in a logical way that enables you to solve it."

Amyus Crowe left before dinner, and Sherlock returned to his room to think about what he had learned. He came back down for dinner and ate in silence, while his uncle read and his aunt talked to herself. Mrs. Eglantine eyed him suspiciously from the side of the room, but he didn't meet her gaze. The only conversation was when his uncle looked up from the book he was reading and said to the housekeeper: "Mrs. Eglantine, what stocks of food do we have within the manor house gardens?"

"For vegetables, we grow enough for our needs," she said, her mouth pinched. "For fowl and for eggs, likewise. As far as meat and fish are concerned, we can probably manage for a few weeks before we run out, if it is carefully husbanded."

Uncle Sherrinford nodded. "I think we must assume the worst. Prepare to smoke or otherwise preserve as much of the meat as possible. Lay in stocks of essentials. If the plague gets hold of Farnham then we may be isolated for some time. I know that Amyus Crowe is counselling caution, but we should take precautions." He turned to Sherlock. "Which reminds me—Mr. Crowe tells me you haven't spent much time on your Latin and Greek."

"I know," Sherlock said. "Mr. Crowe and I have been concentrating on . . . mathematics."

"Mr. Crowe's time is valuable," Uncle Sherrinford went on in a calm, measured manner. "And your brother has gone to some expense to secure his services. You may wish to reflect on that."

"I will, Uncle."

"Mr. Crowe will return tomorrow afternoon. Perhaps you might do some translation for me."

Remembering Matty's estimate that they wouldn't be back until dinnertime, Sherlock winced. He couldn't tell his uncle that he was going to Guildford, however. He might be forbidden to go. Glancing up, he found that Mrs. Eglantine was glaring at him with her small, beady eyes. What did she know?

"I'll be here," he promised, knowing as he said the words that he was unlikely to make it back in time. He would worry about explaining that when it happened.

Finishing dinner, he excused himself and pushed open the door to the library. His uncle was still in the dining room, eating, and he had said a day or two back that Sherlock could go into the library if he wished, but still he felt like an intruder in this hushed room, curtains drawn against the sunlight, with the smell of leather and old paper filling every nook and cranny. Sherlock browsed along the shelves, looking for something related to local geography. He found several different sets of encyclopaedias, bound volumes of ecclesiastical periodicals, myriad books containing collections of sermons from what he presumed were renowned clergymen of the past, and many histories of the Christian Church, and eventually came across several shelves of local history and geography. Choosing a book about the waterways of Surrey and Hampshire, he left the library and returned to his room in the eaves of the house.

For half an hour or so he composed a note explaining that he had gone out early and that he would be back later. His first few attempts were too detailed, specifying various untruths about what he was going to do and where, but he realized after a while that the simpler his note was, and the fewer facts it contained that could be checked, the better. Once he had finished it, he lay on his bed and read the book that he had taken from the library.

Sherlock scanned the book looking for mentions of the River Wey, preferably with a map that he could memorize, but soon found more than he expected. The Wey, for instance, wasn't just a river—it was apparently something called a "navigation." Rivers tended to wind around the landscape in unpredictable directions, whereas canals— built for purposes of trade between towns—were straight where possible and used steplike constructions called "locks" to raise and lower the level of the water depending on the shape of the land. A navigation, he discovered, was a river that had been made more navigable by the building of weirs and locks—converting a natural river into something closer to a canal.

Sherlock's head buzzed with details of the immense feats of engineering that had been required to bend the river to the will of man, and the many years that it had taken. He eventually tried to sleep, knowing that he was going to have a long day ahead of him. Although his mind seethed with ideas, images, and facts, he slipped into a dreamless sleep before he knew it. When he woke it was still dark, but a fresh breeze was blowing through the window and the birds were beginning to sing in the trees and bushes. It was four o'clock.

He had lain down dressed, and so within moments he was slipping through the darkened house, out onto the attic landing and down the narrow wooden stairs, making sure that he stepped on the outside of the treads to avoid creaks, then cautiously along the first-floor landing, past the bedroom of his aunt and uncle, past their dressing room, trying not to breathe too heavily, and then down the main stairs that swept in a curve into the ground-floor hall, hugging close to the wall and sensing the weight of the paintings that hung above him, their ornately carved wooden frames dwarfing the pictures themselves into relative insignificance. The only noise was the ticking of the great clock that stood in the angle where the stairs met the tiled floor.

He paused as he reached the hall. Now he had to cross the expanse of tiled floor towards the front door. No more sliding along the wall—he would be exposed, out in the open if anyone happened to come out of a doorway or looked down from the upstairs balcony. He knelt for a moment, trying to see if there was any light under any of the doors, but everything was dark. Eventually he screwed up his courage and crossed the tiles. By the time he reached the front door his heart was hammering twice as fast as the ticking of the clock.

The door was bolted, but he slipped the bolt and slowly pulled it open. Someone might notice in the morning that the door had been unlocked, but hopefully they would assume that someone else had got there first.

The door was almost closed when Sherlock remembered the note that he needed to leave, explaining that he had gone out early. He threw his weight against the door, pushing it open again, then slipped back inside and left the note on a small side table in the hall next to the hatstand where the morning and afternoon post was usually placed awaiting collection.

The air outside was cool and refreshing compared with the stuffiness within the house, and there was the suspicion of a glow above the trees where the darkness was giving way to the blue of the dawn. Sherlock sprinted as quickly as he could across the stones of the drive, hearing them crunch beneath his feet, before hitting the silence of the lawn.

It took ten minutes for him to get to the riverbank, following Matty's directions. A long black shape lay on the silvery river, moving back and forth as the water undulated. It looked strangely like a long, low hut that had been built on top of a narrow keel. The only gap was at the rear end, where the hut stopped and there was a platform with room for two people to stand, one of them holding the tiller. A rope attached to the front of the boat dipped towards the surface of the water, then rose again to where a horse contentedly ate its way along the grassy banks. Unlike Virginia Crowe's magnificent black stallion, this appeared to be a heavy, thick-legged creature with a shaggy mane. It glanced once, incuriously, at Sherlock, then went back to eating.

Matty was waiting on the front of the narrowboat, a dark shape against the dawn sky, like the figurehead on a ship or a gargoyle on a cathedral. He was holding a boathook—a long wooden pole with a metal hook on one end.

"Let's go," he said as Sherlock clambered onto the boat. "That's Albert, by the way." He made a clicking noise with his tongue. The horse looked round at him with an expression of regret on its long face, then started walking along the side of the river. The rope running between it and the boat pulled taut, then the boat began to move as Albert dragged it along. Matty used the boat hook to push the narrowboat away from the bank so that it didn't get caught in the reeds.

"Does he know where he's going?" Sherlock asked.

"What's to know? He walks along the bank pulling the boat after him. If he comes to an obstruction, he stops and I sort it out. You stay at the back and keep a hand on the tiller. If we start drifting out into the river then steer us back towards the bank. There's a blanket on the deck, if you get cold. It's a horse blanket, but it'll keep you just as warm as a fancy one."

The narrowboat drifted on. Water lapped against its sides in a regular rhythm that lulled Sherlock into a drowsy, almost hypnotic state. The river was empty of anything apart from the occasional duck or goose drifting past.

"What did you find out about the man who died?" Sherlock called forward after a while. "The first man. The one in the house."

"He was a tailor," Matty yelled back. "Worked for a company who were making uniforms for the Army in Aldershot. Big order, apparently, so the company were calling in all the local people who could cut cloth or sew the pieces together."

"How did you find out?"

Matty laughed. "I said I was his son, and that my mam wanted to find out if he had any money coming from an employer. Apparently he's owed some back wages, but his landlord's already got his eye on that for rent."

"Where was the company based?" Sherlock called back.

"They've got a main office near the market, but they've also got a warehouse on the edge of town where the cove worked. That's probably the one that burned down!"

Sherlock reflected as the narrowboat drifted on, pulled by Matty's horse. The man who died had been a tailor, making uniforms. The warehouse where he had worked had been full of boxes, which the thugs had loaded onto a cart. Boxes of uniforms? It seemed likely. But that still didn't explain why the man had died, or how, and it didn't explain the death of the second man, the one in the woods.

The sky to the east was the deep purple of a fresh bruise, and the trees lining the river were just visible as darker shapes against a dark background. A lone star shone brightly, close to the horizon. Ahead, Sherlock could see a black arch crossing their path: probably a bridge. Perhaps even the one that he and Matty had sat on, only a day or two before, watching the fish in the river.

Albert snickered, as if something had startled him. Sherlock stared at the bank, trying to make out the animal's shape against the darkness of the hedges that lined the bank. The sound of its hoofs against the path changed. To Sherlock it sounded as if the horse was trying to move away from something that was getting too close.

Matty said something calming—more a reassuring noise than actual words—but Sherlock could tell from the tone of his voice that he was concerned. What was the problem? Was there a wild dog wandering around, spooking the horse, or had it just smelt something unexpected?

Sherlock was about to call to Matty and ask him what the problem was when something moved on the bridge beyond the black shape of Matty's head and shoulders.

Sherlock switched his gaze onto the dark shape that

was crossing the river ahead of them. Something was breaking the smooth arc of the bridge: a lumpy shadow slightly off-centre. *Two* lumpy shadows, as the first one was joined by a second. They conferred for a few moments, leaning together, and then moved apart.

Locals from Farnham, out and about early? Poachers, perhaps?

Theories that Sherlock abandoned when the flare of a match momentarily illuminated a swarthy face that he recognized from the warehouse.

The thug named Clem.

The flame turned into a warm glow that spilt across the brickwork. Clem held a lamp high, casting its light down onto the approaching narrowboat. As they headed towards the bridge Sherlock could see a cruel smile twisting his mouth. The glow from the lamp outlined Matty's figure as he stood up in the bows of the boat. He seemed as if he was about to say something, but Clem swung the lamp above his head, sending shadows flickering everywhere, and then threw the lamp at Matty's head.

Matty ducked, and the lamp bounced twice before shattering across the back of the narrowboat, spilling burning oil everywhere. Tiny slivers of flame caught hold of the wood, licking hungrily across the veneer. Sherlock glanced around. They were on a river, for heaven's sake, and he could see no way of getting the water to where they needed it!

His gaze snagged on the horse blanket that Matty had pointed out to him, crumpled in the corner of the deck near the tiller. Sherlock swept it up and threw it forward, across the flames, keeping hold of one corner so that the blanket didn't slide off into the water. Smoke rose from underneath, but no flames. Sherlock pulled the blanket back towards him. Half of the fire was out, suffocated by the thick material, but tiny ripples of flame were still investigating the seams in the boat's construction.

Matty cried out as another oil lamp hit the edge of the boat near Sherlock's head and bounced into the river, where it sank, spitting and hissing as the wick touched the water. Sherlock whirled round and dipped the blanket over the side of the boat, making sure he kept a tight grip on it. Before it became too saturated, he pulled it out and heaved it across the wood again. This time the flames hissed as the sodden material extinguished them.

Sherlock glanced up at the bridge as the narrowboat passed beneath it, expecting a third oil lamp to come hurtling down onto his head, but their assailants appeared to have no more. Instead, Sherlock was shocked to see a body plunging down towards him. Clem had jumped. The thug hit the roof of the narrowboat, cracking the wood with his boots. He fell backwards onto the deck. Pulling himself to his feet, teeth clenched and eyes gleaming, he advanced towards Sherlock. Reaching down with his right hand, he pulled a wickedly curved knife from his belt.

"You thought you could break into our barn an' get away with it?" he snarled. "You was seen running off from the blaze like the rat you are." He reached for Sherlock's hair with his left hand. "Prepare to meet your Maker!"

Sherlock backed into the corner of the tiny deck area, feeling the breeze as Clem's flailing fingers passed in front of his eyes. The man was so close that Sherlock could smell the rank, sweaty odour rising from his rough clothes and see the dirt ingrained beneath his chipped fingernails.

Clem lunged forward and wound his fingers into Sherlock's hair, pulling the boy forward. Sherlock couldn't help crying out at the pain as his hair was almost yanked out of his scalp. For a moment, bizarrely, the memory of Albert tearing clumps of grass out of the riverbank filled his mind. Clem grabbed hold of Sherlock's shoulder with his other hand, fingers digging hard into the boy's flesh, and relinquished his grip on Sherlock's hair. Sherlock's entire arm went numb.

Clem pulled Sherlock against his shirt and gazed down into the boy's eyes. Sherlock could feel Clem's right hand coming up towards his throat, holding the knife. He was seconds away from having his throat slit open.

Something slammed against Clem's back. Clem's eyes widened in shock, and Sherlock felt the tight grip on his shoulder relax. He took a step backwards, pushing Clem away with both hands. The man didn't resist, but staggered back before shuffling round, taking exaggeratedly careful steps.

Matty stood behind Clem. He was holding the boat hook raised in both hands. For a moment Sherlock couldn't quite work out what had happened, and then, as Clem turned fully towards Matty, Sherlock could see a deep and bloody gash running down the back of his head from the crown to his thick, bullish neck. The skin was split open, and Sherlock could see white bone beneath the blood. Matty had hit him squarely on the back of the head with the boathook.

Clem took a step forward towards Matty, and then another. He raised the hand that held the knife, but he didn't seem to know what to do with it. He gazed stupidly at the knife, and then he toppled sideways, off the narrowboat and into the river, like a falling tree. The splash as he hit the surface of the water reached up almost as far as the bridge. For a moment Sherlock could see Clem's face as he sank, and the expression of disbelief in his mad eyes, and then he was vanishing into the murk and sediment at the bottom of the river. His hands were the last to disappear, fingers waving like weeds in the current, and then they too were gone.

EIGHT

Sherlock was still shivering by the time the sun was fully above the horizon and hanging in the sky behind the black silhouettes of the trees like an overripe fruit. Clem's grip on his shoulder had left a deep ache that radiated downward into his back. If he looked he was sure he would find bruises there—five oval bruises left by four fingers and a thumb.

After the attack, after Clem had sunk in the water and his companion had run off, Matty and Sherlock had just stared at each other for a few moments, shocked by the sudden violence and the equally sudden cessation.

"He wasn't trying to steal the boat," Matty had whispered eventually. "He was trying to destroy it. I've had coves trying to steal it before, but why would someone want to burn it? I never seen 'em before! What have I ever done to them?"

"They wanted me," Sherlock had said reluctantly. "That was one of the men from the warehouse. I think he was in charge—at least, in charge of the men who were there. The Baron that they talked about is really in charge. He must have seen me leaving the warehouse when it was burning and realized that I'd overheard them. But I don't know how they tracked us down to the barge." He had shaken his head in disbelief. "What is it that they're doing that they're willing to kill us to protect their secret? What is *that* important?"

Matty had just stared at Sherlock as if he'd been betrayed, then he had abruptly turned away and flicked the rope to get the horse moving again.

And now, as the sun was rising and Sherlock's shoulder was aching like a rotting tooth, they were coming into Guildford, and he still hadn't worked out what it was he was meant to know. All he had was questions, and the attack had just added to them.

A small pack of scruffy dogs was following them along the riverbank, watching in the hope that they might throw some scraps of food away. Sherlock smiled briefly, thinking how much like Matty they were in that regard. He glanced forward, to the back of Matty's head, and the smile faded from his face. He had put the boy's boat at risk—the only real home that Matty possessed. Worse, he had put the boy's *life* at risk. And for what?

People were beginning to appear at the side of the river now. Some were obviously on their way into or out of town, using the riverbank as a convenient route, while others were sitting on boxes and dangling makeshift fishing rods into the water, hoping to catch some fish for their breakfast. Smoke was rising into the sky ahead of them, as Guildford's occupants set about their cooking for the day. Buildings began to line the banks: some shacks formed out of wood that had been nailed together at various angles and some more substantial affairs of brick. Stone paving slabs appeared, patchy at first but eventually forming a pavement of sorts along the edge of the water.

After a while, as they approached a collection of warehouse-like buildings clustered together on the riverbank, Matty began to pull on the rope. The horse slowed, and the narrowboat coasted gently into the bank. Matty had timed it well: they ended up coming to a rest just by a large iron ring that had been set into one of the slabs. Sherlock expected him to wrap the rope about the ring, but instead Matty reached into the bows of the boat and pulled out a chain that appeared to be fastened to an eyelet sunk into the wood. He threw it to the bank and jumped after it. Winding the chain about the iron ring, he took a large old padlock out of his pocket and slipped it through several links of the chain.

"Can't trust anyone round here," he muttered, still not looking at Sherlock. "A rope they could cut, but a chain and padlock'll take them a pretty time to get through. More time than the boat's worth, I reckon."

"What about the horse?" Sherlock asked.

"If he can find someone who'll treat him better than me, he's welcome to go," Matty said. He took a step onto the grass, then looked back at Sherlock. His expression wasn't exactly apologetic, but at least he was willing to make eye contact now. "He's too old and lame to pull a plough or a cart," he explained. "A boat's about his limit, and even then he's slow. He's not worth stealing."

"I'm sorry about what happened," Sherlock said awkwardly.

"'S not your fault," Matty said, wiping a sleeve across his mouth. "You've fallen into something, and it's got hold of you. I'm just caught in it as well. Best thing to do is try and get ourselves out as quickly as we can, and move on." He looked around. "This is Dapdune Wharf," he said. "If we get separated, which is likely, then just remember to meet back here. I won't go without you." He looked critically at Sherlock. "An' I'm pretty sure you can't leave without me. Now, what was the name of that cove you was lookin' for?"

"Professor Winchcombe," Sherlock said.

"Then let's go and find him. And maybe we can get some breakfast on the way."

Together, the two boys headed away from the river, along a path that promised to lead them out onto a larger thoroughfare. It took them an hour of walking, and asking several passersby, before they discovered that Professor Winchcombe's house was in Chaelis Road, which led off the High Street, and then another half an hour to find the High Street, which led uphill away from the river and was lined with two- and three-storey shops constructed out of black wooden beams with white plaster infill. Signs hung outside: wooden plaques with paintings of fish, bread, vegetables, and all manner of other goods. The people walking up and down the street and looking in the windows were, for the most part, dressed better than the people in Farnham. Their clothes were made of finer fabrics, trimmed with lace and ribbon, more colourful and cleaner than Sherlock had seen for a while.

A few stalls selling fruit and cold cooked meat were located at the bottom of the High Street, along a waist-high wall that separated the town from the river. Matty was about to creep along the wall behind the stallholders and look for food that had fallen off the stalls, but Sherlock just walked up and used some of the dwindling resources that Mycroft had sent him to buy them both some breakfast. Matty glanced at him suspiciously: Sherlock got the impression that Matty thought food somehow tasted better if he hadn't had to pay for it. As far as Sherlock was concerned, food tasted better if it hadn't been rolling in the dust or if you hadn't had to fight a dog for possession of it.

Chaelis Road was halfway up the High Street, and both boys were out of breath by the time they got to the point where it started. The road curved sharply out of sight and Sherlock set off along it, but paused when he realized that Matty wasn't following. He turned and gazed questioningly at the boy.

"What's the matter?"

Matty shook his head. "Not my kind of place," he said, eyeing the tall houses and well-kept gardens that lined the road. "You go ahead. I'll wait here." He looked around. "Somewhere round here, anyway."

Sherlock nodded. Matty was right—the presence of what Mrs. Eglantine had described as a "scruffy street urchin" would probably cause them problems. Brushing as much dust from his clothes as possible, Sherlock moved on.

The house he was looking for was just round the curve. He pushed the gate open and approached the door, which was protected by a Greek-style portico. A brass plate was screwed onto one of the pillars. Engraved on it were the words: "Professor Arthur Albery Winchcombe. Lecturer in Tropical Diseases."

Before nerves could get the better of him, Sherlock tugged at the bell pull.

A man in a severe black suit and grey waistcoat opened the door. He stared down at Sherlock through tiny glasses that barely covered his eyes.

"Is Professor Winchcombe at home?" Sherlock asked.

The man—Sherlock assumed he was a butler—paused for a moment. "Whom shall I say is calling?" he asked eventually.

Sherlock opened his mouth, about to introduce himself, then hesitated. Perhaps he would be better off invoking someone else's name—someone that the professor had heard of. Mycroft, perhaps? Or Amyus Crowe? Which one would be best?

In the end, he chose one at random. "Please tell the

professor that a student of Mr. Amyus Crowe wishes to consult him," he said.

The butler nodded. "Would you care to wait in the sitting room?" he asked, holding the door open. Treating Sherlock as if he were royalty rather than just a somewhat dishevelled and nervous boy, he gestured towards a door across the hall.

The wallpaper lining the room was covered in paintings of tall, thin plants that Sherlock didn't recognize, like massive grasses. They seemed to have rings round their stalks, set at equal distances all the way up. He found himself fascinated by them, and he was still looking at them when the door opened and a man entered the room. He was small—smaller than Sherlock—and his stomach protruded as if he had a cushion shoved under his jacket. He wore a funny little red hat on his head with no brim or peak: just like a short, fat tower made of red silk.

"Bamboo," he said.

"Pardon?"

"Those plants on the wallpaper. Bamboo. It's a woody perennial evergreen of the grass family. I spent quite some time in China in my youth, and became very familiar with it. Bamboos are the fastest growing woody plants in the world, you know. The bigger ones can grow up to two feet a day, under certain conditions. The wallpaper itself is Chinese, by the way. Rice paper."

Sherlock wasn't sure he understood. "Paper made from *rice*?"

"A common misconception," the professor replied. "In fact, rice paper is made from the pith of a small tree, *Tetrapanax papyrifer*." He cocked his head to one side. "You say you are Amyus Crowe's student?" he asked. His eyes, behind his glasses, were bright and birdlike, alive with curiosity.

"Yes, sir," Sherlock replied, feeling strangely as if he was back at Deepdene School.

"I received a letter from Mr. Crowe this morning. Very odd. Very odd indeed. Is that why you are here?"

"Was the letter about the two dead men?"

The professor nodded. "Indeed it was."

"That's why I'm here. I heard Mr. Crowe say that you were an expert on diseases."

"I specialize in tropical diseases, but yes, my area of expertise covers most of the serious contagious illnesses, from Tapanuli fever and the Black Formosa Corruption to cholera and typhoid. I understand that these two men may have died of some unknown illness."

"I'm not so sure." Sherlock scrabbled in his jacket pocket and pulled out the envelope that had contained Mycroft's letter, and now contained a sample of the yellow powder. "I collected this from near one of the bodies, but I know it was present on both of them," he said in a rush. "I don't know what it is, but I think it's connected to the deaths. It might be poisonous."

The professor held out his hand for the envelope. "In that case I will treat it carefully," he said.

"You believe me?" Sherlock asked.

"You've come all this way to see me, so I assume you are taking this seriously. The least I can do is to take it as seriously as you. And besides, I know Amyus Crowe and I believe him to be a man of integrity. I cannot imagine him taking on a student who would indulge in practical jokes." He smiled suddenly, and his face was transformed into something cherubic. "Now, let's go and take a look at this sample that you've brought me."

He led the way across the hall and into another room. This one was lined with books, and had a large desk over by the window where the light was best. Sitting on a pad of green blotting paper on the desk, among scattered papers and journals and a burning candle, was a microscope.

Professor Winchcombe sat in a leather-backed chair behind his desk and gestured for Sherlock to pull up another chair by his side. He pulled a sheet of blank parchment from a drawer and put it on the blotter beside the microscope, then cautiously teased the flap of the envelope open with a paperknife and poured the contents onto the parchment. Within moments he had a pile of yellow powder in front of him. With the tip of the paperknife, he collected a few grains of the powder and transferred them to a glass slide that was already clipped to the stage—the flat plate beneath the objective lens. He adjusted a mirror beneath the stage, angling it so that it reflected the light from the candle up through a hole in the stage and through the glass slide to the lens. As Sherlock watched, trying not to breathe too hard so that he didn't disturb the powder, the professor stared into the microscope, twisting the coarse and then the fine adjustment knobs, bringing the grains into focus.

"Ah," he said, and then, "Um." He took his red hat off, scratched his head, and replaced the hat exactly where it had been.

"What is it?" Sherlock whispered.

"Bee pollen," the professor said. "Quite unmistakable."

"Bee pollen?" Sherlock repeated, not sure whether he'd heard correctly.

"Have you ever studied bees?" the professor asked, leaning back in his chair. "Fascinating creatures. I commend them to you as a subject for serious investigation." He removed his glasses and rubbed his eyes. "They collect pollen from flowers and carry it to their hive."

"What *is* pollen?" Sherlock asked, feeling strangely disappointed. "I've heard the word before, but I've never been quite sure what it meant."

"Pollen," the professor said, "is a powder consisting of microgametophytes, which produce the male gametes, or reproductive cells, of seed plants. The pollen is produced by the stamen, or male reproductive organ, of a flower and carried by the wind, or by foraging insects, to the pistill, or female reproductive organ, of another flower of a similar nature. There they fuse to form a seed." He examined his glasses, then slipped them back on his nose. Sherlock tried to sort through what the professor had told him, but realized that the man was speaking again. "In the case of bees, they collect pollen from flowers and carry it back to the hive in ball-like masses on their hind legs. The benefit to the plant, of course, is that as the bee travels from flower to flower it drops some of the pollen from the stamen of one flower onto the pistil of another, thus assisting the reproduction. Now, on the bees' upper hind legs they have minute hairs that act as a basket where the bee rolls up the pollen dust grains and mixes them with nectar to form a ball. And that is what we call 'bee pollen.'"

"And it's safe?"

"For most people, yes, although a few unfortunates do have a physical aversion to it." He leaned back and thought for a moment. "Could that have caused the boil-like swellings that Mr. Crowe described in his letter? Hmm, I doubt it. Reactions to pollen tend to be more like rashes than boils, and to find two men chosen presumably at random who have such a sensitivity would be unlikely." Suddenly he hit the desk with his hand. Sherlock jumped. "Of course! I'm ignoring the obvious answer!"

"Obvious?" Sherlock racked his brains. What was the obvious explanation for boil-like swellings when bees were involved? And then the realization burst on him like a flash of lightning. "Stings!" he cried out.

"Well done, my boy. Yes, bee stings. Very virulent stings, at that. Most bees, in this country at least, have stings that cause pain and a slight raised spot, but nothing like the boils that Mr. Crowe described." He glanced at Sherlock. "You must have seen them too. How large were they?"

Sherlock held up his right hand. "About the size of the end of my thumb," he replied.

"Indicating a very virulent strain of venom, and perhaps a very aggressive form of bee."

"How do you know so much about bees?" Sherlock asked.

The professor smiled. "I told you that I spent some years in China. The Chinese have been keeping bees for several thousand years, and I discovered that honey is highly prized by them for its medicinal benefits. According to the records in the great medical work *Bencao Gangmu*, or *The Compendium of Materia Medica*, which was written by a man named Li Shizhen three hundred years ago, honey has the ability to tone the spleen, alleviate pain, remove toxic substances, reduce vexation, brighten the eye, and prolong life." He looked away from Sherlock, towards the wall, and Sherlock got the impression that he was remembering things that had happened many years before. "Here in Great Britain we are used to the rather docile European honeybee, *Apis mellifera*. The Asian rock bee, *Apis dorsata*, is considerably more aggressive and has a much more painful sting, and yet still the Chinese keep them and harvest honey from their hives. Unlike our hives, which are shaped like bells, the

Chinese use hollowed-out logs or woven cylindrical baskets to keep the bees in. Sometimes you could see the Chinese peasants carrying their beehives up into the mountains, two at a time, slung on the end of bamboo poles that they balanced on their shoulders. I remember watching them climb, with the bees buzzing around them like a cloud of smoke."

A cloud of smoke. The words hit Sherlock like a blow between the eyes.

"*That's* what it was," he breathed.

"What?"

"I saw a shadow moving away from one of the bodies, and my friend saw the same thing coming out of a window where the other body was discovered. It must have been the bees!"

The professor nodded. "They would have had to be pretty small for you to mistake them for a shadow, and probably dark in colour, rather than the bright yellow and black of your typical bumblebee. I believe there are African bees that are small and virtually black. They too are very aggressive."

"Would you do something for me?" Sherlock asked.

"Of course."

"Would you write a letter to Amyus Crowe, telling him what you believe caused the deaths of those two men? I'll take it back to Farnham and give it to him." He looked away from the professor, feeling his face flush. "I think I'm going to be in trouble with my aunt and uncle when I get back, and that might save me from getting punished."

The professor nodded. He tipped the yellow powder—the harmless yellow powder, Sherlock had to remind himself—from the sheet of parchment onto his blotter. Reaching for an inkwell on the edge of his desk, he withdrew a quill and began to write on the parchment. His handwriting was spidery but Sherlock could just make out the words.

Dear Mr. Crowe,
I have had the pleasure of making the
acquaintance of your student—

"What is your name, young fellow?" he asked, turning to Sherlock.

"Holmes, sir. Sherlock Holmes."

Master Sherlock Holmes—who has brought
me a sample of a yellow powder that he
tells me was found near the unfortunately
deceased fellows whose demise you described
to me in your letter, which arrived this morning.
Having examined the powder, I recognize it
to be simple bee pollen, and thus I
deduce that your two men were killed not
by bubonic plague or some such illness, but by

bee stings. If you request a local Doctor to examine the supposed "boils" I suggest he will find small stingers embedded in each one, or at the very least the marks left by such stingers. I commend this young man for bringing the sample of powder to me. Had he not, rumours of a fatal fever sweeping the county might have caused great panic.

I look forward to renewing our acquaintance at some time convenient to you.

Yours sincerely,
Arthur Winchcombe, Esq (PhD)

Folding the sheet, he slipped it into an envelope that he took from a drawer of the desk, sealed the envelope with a blob of wax from the candle that he had been using to illuminate the microscope, and handed the envelope to Sherlock.

"I trust this will save you from too painful a punishment," he said. "Please convey my respects to your tutor."

"I will." Sherlock paused, then continued: "Thank you."

Professor Winchcombe rang a small bell that sat on the blotter by the microscope. "My butler will show you out. If you want to know anything more about tropical diseases, beekeeping, or China, feel free to call on me again."

Outside, Sherlock was surprised to see that the sun hadn't changed its position in the sky by more than a few degrees. It had felt as if he had been in Professor Winchcombe's house for hours.

Matty was sitting on the garden wall. He was eating something from a paper cone. "Done what you came for?" he asked.

Sherlock nodded. He gestured towards the cone of paper. "What have you got there?"

"Cockles and winkles," the boy replied. He tipped the mouth of the cone towards Sherlock. "Want some?"

Inside the cone, Sherlock saw a pile of seashells. "Are they cooked?" he asked.

"Boiled," Matty replied succinctly. "I found a fishmonger's stall. He was selling them. Prob'ly came up from Portsmouth overnight. I helped out for a while, tidying up his boxes, fetching more ice and stuff. He gave me a twist of them in payment." He reached into the cone and picked out a shell. Resting the cone on the wall, he retrieved a folding knife from his pocket and fiddled around inside the shell with the point, spearing whatever was inside. After a few seconds he pulled out something dark and rubbery, then popped it into his mouth. "Lovely," he beamed. "Don't get these very often, 'less you live near the sea. Bit of a treat when you do."

"I think I'll pass," Sherlock said. "Let's go home."

This time they walked down the High Street to the river, then walked along the riverbank until they found the narrowboat. As Matty had predicted, both it and the horse were still there. Sherlock wondered how they were going to turn the narrowboat round, but Matty led the horse along the bank towards town until they got to a bridge, then led the horse across the bridge to the other side, pulling the nose of the boat round while Sherlock used the boathook to stop it hitting the banks on either side. And then it was a case of making their slow way back, Sherlock in front this time, keeping the horse moving, and Matty in the back operating the tiller.

The two boys talked as the boat slowly moved downstream. Sherlock told Matty about Professor Winchcombe and his explanation concerning the bees and the stings. Matty was dubious at first, but Sherlock eventually persuaded him that no supernatural explanation was required for the cloud of death. Matty seemed to be caught between relief that the plague hadn't come to Farnham and irritation that the explanation was so prosaic. Sherlock didn't say anything, but as they travelled he became more and more certain that they had just removed one mystery to reveal another. Why had the bees stung those two men in different locations but nobody else? Why were African bees in England in the first place? And what did any of this have to do with the warehouse, the boxes that had been loaded onto the cart by the ruffians, and the mysterious Baron?

After a while, Sherlock became aware that another horse had joined theirs on the riverbank. It was a glossy black stallion with a brown patch on its neck, and Virginia Crowe was riding it. She was still wearing riding breeches and a blouse, with a jacket over the top.

"Hello!" Sherlock called. She waved back.

"Matty, this is Virginia Crowe," he called over his shoulder. "Virginia, this is Matthew Arnatt. Matty."

Matty nodded at Virginia, and she nodded at him, but neither said anything.

Sherlock stood, balanced precariously on the bows of the boat for a moment, feeling it rock beneath him, and jumped to the bank. He took Matty's horse's rope collar and guided him forward, walking alongside Virginia and her horse.

"This is Albert," he said eventually.

"This is Sandia," Virginia replied. "You really should learn to ride, you know."

Sherlock shook his head. "Never had the chance."

"It's simple, but you fellows always make a fuss over how difficult it is. Guide with your knees, not the reins. Use the reins for slowing the horse down."

Sherlock couldn't think of a suitable response to that. They kept walking in awkward silence for a while.

"Where have you been?" Virginia asked eventually.

"Guildford. There was someone I wanted to see." Remembering, he delved into his jacket and took out the letter that Professor Winchcombe had written. "I need to get this to your father. Do you know where he is?"

"Still looking for you. You were supposed to have a lesson."

Sherlock glanced at her to see whether she was serious, but there was a slight smile on her lips. She looked down at him, and he turned his face away.

"Give me the letter," she said. "I'll see he gets it."

He held the letter out to her, then pulled it back. "It's important," he said hesitantly. "It's about the two men who died."

"Then I'll see he gets it straightaway." She took the letter from his outstretched hand. Her fingers didn't touch his, but he could almost imagine that he felt their heat as they passed close. "Those men died of the plague, didn't they? That's what people are saying."

"It's not the plague. It was bees. That's why I had to go into Guildford—I needed to talk to an expert in diseases." He realized he was talking faster, but he couldn't seem to stop himself. "I found a yellow powder near both bodies. I wanted someone to tell me what it was, so I took some of it into Guildford. It turns out it was pollen. That's why we decided that bees were responsible."

"But you didn't know that when you found the powder," Virginia pointed out.

"No."

"Or when you collected the powder and carried it all the way to Guildford."

"No."

"For all you knew, it might have been something that *caused* the plague. Something contagious."

Sherlock felt he was being backed into a corner. "Yes," he said, drawing the word out to something that sounded more like "Ye-e-e-s."

"So you risked your life based on the fact that you thought everyone else was wrong and you could *prove* them wrong."

"I suppose so." He felt obscurely embarrassed. She was right—getting to the bottom of the mystery had been more important to him than his own safety. He might have been wrong—he didn't know much about diseases or how they were transmitted. The yellow powder might have been something the men's bodies had produced as a result of an illness, like dry, infected skin—something that could have contained the disease and passed it on. He'd been so consumed by puzzle-solving that he hadn't thought of that.

The rest of the journey back to Farnham was conducted in silence.

NINE

"You disappoint me, boy."

Sherrinford Holmes was sitting at the massive oak desk in his study, Amyus Crowe stood behind his left shoulder, and Mrs. Eglantine stood behind his right shoulder, her black clothes blending so well with the shadows that only her face and hands were visible. What with Uncle Sherrinford's long white beard and the various Hebrew, Greek, Latin, and English Bibles that were stacked all over his desk it was, Sherlock reflected, like being disciplined by God, with two avenging angels standing behind his throne, an effect spoilt only by the fact that Uncle Sherrinford was wearing his dressing gown over his suit.

Sherlock's face burned with shame and with anger. He wanted to protest that he'd done what he did for the best reasons, but one look at his uncle's face told him that arguing wouldn't help. "I'm sorry, sir," he said after a long moment passed and he realized that his uncle was awaiting a response. "I won't do it again."

"Your brother—my nephew—entrusted you into my care, with an understanding that I would continue with your moral education and prevent you from falling into bad company or bad ways. I am mortified to find that I have failed in both of those tasks."

Another long pause. Sherlock felt under pressure to say that he was sorry again, but he had a feeling that repeating himself would be taken as a sign that he was being cheeky. "I know that I shouldn't have gone all the way into Guildford by myself," he said eventually.

"That is the least of your trespasses," Uncle Sherrinford pronounced. "This very morning you crept out of this house before the sun was up like a common criminal—"

"His bed wasn't even slept in," Mrs. Eglantine interrupted. "He must have left before midnight."

Sherlock could feel his shoulders trembling with the effort of keeping his anger in check. He knew that she was lying—he *had* slept, for a few hours, and had left just before dawn—but he couldn't contradict her despite a burning desire to tell the truth. She was trying to get him deeper into trouble, and arguing with her would just be taken as defiance and punished appropriately.

"I will write to your brother," Sherrinford continued, "telling him that the trust I placed in you has been betrayed. And you will not be allowed to leave this house for the next week."

"If I may," Amyus Crowe drawled from behind Sherrinford, "I'd like to say a word or two on the boy's behalf." He reached into his dazzlingly white jacket and removed an envelope. "The letter that the boy brought back from the eminent Professor Winchcombe has calmed fears of an outbreak of bubonic plague in the area. Taking that sample of pollen to be identified shows evidence of a strong will, an independent turn of mind, and a reluctance to take things on trust—all attributes that should be encouraged, I would say."

"Are you suggesting that the boy should escape punishment, Mr. Crowe?" Mrs. Eglantine asked in a silky voice.

"Not at all," Crowe rejoined. "I would suggest that rather than ban him from leavin' the house entirely, you make it so that the only time he can leave is with me. That way *I* can continue to uphold the agreement I made with his brother."

Sherrinford Holmes considered for a moment, stroking his beard with his right hand. Then, "Very well," he pronounced. "We will effect a compromise. You are confined to this house for the rest of this day and the next. Following that, you will stay in this house at all times except when you are being tutored by Mr. Crowe. When in the house you are to stay in your room except for mealtimes." His lips twitched. "Although I will allow you to take any books you wish from my library to pass the time. Use them wisely to improve yourself, and to reflect upon your actions."

"I will, sir," Sherlock said, having to force the words out. The tension in his shoulders eased somewhat. "Thank you, sir."

"Now go, and do not return until dinner."

Sherlock turned and left the study. He desperately

wanted to argue, to point out that what he had done had been *right*, but he knew enough about the way the adult world worked to realize that arguing would just make things worse. *Right* didn't matter. *Obeying the rules* did.

He headed up the wide, carpeted stairs to the first floor, then the narrower wooden ones to the eaves, where his room was located. He lay on his bed, staring at the ceiling, letting his thoughts churn and roil inside his head.

The rest of that day and the whole of the next passed in a blur. Sherlock's body, tired and battered by his adventures, took the opportunity to repair itself through as much sleep as it could get, but when he was awake he found his thoughts fluttering aimlessly, like moths around a candle flame. What was going on? What exactly was Baron Maupertuis planning, and who was going to stop it?

He spent some time trying to compose a letter in his head to his brother, not because he expected Mycroft to do anything but because he wanted to tell someone he trusted what had been happening. Eventually, when he had got the wording the way he wanted it, he set it down on paper.

Dear Mycroft,
*   I wish I could tell you that I have been following your advice, and throwing myself into a mixture of studies in Uncle Sherrinford's library and ramblings around*

the local countryside, but I seem to have got myself into trouble and I do not know what to do next. The good news—if there is any—is that I have made two friends. One of them is called Matthew Arnatt, and he lives on a narrowboat on the canal. I think you might like him. The other is Virginia Crowe. She is the daughter of Amyus Crowe, who says he is teaching me about nature and about observing the world around me, but I think he is actually teaching me how to think. I wish you had not thought it necessary to find a tutor for me during the holidays, but of all the tutors you might have found I think Mr. Crowe is the best.

Strange things have been happening here in Farnham, and I wish I could talk to you about them. A man's body was discovered in town, covered in swellings, and another here in the grounds of Holmes Manor. The townspeople thought it might be the plague, but a man named Professor Winchcombe proved that they were killed by hundreds of bee stings. I think the bees are somehow connected to a man named Baron Maupertuis, who owns a warehouse in Farnham, but I do not know how. The warehouse burned down, destroying any evidence. I will tell you how that happened when I see you.

In short, life here is more interesting than I expected—when I can get out of the house. I am presently confined to my room for having gone to Guildford to see Professor Winchcombe, but that is another story that I will tell you when I see you.

Is there any news of Father? Is he still on his way to India, and do you have any more information on when the problems there might be over?

Give my love to Mother and our sister. Please visit soon.

Your brother,
Sherlock

After finishing and blotting the letter, he left it on the table in the hall at lunchtime, to be collected by a maid and delivered to the post office in Farnham. When he came down again for tea the letter was gone. Mrs. Eglantine was passing through the hall, her face appearing to float in the shadows, and she smiled mirthlessly at him. Had she seen the letter? Had she *read* it? Had it even made it as far as the post office, or had she destroyed it? Sherlock told himself that he was being foolish—what reasons did she have for doing that?—but Mycroft's warning echoed in his head. *She is no friend to the Holmes family.*

As he lay in his room, these thoughts kept running through his mind. The distant gong for dinner broke him out of a half doze, and he headed down to the ground floor. Mrs. Eglantine was just leaving the dining room. She glanced at him with a sneer on her lips and walked away.

Sherlock didn't feel hungry. He stared at the door for a few moments, trying to will himself to eat something just to keep his strength up, but he couldn't face it. He turned round and began to head across to the library to see if he could find any books about bees or beekeeping.

Halfway across the hall, he noticed a letter on the silver platter on the side table. Had it not been there before, or had he just not noticed it? For a moment he thought it might be another letter from Mycroft, so he picked it up. His name was on the front, along with the address of the manor house, but it wasn't Mycroft's writing. It was more rounded. More . . . feminine. How could that be?

Sherlock looked around, half-convinced that he would find Mrs. Eglantine standing in the shadows, watching, but the hall was empty apart from him. He took the letter, opened the front door, and stood in the early evening sunlight but still in the doorway so that he couldn't be accused of leaving the house.

There was a single sheet of paper inside. It was a pale lavender in colour. On it, below his name and address, was written:

> Sherlock,
> There is a fair being held on the meadow below the castle grounds. Meet me there tomorrow at nine o'clock in the morning—if you dare!
>
> Come alone.
> Virginia

He felt dizzy for a moment, and took a deep breath. Virginia wanted to see him? But why? On the two occasions they'd met up he'd got the impression that she didn't like him that much. They certainly hadn't said very much to each other. And yet, now she wanted to meet him—alone?

But he couldn't go! He'd been forbidden to leave the house!

His thoughts raced, trying to come up with a justification that would allow him out of the house the next morning without getting into trouble. Surely there had to be a logical argument that he could construct that would stand up to scrutiny by Uncle Sherrinford. Virginia had asked him to meet her. From what little he knew about her, he could tell that she was more independent than English girls of her age. She could ride a horse—properly, not just sidesaddle—and she was perfectly capable of going off on her own. But if she had been English, she wouldn't have been going to the fair if she wasn't with her family. And that meant it would be reasonable for Sherlock to interpret the letter as being an invitation to meet her *and her father,* which meant he could leave the house without violating the terms of his agreement with his uncle. Sherrinford would not believe that a girl could arrange to meet a boy without her family being present. Sherlock knew better, but if challenged he wouldn't let on.

A momentary thought threw him—what if someone

from Holmes Manor was at the fair?—but a further thought persuaded him that neither his uncle, his aunt, nor Mrs. Eglantine was likely to be there, and if any of the maids or cooks or workers were there they probably wouldn't even recognize him.

He spent the rest of the evening and much of the night alternately convincing himself that he should go next morning and that he shouldn't. By the morning he still wasn't sure, but as he came down the stairs for breakfast he found himself thinking about Virginia's face, and he decided that he would. He really would.

He checked the time on the grandfather clock. It was a little after eight o'clock. If he started now, and used the bicycle, he could just about get there in time. He knew where the castle was—perched on a hill above the town—and he guessed that the common was a patch of meadow a short distance below the castle.

Should he leave a note? After recent events, he thought it might be wise, so he dashed off a quick explanation on the back of the envelope, saying that he was off to see Amyus Crowe, and left it on the silver platter, then half walked and half ran to where he had left the bicycle, ducking beneath the windows as he passed them and staying behind walls wherever possible.

His head was whirling with thoughts and speculations as he rode. He had never really had a proper female friend before. There was his sister, of course, but she was older than him, and her interests were different—painting, crocheting, playing the piano. And, of course, there was her illness, which had kept her secluded and bedridden for large parts of Sherlock's childhood. He'd never really made friends with anyone in the area around his parents' house, let alone with girls, and Deepdene School was a school for boys. He wasn't entirely sure how to behave with Virginia, what to talk about or how to act.

Cycling into Farnham, he took a side road that headed uphill, towards the castle that he could see perched above the town. He struggled on until his legs began to burn, then dismounted and walked, pushing the bicycle beside him. By the time he got to the castle grounds, he was exhausted.

Spread out across the meadow, illuminated by the morning sun, Sherlock could see a cross section of human life. Like a miniature town in its own right, booths and rope-edged rings had been set up on either side of broad, grassy alleys down which people were wandering and pointing out the sights. A haze of smoke hung above everything, and the smells of cooking meat, animal dung, and people made Sherlock's nose itch. There were areas for jugglers, for boxing, for stick-duelling, and for dog fights. Mountebanks were selling patent medicines made from who knows what, fire-eaters were pushing flaming coals on metal prongs into their mouths, and locals were pulling grotesque faces for the prize of a hat, racing for the prize of a nightgown, and eating hasty puddings with a cash prize for the one who could eat the most.

He scanned the crowd, looking for Virginia's distinctive copper hair, but there were so many people that he couldn't tell one person from another. She hadn't specified where to meet, so his only options were to wait and hope she came to him or to dive into the crowd looking for her. And he had never been very good at waiting.

With some trepidation, Sherlock left his bicycle leaning against a fence on one side of the paddock. He wasn't entirely sure it would be there when he returned, but the sheer press of people meant that he wasn't going to be able to keep it with him.

The first thing he came to as he walked across the meadow was a large barrel filled to the brim with water. People were clustered around it, laughing and urging each other on. The surface of the water appeared to be boiling, leading Sherlock to suspect that something was being cooked inside, but there was no fire underneath. One of the crowd, a thin youth with a spotted handkerchief knotted around his neck, was trying to impress a rosy-cheeked girl in a white frock who stood beside him. He handed a coin over to the man who apparently owned the barrel, grasped the sides with both hands, and abruptly thrust his head into the water.

Sherlock gasped, still half-convinced that the water was boiling, but the boy seemed to be coming to no harm. He was wiggling his head from side to side in the water, apparently searching for something, darting it forward every few seconds and then pulling it back. At last he withdrew his head entirely. Water streamed down his face and neck and onto his clothes, but he didn't seem to care. There was something clenched between his teeth—something silvery that wriggled frantically, trying to escape. For a moment Sherlock couldn't work out what it was, and then he realized. It was an eel, barely longer than a man's finger. Sherlock moved on, amazed. He'd heard of bobbing for apples, but bobbing for eels? Incredible.

"See the most extraordinary sheep in the world!" a barker cried from in front of a booth. "See a sheep with four legs and the half of a fifth 'un. You'll never see another one like it!" He caught Sherlock's gaze as the boy passed by. "You, young sir—see the most amazing sight on God's green earth. You'll never forget it. Girls will hang on your every word as you describe the incredible sheep with four legs and half of a fifth 'un."

He passed a booth where two puppets were on display in a window, operated by a puppeteer whose body was hidden inside the booth. Their heads were carved out of wood, with exaggerated noses and chins, and their clothes were made out of bright ribbons. As Sherlock watched, one puppet laid its head on the edge of the window—nearly doubling up to do so—and the other puppet then instantly chopped it off with a miniature axe. The head fell away and bright red ribbons exploded outward, simulating the spurting of blood. The crowd cheered and waved their hats.

There was a pond over to one side of the fair, and a duck being thrown in by a man in a brightly coloured waistcoat and top hat. Its leg was tied to a weight by a thin length of cord, and the weight was holding it down. Around the edge of the pond, dogs were snarling and slavering at the end of ropes and leather leashes. Seeing money being exchanged all around the crowd, Sherlock had a terrible feeling that he knew what was coming next. The man in the waistcoat stepped backwards and raised his hand. The crowd grew quiet, expectant. The dogs redoubled their efforts to get free, and their growling was enough to cause the ground to shake. The man's hand dropped to his waist, and the dogs were let loose by their owners. As a mass they plunged into the pond, trying to seize the quacking bird and sending water spraying everywhere. Terrified, the duck fluttered back and forth across the water as far as the cord and the weight would let it, evading their lunges. For their part the dogs avoided going too far out of their depth, with the exception of one brave terrier that paddled frantically across the pond, chasing the duck. Sherlock turned away before it sank its teeth into the duck's neck. It was a foregone conclusion, the only uncertainty being which owner would win the prize.

Sickened, Sherlock turned away.

He walked past stalls selling hot sausages and cold

toffee-covered apples on sticks, orange-flavoured biscuits, and puffy, salted pork crackling. He wasn't sure if the feeling he had in his stomach was hunger or nervousness. Or both.

The crowd was growing thicker and more raucous, and Sherlock felt himself pushed and jostled from behind. People around him were jeering and grumbling. A voice rose above them, shouting: "Who will take on the undefeated champion? Who has the courage to pit themselves against Nat Wilson, the Kensal Green Wonder? A sovereign if you win; nothing but scorn and derision if you lose!" Sherlock stumbled to one knee. Pulling himself to his feet, he was knocked sideways. Something hard slammed into his back. He turned, and found that he was suddenly at the front of the crowd. The thing that he had stumbled against was a wooden pole, one of four that marked out the corners of a square. Ropes had been strung between the poles. A man wearing nothing but leather breeches stood in the centre of the ring, posturing and gesturing to the crowd. His chest and arms were corded with muscle. Another man, this one in a dusty suit and a battered hat, was staring straight at Sherlock.

"We have a challenger!" he cried. The crowd applauded.

Sherlock tried to back away, but people were pushing him from behind. Hands pulled the ropes apart to form a gap, and Sherlock was pushed through into the grassy enclosure.

"No!" he shouted, realizing that somehow *he* was the challenger. "I don't—"

The barker cut across him. "Standard Broughton Rules," he chanted. "No padding and no knuckledusters. Anything goes except hitting a man when he's down. When a man *is* down he gets thirty seconds to rest and eight additional seconds to come to scratch. The fight is over when one man can't stand up." He glanced at Sherlock, who was looking wildly around, trying to find a gap in the crowd through which he could escape. "Kid," he murmured, "I don't rate you for more than a minute unaided. If you can last five, I'll double the prize. Got to keep the punters entertained."

"I shouldn't be here!" protested Sherlock.

"It's a little late for that," the barker replied.

"But this is an accident!"

"No." The barker smiled, revealing black, rotting teeth. "This is a massacre."

The barker headed for the side of the ring, where more people held the ropes apart for him. Sherlock tried to follow him, but the ropes snapped back up into place and the men, women, and children in the crowd jeered as he approached. Stones were flung at him, causing him to back away into the centre of the ring.

The other fighter strode over, his gaze flickering around the crowd and drawing their applause. He was at least six inches taller than Sherlock, and bigger around the chest. His hands looked like two leather bags filled with walnuts. "Up to scratch," he grunted.

"What?"

The fighter indicated two parallel lines that had been cut into the grass, about three feet apart. "You stand behind one; I stand behind the other. When the bell goes, we fight. That's the way it goes."

"I don't want to fight," Sherlock protested.

"That's your choice, boy," the fighter snarled. "I still got to make it last five minutes, an' your head'll look like minced meat if you don't protect yourself." He eyed Sherlock critically. "An' it'll prob'ly look that way even if you do," he added. He shoved Sherlock towards the nearest line in the grass. "Hands up, protect your face. An' keep standin' up. If you fall, I'll kick you till you stand again."

"I thought the referee said no hitting a man when he was down."

The fighter shrugged. "Didn't say nothin' about kickin'."

Sherlock, disbelieving, moved to his mark. The fighter stood with his booted feet on the other line. Sherlock glanced around, looking for someone, anyone who might help, but the faces looking back at him were flushed, sweaty, and distorted by aggression. There was no way out.

A bell rang.

Sherlock stepped back just as his opponent's fist

swished past his nose. He brought his hands up to defend himself, backing away as the other man stepped forward. The crowd roared. He'd seen pictures of boxers in books, watched a few fights in the Deepdene gymnasium, even sparred a little himself, and he took up the position that he remembered—hands clenched into fists and held high in front of him—but his opponent obviously hadn't read the same books and lumbered forward, swinging his arms in sideways from shoulder height. Sherlock took a blow to his own left shoulder—the one that Clem had hurt the other night—and felt agony pouring down his arm like liquid metal. His hand dropped uselessly to his side. How had this happened? Only a minute ago he'd been anonymous in the crowd, and now he was the centre of all attention! It was almost as if something, *someone*, had been guiding the crowd, pushing them to this very moment.

The fighter stepped closer, ready to punch upward into Sherlock's face, so Sherlock stepped backwards and lashed out with his right fist. Incredibly, he connected with the man's nose. He felt something crack under his fingers, and blood waterfalled down the man's chin and chest. The other fighter jerked back and breathed out explosively, spraying blood over Sherlock's shirt, then punched his right hand straight out into Sherlock's chest. The impact knocked Sherlock backwards. Pain radiated across his ribs. For a moment he thought his heart had stopped. He tried breathing in, but his lungs wouldn't work. He bent double, trying to force some air into his throat. A hand grabbed him by the back of the neck and threw him across the grass. The impact of his body on the ground forced the last remnants of air from his lungs, and he was suddenly sucking great breaths again. He rolled away as a foot smashed into the ground where his head had been, and scrambled to his feet.

The other fighter's face was a mask of blood, broken only by two narrowed and furious eyes and the snarling line of his teeth. He stepped towards Sherlock and punched twice, left hand to Sherlock's ribs and right hand to the side of Sherlock's head. Pain filled Sherlock's world, red and raw. Everything seemed so far away. He was falling, but he didn't feel the impact as he hit the ground.

Darkness claimed him, and he went willingly.

TEN

When Sherlock woke up, his head was aching. The pain seemed to be centred around his right temple, and it pulsed sickeningly in time with his heartbeat. It was like a massive soft, throbbing lump that he couldn't see past and couldn't climb past. He lay in the dark for a while, not thinking, but just drifting back and forth with the pain, waiting for it to recede. Eventually, it did.

The last thing he remembered was being knocked unconscious on the meadow beneath Farnham Castle by the fairground fighter. And now he was in a comfortable bed, with his head supported by feather pillows. That meant he wasn't still at the fairground, lying on the muddy grass ring or bundled into a tent to recover. Unless, of course, he was hallucinating, which was a distinct possibility given the fact that he'd suffered a head wound.

No, he told himself firmly: he had to work on the assumption that what he was feeling, hearing, and seeing was true, and not just some fabrication of a bruised brain.

The diffuse light filtering through the curtained windows told him that it was still morning. He wasn't in his own bed; that was for sure. His own bed was harder, and his pillows were lumpier. He must have been found by someone from Holmes Manor and brought back there, but left in a more comfortable bed: one that the doctor and the maids could get to more easily, perhaps. He strained, trying to hear movement outside the window, but there was nothing apart from what might have been distant birdsong.

How much trouble was he in? The thought brought an unplanned groan to his lips. He'd disobeyed his uncle's clear instructions, and he suspected that any attempt to explain that he thought he was meeting Amyus Crowe would be dealt with harshly. Worse, he had become involved in a common fistfight. Worse than *that*, he had lost. That might not have concerned Sherrinford or Anna Holmes, but if Sherlock's father ever got to hear about it he would be furious. One of his favourite sayings was: "A gentleman never starts a fight, but he always finishes it."

If he was lucky, his uncle would confine him to his room for the next month, and restrict his meals to bread and water. If he was lucky. If he was *un*lucky . . . well, he wasn't sure, but he suspected that the punishment would be dire. A thrashing, perhaps? A beating with a cane or a leather belt? His uncle would probably do it in sorrow rather than in anger, but wasn't there some Biblical quotation about "spare the rod and spoil the child"?

This wasn't going to be good.

Sherlock reached up to touch his head. His fingers

encountered swelling, and when he pressed against it a spike of pain shot through him.

He sat up cautiously. Neither his head nor his stomach was happy at the movement, but they didn't complain too much.

The room he was in was lined with wood panelling, and the bed was a four-poster with an embroidered canopy overhead. It wasn't one he was familiar with, and the decoration looked out of step with what he remembered from Holmes Manor. He looked down at himself. He was still dressed, although his jacket had been removed. He glanced around and found it hanging from a clothes hanger on the back of the door.

Throwing back the sheet that covered him, he pushed himself gradually upright. The world seemed to slosh back and forth for a few moments like water in a bucket before stabilizing. His shoes had been removed, but he saw that they were sitting together at the bottom of the bed. He lurched across to them and did his best to slip his feet into them without bending over. Bending over would be a bad idea, he thought.

He crossed to the window and drew back the curtain, but the view that greeted his eyes was nothing at all like the landscape around Holmes Manor.

The ground outside was flat and barren, denuded of grass or plants. The earth was reddish brown and dry, and as far as the eye could see it was covered in wooden boxes on four sturdy legs. They were a bit like chicken coops but smaller, and each one had a small hole at the bottom, just before the point where a wooden base separated the box from its supports. The boxes were spaced apart in a regular grid. A quick multiplication in Sherlock's mind told him that he was staring at something like five hundred boxes.

Smoke seemed to be curling above some of the boxes, but the wind must have been eddying in strange ways because the smoke from different boxes was moving in different directions. Some of the plumes were trailing upward, some to the left and some to the right, and some were just hanging around the entrance to the boxes as if trying to get in or out.

A figure moved from behind one of the boxes. It was clad in a loose one-piece overall that seemed to be made of canvas, and its head was covered in a mask made of muslin thin enough to see through, held away from its face by wooden hoops. The figure moved to another box and carefully lifted the lid. More smoke puffed outward and enveloped its head. It didn't seem to mind. It bent closer, gazing into the box, then closed the lid again and pulled what looked like a wooden tray from underneath. The figure gazed at it for a few seconds, then walked a few steps and placed the tray onto a pile of similar ones.

His brain finally waking up properly, Sherlock realized what he was watching. The cloud he had seen leaving the body of the man in the woods around Holmes Manor, the smoke Matty had witnessed, the pollen he'd taken to Professor Winchcombe—it was finally making sense. This was not smoke but bees. Small black bees. And that meant the boxes were beehives and the man in the mask was a beekeeper.

But what kind of bees were they, and what were they for? Making honey? Defence? Or something else?

More important, where in heaven's name was he?

Behind him, the door to the bedroom opened. He turned quickly. Two men were standing inside the doorway. They were dressed in immaculate black velvet clothes of an old-fashioned cut—breeches, stockings, waistcoats, and short jackets—and their faces were covered with black velvet masks with slits cut in at eye level for them to see through.

One of them gestured over his shoulder. His meaning was clear—Sherlock was to go with them. For a moment he rebelled—he'd never been good at following orders given with no explanation—but a moment's thought suggested that if he didn't do what they said then they would just pick him up and carry him. And they probably wouldn't be careful either.

It also occurred to him that going with them was probably the only way to find out what was going on.

Heart pounding, but keeping a calm, even bored expression on his face, Sherlock walked over to the door. The two footmen backed away to let him through.

The hall outside the bedroom door was opulently

decorated in rich reds and purples, with a distinctive coat of arms woven into the wallpaper and embroidered on the velvet curtains. One footman led Sherlock down a wide flight of white marble stairs, while the other one followed behind. Sherlock's footsteps were the only noise: the footmen's shoes were muffled and barely produced a whisper on the treads.

At the bottom of the stairs the first footman led Sherlock towards a closed door beside a heavy teak cabinet. He pulled it towards him, and gestured Sherlock through. With only a moment's hesitation, the boy complied.

The door shut behind him with a faint but definitive *thud*.

The room inside the doorway was large, shadowy, and cool. All the windows were covered with thick curtains. Only a few diagonal shafts of light penetrated the gloom, and in their meagre light Sherlock could just make out one end of a massive wooden table with a heavy chair set in front of it. All else was darkness apart from the glint of what might have been objects made of metal hanging on the stone walls.

It seemed obvious what was expected of him. Feeling nervous beads of sweat trickling down his back, he walked forward and sat in the chair.

For a long while there was silence, apart from the rapid beating of his heart. He strained his eyes against the darkness, but he couldn't make out anything other than the surface of the table immediately in front of him. And then, gradually, he began to distinguish a faint noise: a rhythmic creaking, like the rigging of a ship as it pitched and tossed on the waves of some phantom ocean. It seemed to come and go, almost as if a faint breeze were pushing intermittently against canvas, and pulling the wet ropes tight and then letting them hang loose again. He couldn't work out what it was. Surely he couldn't be on a ship? He'd seen ground outside the bedroom window, and the floor wasn't rising and falling. So what was that noise?

"You were at the warehouse." A man's voice, barely more than a whisper, spoke from the darkness at the other end of the table. There seemed to be a trace of an accent there—the word "the" came out more like "zee"—but Sherlock couldn't work out which country the speaker hailed from. "*Why* were you at the warehouse?"

"Who are you?" Sherlock said firmly, his voice underpinned by a bravado that he didn't feel.

"*Why* were you at the warehouse?" the voice persisted. Sherlock had to strain to make out the words above the creaking.

"My uncle will be worried about me," Sherlock blustered. "There will be search parties out, looking." He didn't know if that was true or not, but it seemed like a good thing to say. It might throw his mysterious interrogator off his stride.

"I will only ask you once more, and then there will be consequences. *Why* were you at the warehouse?"

"I don't know what you're talking about."

Something came flashing out of the darkness, thin and black and uncurling like a striking snake. It caught his right cheek before withdrawing into the dark. He flinched, feeling blood trickling down his skin a moment before the pain blossomed through his flesh.

"*Why* were you at the warehouse?" the voice insisted.

Sherlock touched his hand to his burning cheek, then took it away and looked at it. Blood stained the lines on his palm. "You hurt me," he said, not quite believing it.

The whip flicked out of the darkness again. This time he caught sight of the tip just as it whistled past his face. There was a knot in the thin leather lace. The *crack* of the knot hitting its full extent and pulling back coincided with the agony of it slicing through the top of his right ear. He cried out, clapping a hand to the side of his head. This time he could feel blood pooling in his palm and trickling down his wrist.

"*Why*—"

"I followed a man from a house in Farnham!" Sherlock yelled. "He went to the warehouse!"

The voice was silent for a moment, thinking. Then: "Why were you following the man from the house?"

Blood from Sherlock's ear was wet and warm against his neck now. The whole right side of his face throbbed sickeningly. "Someone died in that house. I wanted to find out how."

"They died from the plague, surely?" the voice whispered. "That's what people are saying,"

Sherlock bit his tongue before he could say anything about the bee stings, but the whip lashed out of the darkness again and bit into his forehead above his left eye. His head jerked back against the chair, sending waves of agony crashing through his skull. When he tried to open his eye he found it was glued shut by blood dripping down from the cut that had been laid open.

If he kept on like this his head would be slashed to ribbons.

"He died of bee stings," he shouted. "Hundreds of bee stings."

Silence. The pain from the three slashes in Sherlock's skin flowed together into one red-hot centre of agony that throbbed with the rapid beating of his heart.

"Who else knows about the bees?"

"Just me!" he lied.

Again the whip *cracked* out of the shadows like a striking serpent, hitting just to the side of his left eye, a hair's breadth from cutting into the soft jelly of the eyeball itself. Blood flecked his eyelashes: black globules hanging in his field of vision.

"The next time my whip-master strikes, he will blind you in your left eye," the voice said. "The time after that he will remove your right ear. Answer my questions fully, and do not lie to me."

My whip-master? Sherlock thought. That meant whoever was asking the questions and whoever was handling the whip were two different people. How many more were hidden there, in the darkness, watching and listening?

"I already know some of the answers to the questions that I ask you," the whispering voice went on, "and if your answers are different then you will suffer, both now and for the rest of your life. Who else knows about the bees?"

"Professor Winchcombe in Guildford and Amyus Crowe in Farnham." Sherlock's voice was trembling with the effort of keeping the pain under control. "My uncle Sherrinford. Amyus Crowe told the local doctor. I don't know who else." Deliberately, Sherlock left Matthew Arnatt's name off the list, hoping that the man in the shadows didn't know about him, or was discounting him as anyone important.

"Too many," the voice said. Sherlock got the impression that it was talking to itself rather than him. Or perhaps to someone else, someone who was remaining silent. "We must accelerate the operation." A pause, as if the man behind the voice was thinking, and then: "Take the boy away and kill him. Make it look like an accident. Run him over with a horse and cart. Make sure the wheels crush his neck."

Sherlock had a sudden horrific vision of the dead badger he had seen outside the warehouse—the one whose midriff had been flattened by a passing cart. And now the same thing was going to happen to him.

Hands grabbed his shoulders and hauled him out of the chair. He stumbled across to the door, pushed by the two footmen who had been standing silently behind him all this time. His mind flashed through a kaleidoscope of ideas for how to escape, but all of them depended on the first step of getting away from those clutching, pushing hands. Light suddenly spilt across the three of them as the door opened outward, pushed by one of the footmen who had momentarily released Sherlock's shoulder. Sherlock turned, lashing out with a foot, hoping to hurt the other one enough that he would let him go, but his shoe just connected with the side of a leather boot and bounced off. A fist lashed out and cuffed the side of his head. Galaxies of light pinwheeled across his vision.

The door to the darkened room closed behind them, revealing Matty Arnatt standing there, holding a studded metal club. It looked like something an old-fashioned knight would have used on the field of battle.

He whacked it down on the head of the nearest footman. The man fell with all the grace of a sack of coal flung into a cellar. The other footman let go of Sherlock and took a step towards Matty, scowling, his burly hand reaching for Matty's head. Sherlock stepped around him and punched him hard in the groin. The man folded, gasping for breath.

"This way," Matty hissed, gesturing to Sherlock to follow him.

The two of them raced through the corridors of an

unfamiliar house, all dark oak panels and black velvet curtains and startlingly white alabaster statues of naked Greek nymphs.

"Where did you get that mace?" Sherlock yelled as they ran. He could hear sounds of pursuit behind them.

"There's suits of armour and stuff all over the house," Matty called back over his shoulder. "I just took it."

"And what are you *doing* here?"

"I was at the fair. I saw how you got suckered into that fight. I went to help, but you were being dragged off by two big coves. They threw you into the back of a cart and drove you here. I hung on to the back of the cart where they couldn't see me, and then hopped off when it turned into this place. I've been looking for you ever since."

"Right," Sherlock gasped. "Where *are* we?"

" 'Bout three miles from Farnham. Other side from Holmes Manor." Matty led the way through an unremarkable door into what was probably the servants' area, and from there to a bare brick corridor that led to a door into the garden. They emerged into blessedly fresh air and bright sunlight.

"And you didn't bring the bicycles?"

"How could I?" Matty shouted, affronted. "I was hanging off the back of a cart! I could hardly carry them, could I?"

"Good point!" Sherlock glanced around as they ran. They were at the back of the house. Instead of a garden, past a wide paved veranda and a short wall was the field full of beehives that he had seen earlier. "So how are we going to get out?"

"I found a stable, didn't I," Matty said, still aggrieved. "There's 'orses!"

"I can't ride!"

Behind them, three men wearing black masks and black clothes erupted from an open set of glazed doors that probably led into a drawing room. They scattered in different directions. One of them saw Sherlock and Matty and let out a yell.

Matty scowled at Sherlock. "Well, you ain't got much time to learn, mate!" he said.

Matty led the way round the corner of the house. A large barn lay ahead of them. The two boys raced across the open ground, hearing the rapid *thump thump thump* of running footsteps from behind them. They got to the barn and sprinted in through the open doors.

Inside, the barn was in shadow, and Sherlock's eyes took a moment to adjust. Matty, who had been there before, immediately moved across to where two horses had been tied to wooden pillars outside their stalls. Both were already saddled.

"Get on," Matty said. "Use the side of the stalls as a step."

The pounding footsteps outside were getting closer. As Matty grabbed the saddle of the smaller horse, placed his foot in a stirrup, and hoisted himself up, Sherlock half climbed up the wooden side of the stalls with his right foot, slipped his left foot into the stirrup, and tried to copy Matty's smooth action on the other horse, a large chestnut mare. He ended up sitting in the saddle more through luck than judgement. The horse looked back at him calmly. It seemed unfazed by having a stranger suddenly jumping on its back.

"Let's go!" Matty called. He'd taken the reins in one hand and was untying his horse with the other. Sherlock grabbed at his own reins and tried to remember what Virginia had told him about riding horses. *Guide with your knees, not the reins. Use the reins for slowing the horse down.*

Without glancing backwards, Matty urged his horse out of the barn doors. He seemed to assume that Sherlock would just follow. Sherlock shook loose the rope that kept his own horse from wandering off. A sudden wave of panic swept over him as he realized that Virginia had told him how to steer and how to stop, but not how to start. Tentatively, he pressed both knees into the horse's sides. Obediently, the horse began to walk. Sherlock leaned forward in the saddle to compensate for the swaying movement. He pressed harder with his knees and gave the reins an experimental shake. The horse broke into a trot, then a canter. Why did people make out that riding was so hard? It was just a series of signals and actions!

The scene outside burst upon Sherlock in a blaze of colour and action as they left the barn. Matty was racing off, with a group of masked servants chasing him on foot and falling behind. Two masked men were standing in front of Sherlock, trying to block his path. One of them was waving a revolver. He fired in Sherlock's direction, and Sherlock felt something hot brush past his hair. He urged his horse into a gallop. The horse ploughed straight through the middle of the two men, knocking them to the ground. Using his knees, he pushed his horse into speeding up. It seemed as if they were flying across the ground, catching up with Matty.

Within moments they were approaching the boundary wall of the estate. It must have been ten feet high. The two boys guided their horses into a curve, towards the main gates. The two horses pounded across the ground, the sound of their hoofs changing as they went from soft earth to the stones of the drive. Sherlock's heart sank as he saw that the main gates of the estate were being pushed closed. Two masked servants with shotguns were standing in front of them, aiming at the horses. At the same moment, Sherlock and Matty hauled back on their reins. With a spray of stones, the horses skidded to a halt.

One of the men fired his shotgun. The blast echoed across the grounds. Sherlock glimpsed the buckshot flying past them in an expanding cloud, like an explosion of midges.

Using his knees to guide the horse, and instinctively tugging on the left side of the reins for emphasis, Sherlock pulled the animal around. Matty did likewise. The boys urged their horses forward into a gallop again. The house loomed before them, dark and forbidding.

Glancing to left and right, Sherlock saw masked men coming round both sides of the house, armed with a collection of revolvers, shotguns, fowling pieces, and pitchforks. The only direction was straight on, towards the main doors of the house.

Matty began to slow. He glanced round uncertainly.

Sherlock galloped past his friend, yelling: "Follow me!" Left and right were blocked, as was behind. He could almost hear his brother Mycroft's voice saying: "When all other options are impossible, Sherlock, embrace the one that's left, however improbable it might be."

His horse, sensing his intentions, jumped the few steps up to the portico in front of the house and headed unerringly for the wide front doors.

Sherlock ducked as his horse galloped through the open doors and into the entrance hall, feeling the lintel of the doorway brush his hair. The horse's hoofs skidded and clattered on the tiled flooring, nearly unseating Sherlock before the animal could get its footing again. The darkness of the hall confused him for a moment, but his eyes adjusted within seconds and he urged the horse forward, past the marble stairs and towards the back of the house. Matty was close behind. Masked servants ran out of doorways and then fell back, terrified by the two horses that almost filled the space. Rather than head for the servants' areas, Sherlock guided the horse sharply right, pushing open a door into what he suspected—based on its placement and comparing it with Holmes Manor—was a drawing room. He was right.

The room was spacious and bright, with large glazed double doors leading out onto a veranda. And, as Sherlock remembered from the escape earlier, the doors were open!

Within seconds, he and the horse were galloping through the drawing room and out onto the veranda. He heard a commotion as Matty's horse knocked aside furniture in the room behind him, and then the clatter of hoofs on the flagstones of the veranda.

Ahead, across the field of beehives, he caught sight of a smaller back gate, through which provisions and supplies were probably delivered. It looked unguarded. He raced for it, the horse's mane whipping against his face and the breeze rushing past his ears. The boxy shapes of the beehives formed a geometrical grid through which the horse galloped in a straight line. Clouds of bees took flight behind them, but the horse was too fast for them and they just milled and roiled in confusion.

The back gate was locked, but it only took a moment for Sherlock to dismount and throw the bolt back. He turned and looked across the grounds of the house as Matty cantered up beside him. Masked men, armed, were massing on the other side of the field of beehives. They obviously didn't want to risk entering the area. One or two of them were already batting at the air as the angry bees attacked the first thing that came to hand.

"I thought that went well," said Matty. "Shall we stay and watch?"

"Let's not," said Sherlock.

ELEVEN

Amyus Crowe finished cleaning the cuts on Sherlock's face with a flannel and a liquid that smelt sharp and stung wherever he touched it, then walked across his cottage and sat in a wicker chair. It creaked beneath his weight. He pushed with his feet, balancing the chair on its two back legs, and rocked it gently. All the time his eyes were fixed on Sherlock.

Beside Sherlock, Matty shifted uncertainly, like an animal that wanted to run but didn't know which direction was safe.

"Quite a story," Crowe murmured.

Assuming that Crowe's words were just a way of breaking the silence while he was thinking, Sherlock kept quiet. Crowe rocked back and forth, all the while staring at Sherlock. "Yep, quite a story," he said after a while.

Crowe's level gaze was making Sherlock edgy, so he looked away, letting his eyes drift around the room. Amyus Crowe's cottage was cluttered, full of books, newspapers, and periodicals that had been left wherever he had set them down. A pile of letters was fixed to the wooden mantelpiece with a knife through their centres, next to a clock that indicated that it was coming up to two o'clock. Beside them sat a single slipper, from which a handful of cigars protruded like grasping fingers. It should have looked squalid, but there was no dust, no dirt. The place was clean but untidy. It just seemed as if Crowe had a different way of storing things.

"What do *you* make of it all?" Crowe challenged eventually.

Sherlock shrugged. He didn't like being the object of Crowe's attention. "If I knew that," he countered, "I wouldn't have had to come to you."

"It would be nice if one person could always make a difference," Crowe replied without a trace of irritation, "but in this complicated world of ours you sometimes need friends, and you sometimes need an organization to back you up."

"You think we should go to the peelers?" Matty asked, obviously nervous.

"The police?" Crowe shook his head. "I doubt they'd believe you, and even if they did there's little they could do. Whoever lives in this big house of yours will deny everythin'. They've got the power and the authority, not you. And you got to admit, it's a preposterous story on the face of it."

"Do you believe us?" Sherlock challenged.

Crowe's face creased up in surprise. "Of course I believe you," he said.

"Why? Like you said, it's a preposterous story."

Crowe smiled. "People do things when they lie," he replied. "Lyin' is stressful, 'cause you got to keep two different things straight in your head at the same time—the truth that you're tryin' to keep secret and the lie that you're tryin' to tell. That stress manifests itself in certain ways. People don't make eye contact properly, they rub their noses, they hesitate and stammer more when they talk. And they go into more detail than is necessary, as if it makes their lie more believable if they can remember what colour the wallpaper was, and whether the people had beards or moustaches or suchlike. You told your story straight, you looked me in the eye, and you didn't add in extraneous details. Far as I can judge, you're tellin' the truth—or at least, what you believe to be the truth."

"So what do we do now?" Sherlock asked. "There's something going on around here. It's got to do with clothes that are being made for the Army, and bees, and that warehouse in Farnham. And that man in the big house—the Baron, I think—is behind it all, but I don't know what he's doing."

"Then we need to find out." Amyus Crowe let his chair settle down onto its four legs and stood up. "If you haven't got enough facts to come to a conclusion, then you go out and get more facts. Let's go and ask some questions."

Matty shifted uncomfortably. "I gotta go," he muttered.

"Come with us, kid," Crowe said. "You were part of this adventure, and you deserve to find out what's goin' on. And besides, young Sherlock here seems to trust you." He paused. "If it helps make your mind up, I'll get us some food on the way."

"I'm in," Matty said.

Crowe led the way outside. In the meadow beside the cottage, Virginia Crowe was brushing down her horse, Sandia. Beside it was a larger bay mare. Sherlock assumed it was Crowe's horse. The two horses that Sherlock and Matty had ridden away from the Baron's mansion were quietly cropping the grass off to one side.

Virginia looked up as they approached. Her gaze met Sherlock's and she glanced away quickly.

"We're goin' for a ride," Crowe announced. "Virginia, you come along too. The more people askin' questions, the more chance of some half-decent answers."

"I don't know what questions to ask," Virginia protested.

"You were outside the door, listenin'," Crowe said with a smile. "I heard Sandia whinnying. He only ever does that if you're within sight but not actually with him. And I could see somethin' movin' about, blockin' the sunlight 'neath the door."

Virginia blushed, but kept gazing at her father, half defiantly. "You always taught me to take advantage of my opportunities," she said.

"Quite right too. The best way of learnin' is to listen."

Crowe pulled himself up onto his horse, and Virginia did the same. She watched, smiling, as Sherlock and Matty mounted their own horses, and nodded to Sherlock with approval. "Not half bad," she said.

Together, the four of them cantered along the road, reversing the route that Sherlock and Matty had taken to get to the cottage. The sun was shining, the smell of woodsmoke hung in the air, and Sherlock had to try hard to convince himself that he had ever been knocked out, taken prisoner, questioned, and then casually sentenced to death. Things like that just didn't happen, did they? Not on a sunny day. Even the cuts on his face had stopped hurting.

Virginia nudged her horse closer to Sherlock's. "You ride well," she said, "for a beginner."

"I had good advice," he said, glancing at her and then away again.

"That stuff you said, back in the cottage. That was all true?"

"Every word."

"Then maybe this country ain't as boring as I thought."

The nearer they got to the big house in which Sherlock had been imprisoned, the edgier he got. Eventually Amyus Crowe reined his horse to a halt within sight of the gates to the house. There was nobody in sight.

"Is this the place?" Crowe called.

Sherlock nodded.

"There's rutted tracks leadin' out of the gates and along

the road," Crowe continued. "Looks to me like they've skedaddled."

Sherlock looked in confusion at Virginia. She smiled. "Left," she explained. "Run away."

"Oh. Right." He filed that one away for the future.

"Let's head down the road and see what we find," Crowe shouted, and urged his horse on. Virginia was right behind him. Sherlock and Matty exchanged glances and followed.

About five minutes further on, they found a tavern— red brickwork, laid in that distinctive herringbone style that Sherlock had noticed before, white plaster, and black beams. Trestles and benches had been set out on the grass outside. Smoke trailed out of the chimney and Sherlock could smell roasting meat. He was instantly hungry.

Crowe stopped and dismounted. "Late lunch," he called. "Matty, Virginia, you stay out here and watch the horses. Sherlock, you come in with me."

Sherlock followed the big American into the tavern. The ceiling was low, almost hidden by a layer of greasy smoke from the lamb that was roasting on a spit in the fireplace. Fresh sawdust covered the floor. Four men sat together at a table, eyeing the newcomers suspiciously. A fifth man sat on a stool at the bar and paid them no attention, being more concerned with gazing into his drink. The landlord, standing behind the bar and polishing a tankard with a cloth, nodded at Amyus Crowe.

"Afternoon, gents. Will it be drink or will it be food or will it be both?"

"Four plates of bread and meat," Crowe said, and Sherlock was amazed to hear him speaking without his normal American accent. His voice, as near as Sherlock could tell, was pitched as if he was a farmer or labourer from somewhere in the Home Counties. "And four tankards of ale."

The landlord pulled four tankards of beer and set them on a pewter tray. Crowe picked one up for himself and nodded to Sherlock. "Take 'em outside, lad," he said in his gruff "English" voice. Sherlock picked the tray up and cautiously carried it to the door. Crowe, he noticed, was settling himself on a stool by the bar.

Outside, Sherlock saw that Matty had found a table and benches near the tavern. Virginia was still standing with her horse. He joined Matty and sat where he could see through one of the windows. Matty took one of the tankards and started drinking thirstily, holding it in both hands.

Sherlock sipped at the dark brown liquid. It was bitter and flat and left an unpleasant aftertaste in his mouth.

"Hops aren't edible, are they?" he said to Matty.

The boy shrugged. "You can eat them, I s'pose, but nobody does. They don't taste too good."

"So why on earth does anyone think you can make a drink out of them then?"

"Dunno."

Looking through the window into the tavern, Sherlock could see Amyus Crowe chatting with the landlord. From the tilt of his head Crowe appeared to be asking questions and the landlord was answering them, still polishing tankards with his increasingly dirty cloth.

A girl in a pinafore emerged from the tavern carrying a tray with four plates of steaming meat. She walked across, put the plates and cutlery down on the table without a word, and left.

Virginia wandered across to join them, and Sherlock edged up to make room for her. She picked at the hot slices of lamb with a fork. She paused for a moment, fork held near her lips. "You know I didn't write that note, don't you?"

"I know that now." Sherlock looked away, across the countryside, unable to meet her direct gaze. "I thought it was you at the time, but I suppose that's because I wanted it to be you. If I'd thought about it, I should have known it wasn't."

"How so?"

He shrugged. "The paper was delicate and feminine, and the writing was very precise. It was as if someone was trying to pretend to be a girl." He caught himself. "I mean a woman. A young woman. I mean—"

"I know what you mean." She smiled slightly. "So what makes you think I don't normally use feminine writing paper and neat handwriting?"

This time he could meet her eyes, and the contact held

for a long moment. "You're not like any girls I've met in England," he said. "You're unique. I'm still trying to work you out, but I think if you wanted me to go somewhere, like a fair, you'd just come and ask me." He stopped for a moment and considered. "Or, more likely, just tell me," he added.

This time it was her turn to blush. "You think I'm too bossy?"

"Not too bossy. Just bossy enough."

Matty's gaze was flicking between them. "What are you two talking about?"

"Nothing," Sherlock and Virginia chorused.

Looking through the window again, Sherlock noticed that Crowe had joined the four men who were sitting together. They all appeared to be getting along well. Crowe gestured to the landlord, who began pouring more tankards of beer from a pewter jug on the counter.

"Your father's an interesting man," Sherlock said, turning to Virginia.

"He has his moments."

"What did he do, back in America?"

She kept her gaze fixed on her plate. "You really want to know?"

"Yes."

"He was a tracker."

"You mean he hunted animals?"

She shook her head. "He hunted men. He tracked killers who had escaped justice, and he tracked Indians who had attacked isolated settlements. He'd follow them for days through the wilderness until he got close enough to take them by surprise."

Sherlock couldn't quite believe what he was hearing. "And what—he brought them back to face justice?"

"No," she said quietly. Abruptly she stood upright and walked away, back towards the horses.

Sherlock and Matty sat in silence for a while, each occupied with his own thoughts.

Eventually Amyus Crowe left the tavern and joined them, squeezing his bulky form between the bench and the table. "Interestin'," he said, back in his "American" persona again.

"What's happened?" Sherlock asked. "What do they know about the house?"

"And how did you get them to answer your questions?" Matty added. "You're a stranger around here, and people don't usually open up to strangers."

"Best thing to do is not be a stranger then," he replied. "If you just sit there for a while, makin' conversation with the barman, you become part of the furniture. Then you join in with the conversation, if you see an openin', an' tell them somethin' about yourself—who you are, why you're there. I told 'em I was lookin' to buy a farm an' raise pigs, on the basis that the new soldiers in Aldershot are goin' to need a lot of feedin'. They was interested to know how many soldiers are goin' to be garrisoned there, and we got talkin' about the business opportunities. I asked if there was anyone around here who might be interested in investin' in a business opportunity, or who might have some land to spare, an' they told me 'bout the estate down the road. Owned by a man named Maupertuis—some kind of baron, apparently, and a foreigner to boot."

Sherlock glanced across at Matty and smiled. Crowe seemed oblivious to the fact that he was a foreigner in this country himself.

"Nobody's ever seen this Baron Maupertuis, an' his staff were all brought with him, not hired locally, which didn't endear him to the villagers much. All their supplies and whatever were brought in from somewhere else, not purchased nearby. Anyway, the landlord was listenin' to us and said that the Baron had moved out earlier today. Apparently there was a convoy of carts went down the road, all stacked up with boxes and furniture, with a black two-wheeler bringin' up the rear. An' then a while later, there was more carts, this time stacked up with large boxes covered with sheets. I suspect those were the beehives you mentioned, young man."

"They took the beehives with them? Why?"

Amyus Crowe nodded. "That's a very good question. If you're evacuatin' in a hurry, why take all the beehives with you? It's only goin' to slow you down, an' it's not like you can't get more bees elsewhere." He mused for a moment. "It looks like your escape has spooked them.

They couldn't take the chance that you might go to the police and the police would come to investigate. They've relocated somewhere else, and we need to know where."

"We could follow them," Sherlock said.

Crowe shook his head. "They've got too good a start."

"They'll have to travel slowly," Sherlock insisted. "They've got the beehives with them. One person on a horse could catch up with them."

"Too many roads they could have taken," Crowe persisted.

"A long convoy of carts? People would spot them and remember. And they're not going to be taking country roads in bad condition—they'll be sticking to main routes. That cuts down the options."

Crowe grinned. "Well thought through, lad."

"You'd already thought of that?" Sherlock asked, frowning.

"Yeh, but I didn't want to spoon-feed you with the answers. I wanted to see if you were capable of thinkin' something through, especially if I was pushing you in the opposite direction." Crowe stood up. "I know some lads near our cottage who have horses and could do with a few shillings. I'll send them out looking for this convoy. I suggest you go back to Holmes Manor and make your peace with your family. Tell them you were with me all the time—that should calm things down. I'll swing round tomorrow and let you know what I've discovered."

The four of them trotted back along back roads and cross-country paths until they were close to Farnham, where they said their goodbyes. Matty headed off towards wherever he'd left his boat, while Crowe and Virginia trotted in the direction of their cottage. Sherlock let his horse stand quietly for a moment, allowing the events of the past day to settle in his mind, becoming memories rather than a jumble of sensory impressions. Eventually, when he felt calmer, he guided the horse towards Holmes Manor.

When he arrived, he wondered for a moment where to leave the horse. It wasn't his, after all. On the other hand, its previous owner seemed to have abandoned it, and it was definitely a step up from the rackety old bicycle that Matty had found for him. In the end he unsaddled it and left it in the stable with a bale of hay. If it was there tomorrow, he would take it as a sign that he was meant to keep it.

Dinner was just being served as he walked into the house. Normal behaviour, as if nothing had happened, as if the world was exactly the same as it had been that morning. He glanced at his clothes, dusted his jacket down, and headed into the dining room.

The meal was an unreal experience. His aunt chattered on about nothing in particular as usual, and his uncle read from a large book as he ate, muttering beneath his breath every now and then. Mrs. Eglantine stared at him from her position over by the wall. It was hard to reconcile the calm, civilized atmosphere with the fact that he'd been knocked out, abducted, sentenced to death, and had escaped, all within the past few hours. He was famished, despite the meat he had eaten at the tavern, and he hungrily piled his plate with steaming slices of chicken and vegetables, then covered the whole lot with gravy.

"You look as if you've been in the wars, Sherlock," his aunt said during dessert—the closest she'd ever got to asking him a direct question.

"I . . . fell down," he said, aware of the stinging cuts on his face and ears. "I'm not used to riding a bike."

It seemed to satisfy her, and she went back to murmuring to herself, continuing her perpetual monologue.

As soon as was polite, Sherlock broke away and headed for his room. He had intended to read for a while and then perhaps write some of the day's events down in a journal so that he didn't forget them, but as soon as his body hit the bed he found it difficult to keep his eyes open, and within moments he was asleep, still fully dressed.

He woke once when it was dark outside and owls were hooting somewhere in the distance. He slipped his clothes off and slid beneath the rough sheet. He fell into a deep sleep like someone diving into a dark and mysterious lake.

The next day dawned bright and sharp. Amyus Crowe was standing downstairs in the hall when Sherlock descended for breakfast. Amyus was wearing a white linen suit and a broad-brimmed hat.

"We're going to London," he boomed when he saw Sherlock. "I have to go on business, and your uncle has given me permission to take you with me. It'll be an education. We'll see some art galleries, and I'll teach you some of the history associated with that great city."

"Is Virginia going too?" Sherlock asked without thinking, and immediately wished that he could pull the words back out of the air, but Crowe just grinned, his eyes twinkling. "Why, yes," he said. "I could hardly leave her alone in the countryside now, could I? What kind of father would that make me?"

"Why London?" Sherlock asked more quietly as he reached the bottom of the stairs.

"That's where the convoy of carts was heading," Crowe replied equally quietly. "I suspect he has another house there somewhere."

With a barely audible rustle of her skirt, Mrs. Eglantine stepped out of the shadows at the end of the hall. "You should eat your breakfast before I have to clear the table, young Master Sherlock," she said, her voice laden with just enough dislike to be audible but not enough for Sherlock to take any active offence.

"Thank you," he said, then turned back to Crowe. "Are we leaving straightaway?"

"Get some victuals inside you," Crowe answered. "You may need them. Pack a small bag for two days away.

I'll wait in the carriage outside." He turned to Mrs. Eglantine and removed his hat with an exaggerated flourish. "Ma'am," he said, and left.

Sherlock ate his breakfast as fast as he could, barely tasting it. London! He was going to London! And if he was really lucky he might be able to see Mycroft while he was there!

Amyus Crowe was waiting in a four-wheeler carriage outside the manor house. Virginia was sitting beside him. She looked uncomfortable, either because of the frilly dress and bonnet that she was wearing or because she was cooped up inside the carriage rather than being outside in the open air.

"You look nice," Sherlock said as he sat opposite her and as the driver stacked his bag up with the rest. She scowled at him.

The clatter of wheels on gravel as the cart pulled off covered her reply, but Sherlock wasn't sure he wanted to hear it anyway.

When they got to Farnham station, Matty was waiting for them. Amyus Crowe smiled at him. "You got my message, then?"

"Got woken up by the bloke delivering it. How did you know where my boat was moored?"

"It's my business to know where everything is. My business and my particular pleasure too. Fancy a journey, youngster?"

"I ain't got no change of clothes or nothing," Matty said.

"We'll buy you whatever you need in London. Now, let's get our tickets."

Crowe bought four tickets to London, second class, and the party descended to the station platform while the driver of the cart off-loaded their bags. He'd timed it perfectly. The train arrived within ten minutes, a great behemoth of a thing, its tubular front end venting steam, pistons pumping up and down like clockwork arms, and its metal wheels, almost as big as Sherlock, squealing against the track.

"A Joseph Beattie 'Saxon' class locomotive," Amyus noted. "Generically referred to as a 2-4-0. Sherlock, can you tell me why?"

"Why the 'Saxon' or why the '2-4-0'?"

Amyus nodded. "The collection of proper information depends primarily on the proper phrasing of the question," he noted. "I meant the '2-4-0' designation. I suspect the 'Saxon' part was just a piece of historical fancy on the part of the engineer. He also designed an engine he called the 'Nelson.'"

Sherlock let his gaze wander across the engine. The wheels, he noticed, weren't equally spaced, but grouped together in clusters. "I'd say because that's the way the wheels are arranged," he ventured, "but that can't be the case."

"Actually, it is," Crowe replied. "There are two wheels on a single axle at the front, independently swivelling to allow the engine to transit curves. Then there are four wheels attached to the engine proper, on two axles. Those are the powered wheels."

"And the 'o'?" Sherlock asked.

"Some engines have a set of wheels at the rear," Crowe replied. "The 'o' indicates that this engine doesn't have that third set of wheels."

"So it's got a number to indicate that there is no number," Sherlock said.

"Correct." Crowe smiled. "It may not be sensible, but it's eminently logical, if you accept the system they've chosen to use."

They found a carriage to themselves and settled down for the journey. Sherlock had never been on a train before, and everything was new to him: the vibration of the seats and the walls and the windows as they moved, the strangely sweet-smelling smoke that drifted in, the way the countryside flashed past, ever-changing and yet strangely consistent. Matty was wide-eyed and nervous; Sherlock suspected that the boy had never experienced even the meagre luxury such as that of a second-class compartment before.

Woods flashed past and gave way to fields, but the plants grown in these fields weren't corn or wheat or barley; they were brown, spindly plants with small green leaves, curling around sticks that had been fixed in the ground up to a height of five or six feet. Sherlock was just about to ask Crowe what they were when Matty, noticing his interest, leaned forward to take a look.

"Hops," Matty said succinctly. "For the breweries. This area's noted for the quality of the beer it brews. There's thirty pubs and taverns in Farnham alone."

And so the journey went on, punctuated by a change of trains at Guildford, until they reached the great terminus of Waterloo Station in that busy metropolis of London.

The place where Mycroft Holmes lived and worked.

TWELVE

Waterloo Station was a bustling mass of humanity heading in all directions and carrying all kinds of boxes, parcels, suitcases, and trunks, all beneath a massive roof of arched metal and glass. The warmth of the sun was magnified by the glass, making the station hotter than the streets around it. Trains heaved themselves into their platforms and disgorged clouds of steam and even more people, which added to the warmth. Sherlock could feel sweat gathering beneath his collar.

Amyus Crowe engaged a porter straightaway and got him to retrieve their bags from the train. The porter then led them outside, to where a line of hansom cabs were picking up passengers from a long queue. An additional halfpenny tip persuaded their porter to take them along the line to where newly arrived cabs were letting out their passengers before joining the line of waiting ones. A few moments' dickering and they were climbing aboard a cab through one door as its previous occupants were exiting the other.

Amyus Crowe seemed to be familiar with London, and told the cabbie to take them to the Sarbonnier Hotel. The cab trotted off, with Sherlock leaning out of one window to see the sights and Matty leaning out of the other.

The scale of buildings was immense compared with Farnham, Guildford, and the other towns that Sherlock was used to. Many of them reached up five or six storeys. Several had columns supporting porticoes above their front doors and rows of sculptures along their rooflines, some obviously of human figures and others of mythical creatures with wings, horns, and fangs.

Within a few moments they were heading across a bridge that spanned a wide river.

"The Thames?" Sherlock asked.

"It is," Crowe agreed. "One of the most dirty, congested, and evil rivers it has been my displeasure to experience."

Clattering off the bridge on the other side of the river, the hansom made a few turns and ended up outside a long building constructed of orange stone. The driver hopped down and helped unload the bags. Three porters emerged from a door at the front of the building and took the bags away.

Once inside the impressive lobby—white pillars with sculpted bases, a mosaic set into the ceiling, and rose marble tiles on the floor—Amyus Crowe strode across to a long wooden desk.

"Three rooms, for two nights," he said to the uniformed man behind the desk.

The man nodded. "Of course, sir," he said, reaching up to retrieve three keys from a board behind him. Turning back, he added, "Perhaps you would care to sign the guest book, sir."

Crowe signed with a flourish, and the concierge handed him the keys. They were attached to large brass balls, probably so that they couldn't be lost easily, Sherlock guessed.

"Sherlock and Matthew, you will have one room," Crowe said, handing them a key. "Virginia will have a room to herself and I will have the third room. Your bags will be taken up to your rooms. Matthew, I suggest you and I head for somewhere we can get you some clothes and toiletries." He gazed critically at Matty. "And a haircut," he added. "Sherlock, Virginia—I suggest you take a walk outside. Turn right and walk to the end of the street, and you'll find something that might interest you. Be back in an hour for lunch. If you get lost, ask someone to direct you back to the Sarbonnier Hotel."

Taking Crowe at his word, Sherlock led Virginia outside and turned right. The two of them were immediately dragged along by the throng of people who were heading in the same direction. Worried that they might be separated, Sherlock reached out his hand to guide Virginia closer to him. Instead, her hand clasped his, warm and soft, for a moment. His heart felt like it was beating twice as fast. He glanced at her, startled. She smiled back, uncharacteristically shy.

It only took a few minutes before they were at the end of the block of buildings. The road widened out into a vast open plaza which was dominated by a tall column that rose up from a central pedestal. For a moment Sherlock thought that a man was standing on top of the pillar, and his mind suddenly ricocheted back to Holmes Manor, and his uncle talking over dinner one night about the ascetic religious hermits who abandoned their lives and their families to live on top of poles, meditating on the nature of God and eating only what was thrown up to them by passersby. A moment's attention showed him that the figure on top of the column wasn't a man, but a statue that had been carved to look as if it was wearing naval uniform.

"Who is it?" Virginia asked, entranced.

"I think it's Admiral Nelson," Sherlock replied. "Which makes this Trafalgar Square. It commemorates a famous naval victory in 1805."

At the base of the pillar were two fountains whose spray glowed with all the colours of the rainbow in the bright sunlight. This was the heart of London. This was the central point of an empire that stretched to the other side of the globe.

And somewhere nearby, Sherlock's brother, Mycroft, was probably sitting at his desk, helping to run it.

They wandered around Trafalgar Square for a while, watching the people and looking at the fine buildings that lined the roads around, and then they headed back to the hotel. They were just in time: Amyus Crowe was standing in the foyer, waiting for them. With him was a boy of about Matty Arnatt's age, but with neat hair and decent clothes and a scowl on his face. It took Sherlock a few moments to realize that this *was* Matty.

"Don't," Matty warned. "Just . . . don't."

Sherlock and Virginia laughed.

Together, the four of them went into the dining room and ordered lunch. They were surrounded by women in silks, crinolines, peacock feathers, and hats and gloves, and men with shining moustaches in frock coats, but nobody gave them a second glance. They were accepted as a family, taking in the sights of the capital city of the most important country on the face of the planet.

Sherlock had lamb cutlets, which were perfectly cooked—bloody in the centre—and came with potatoes and beans. Matty and Amyus Crowe both went for steak and kidney pudding, while Virginia, more adventurous, risked chicken served with a French sauce with peppercorns and cream.

As they were eating, Amyus Crowe brought them up to date on the reason they were there.

"I telegraphed ahead to a man I know in this fair city," he said between mouthfuls of food. "A business associate of sorts."

Sherlock wondered briefly what kind of "business" Crowe was involved with, as he had never mentioned it before, but the American continued speaking.

"I told him which road the carts were coming in on and asked him to intercept them and find out their ultimate destination. I told him where I'd be stayin', and he's just sent a telegram back to tell me that the carts ended up unloading their various boxes and suchlike at a warehouse in a place called Rotherhithe. He told me where the warehouse was located."

"Rotherhithe?" Sherlock asked.

"It's a few miles downriver—an unsavoury location where sailors take their entertainment between voyages and goods are stored before being loaded onto ships. Not a place where you want to be after dark." He shook his head unhappily. "I wouldn't normally risk taking you there, but this is too big. The Baron's up to something, an' it's important enough that he's willing to kill for it. Already has. He'll no more baulk at disposin' of the two of you than he would steppin' on a spider. The trouble is that we need to check that the boxes on the carts are the beehives you saw back in Farnham, and that means I need you to come to Rotherhithe to take a look, Sherlock. But I warn you—it might be dangerous. Really dangerous."

Sherlock nodded slowly. "I'll take the chance. I want to find out what's going on—why he keeps trying to kill me."

Crowe glanced across at Matty, who was shovelling peas into his mouth with a spoon. "As for you, young man, I guess that you've seen your fair share of wharves and warehouses, given that you spend your life travelling around in a narrowboat. And I guess too that you can handle yourself in a fight."

"If a fight starts," Matty said through a mouthful of peas, "I run. If I can't run, I punch low and I punch hard."

"I couldn't have put it better myself." Crowe nodded. "I'll come with you, of course, but we may have to separate to watch different areas."

"And what about me?" Virginia's voice was high-pitched with indignation, and her violet eyes flashed dangerously. "What do I do?"

"You stay here," Crowe said darkly. "I know you can handle yourself in a scrap, but you don't know what can happen to a young woman in Rotherhithe. The people who live there are worse than animals. I'd never forgive myself if anything happened to you, not after—" He stopped abruptly. Looking across at Virginia, Sherlock saw her eyes suddenly glisten. "Stay here," Crowe repeated. "If we get separated, we need to know that there's someone back here who can take messages and pass them on. That's your job."

Virginia nodded, not saying anything.

Crowe looked back at the two boys. "When you're ready," he said, "we'll head off."

As they crossed the foyer of the hotel, Sherlock turned and looked back at Virginia. She was staring at him. She tried to smile, but the expression turned into a worried twist of her lips. He smiled back at her reassuringly, but he suspected that the expression on his own face wasn't much more convincing.

Instead of taking a hansom cab to Rotherhithe, Crowe led the two boys to the side of the Thames, where stone steps stained green with algae led down into a foul-smelling brown river. The far bank was hidden by a haze of smoke and a brownish miasma that seemed to be rising from the river itself. A boat was bobbing up and down on the water. Its owner sat in the bows, smoking a pipe.

"Rotherhithe," Crowe said grimly, tossing a coin. The boatman nodded, catching the coin deftly and biting it to make sure it was real. Crowe and the boys settled into the stern while the boatman set to, facing backwards and pulling the boat through the water with his oars.

Sherlock found the journey strange and disturbing. Water sloshed in the bottom of the boat and there were things floating in the river that he tried hard not to look at: human waste, dead rats, and lengths of sodden wood covered in weeds. The smell was so appalling that he had to breathe through his mouth, and even then he was sure he could taste the smell as it coated his tongue and the back of his throat. It made him gag. At one point another boat emerged from the murk and passed close to them. Someone shouted a curse, and their boatman replied with a gesture that Sherlock had never seen before but could translate pretty well.

It took twenty minutes or so to make the journey to Rotherhithe, and they disembarked on a set of steps that were almost indistinguishable from the ones that they had started from. Crowe led the way up to the top.

A narrow alley cobbled with rough stones ran along the riverbank, curving away to either side. Crowe led Matty and Sherlock along it, past the towering edifices of warehouses and brick walls, following the edge of the malodorous Thames and keeping to the shadows wherever possible. After ten minutes or so he stopped. Opposite them was one of the taverns that could be found everywhere across the metropolis. The jangly music of a badly tuned upright piano emerged through the doorways and the windows, along with a jumble of voices singing different words to the same tune. Several women stood in a doorway and eyed Amyus Crowe with interest before turning away when they saw Sherlock and Matty.

"I believe the warehouse is just around the corner," Crowe murmured. His attention was focused all around them, looking for threats. "I suggest we check out the lay of the land and settle down for a while."

"What if we're seen?" Sherlock asked.

"I used to be a hunter, back in Albuquerque," Crowe said. "I tracked some of the most dangerous beasts around. There's things you can do to minimize the chances of gettin' discovered. Don't make eye contact, for a start, 'cause all animals spot eyes straightaway. Look at things out of the corner of your eye—it's more sensitive than lookin' straight, although you don't make out colours too well. Don't move if you can help it, 'cause the eye is set up to spot movement, not things that are still. Wear dull clothin' that doesn't have any colours that you wouldn't see in nature—grey for stone, green for moss, brown for earth. And don't wear any metal, 'cause metal ain't found in nature in any great quantities. Follow those rules and you can stand against a brick wall and folk'll just let their eyes move over you an' on till they find somethin' more interestin'."

"It sounds like magic," Sherlock said, unconvinced.

"Most stuff does till you know how it's done." He glanced critically at the two boys. "Those cuts on your face will help you blend in, Sherlock, but you're both a mite too neat for this neighbourhood. Need to dirty you up a bit." He looked around. "Okay, I need you to roll around on the cobbles for a while. Get some dust into your clothes."

"Won't that be suspicious?" Sherlock asked.

"Not if you got a reason for it," Crowe explained. "Matty, shove young Sherlock here in the chest."

"What?" Matty responded.

"Just do it. An' Sherlock, you punch him on the shoulder right back."

The light of understanding dawned in Sherlock's mind. "And we end up scrapping in the dirt, which helps our clothes to blend in *and* establishes us as part of the area. If we weren't local, we wouldn't be fighting in the road."

"Exactly," Crowe said approvingly.

Sherlock was about to ask how long they ought to

fight for when Matty shoved him hard in the chest. "I *told* you!" he shouted.

Sherlock suppressed the sudden urge to punch Matty in the jaw, and instead hit him on the shoulder. "Don't you dare," he yelled, feeling slightly embarrassed.

Matty launched himself at Sherlock, bringing him to the ground. Within moments the two of them were rolling around, clouds of dust rising around them. Sherlock got a grip on Matty's arm, but Matty's fingers closed in Sherlock's hair and pulled his head back.

Sherlock was on the verge of forgetting that it was a pretend fight when Amyus Crowe's huge hands closed on his and Matty's shoulders and yanked them upright. "All right you two, break it up," he said, using his "English" voice again, but gruffer this time.

The two boys stood facing each other, trying to suppress smiles despite the danger of their situation. Sherlock glanced down at himself. His jacket was torn at the sleeve, and everything was covered in dust and horsehair and stuff that he didn't even want to think about.

"Don't worry," Crowe said. "It'll wash off. And if it doesn't, we'll just buy more clothes. Possessions can always be replaced. A good hunter knows that anything material can be sacrificed in pursuit of the prey."

"What kind of animals did you hunt?" Matty asked.

"I didn't say they were animals," Crowe murmured.

Before either of the boys could ask him to clarify his

statement, he walked off. They followed, exchanging uneasy glances.

Crowe stopped at a corner and glanced round it. "Warehouse is across there," he said quietly. "Sherlock, you stay here. Hunker down on the ground an' play with somethin'—some stones if you can find 'em. Remember—don't make eye contact, but watch what's goin' on out of the corner of your eye. Matty, you come with me. You can cover the back, an' I'll move back and forth between the two of you."

"What are we looking for?" Sherlock asked.

"Stuff that's out of the ordinary. Somethin' that might tell us what's goin' on here."

Crowe and Matty walked off, Crowe's hand on Matty's shoulder, and Sherlock followed instructions, settling down on his haunches and pulling one of the cobbles from the mud. He rolled it back and forth. It was a boring game, but it was enough to make him look like part of the scenery, and he found he was still able to see what was going on around him out of the corner of his eye while ostensibly playing his game.

The warehouse was a brick building with a front made up almost entirely of a large pair of wooden doors, hinged so that they opened outward onto the street. There was nothing obviously suspicious about it, and Sherlock wondered whether they were actually watching the right place, or just a randomly chosen building.

Amyus Crowe wandered back after what seemed like

hours, but was probably closer to half an hour. Although he was wearing the same clothes as before, and he hadn't dirtied them as noticeably as Sherlock and Matty, he looked disheveled. His jacket was buttoned up wrongly, giving him a lopsided appearance, and his shirt was hanging out of his trousers. He was weaving slightly, and staring at the ground directly in front of his feet. He stopped near Sherlock and slumped against the wall.

"Everythin' okay?" he murmured.

"Nothing's happened," Sherlock replied, equally quietly.

"You all right?"

"I'm bored."

Crowe chuckled. "Welcome to the hunt. Long stretches of boredom punctuated by moments of exhilaration and terror." He paused, then went on: "I think I might wander into that there tavern for a while, see what's bein' said."

"Fine. Couldn't send me out a glass of water, could you?"

"Son, you're prob'ly better off drinkin' out of the Thames than the water from any tavern around here. If you're hungry or thirsty just register the fact an' then push it to one side. Don't dwell on it. A human being can go three, four days without water. Just keep tellin' yourself that."

"Easy for you to say."

Crowe laughed.

"Can I ask you something?" Sherlock said, wanting to keep Crowe there for a few moments more.

"Sure."

"What are you doing in England? What *is* that 'business' you mentioned earlier?"

Crowe smiled without humour and glanced away, not meeting Sherlock's gaze. "Not to be a tutor, that's for sure," he said softly, "although that's becomin' an interestin' pastime. No, I was retained by . . . well, let's say the American government to make it easy, to seek out men who'd committed crimes, atrocities, the most terrible things durin' the recent Civil War, an' escaped the country before the hand of justice could come down on their shoulders. That's how I came to know your brother—he signed the agreement that allows me to be here. An' that's why I've been developin' a network of useful people, especially in docks and ports. So when you told me that the Baron was accelerating his plan, whatever that may be, I just sent out the word to look for his carts. An' I got to say, I was surprised that my people found them so easily." He looked back at Sherlock. "Satisfied?"

Sherlock nodded.

"Not many people I've told that to," Crowe added. "Grateful if you'd keep it to yourself." He moved away before Sherlock could say anything more.

Sherlock continued playing his game, rolling the cobble back and forth, as the minutes slid away, one after the other. He kept watch on the warehouse doors, but they were firmly closed and nothing was stirring. He was beginning to think that they were all on a wild-goose chase.

A sudden escalation of noise from behind him almost made him turn and look, but he stopped himself just in time. He let the cobblestone run a little further, turning to retrieve it and letting his eyes drift upward to take in the tavern. One of the doors was open and a group of men were emerging, obviously the worse for drink. They bantered for a moment, then turned and walked towards him. He concentrated on his stone, listening to whether they were saying anything about the warehouse, or the beehives, or Baron Maupertuis, or anything related to the mystery.

"When're we hauling out?" one of them said.

"First light tomorrow morning," another replied. There was something familiar about the voice, but Sherlock couldn't quite place it.

"Who's got the roster?" a third voice asked.

"It's in my head," the second man replied. "You head off to Ripon, Snagger goes to Colchester, the lad Nicholson here gets an easy ride to Woolwich, an' I get to go back to Aldershot."

"Can't I go to Ascot instead?" asked a Northern-accented voice—presumably the lad Nicholson.

"You go where you're told, sunshine," the second man responded. As he was talking, he passed close to Sherlock. His foot caught the cobblestone, kicking it across the alley. Unwittingly, Sherlock glanced up and met the man's gaze.

It was Denny, the man whom Sherlock had followed back to the warehouse in Farnham, the man who had been there when his friend Clem jumped on the narrowboat to attack Sherlock and Matty. The man who worked for Baron Maupertuis.

So much for being invisible. Denny's face instantly flushed with anger.

Sherlock rolled away as hands reached for him. He sprang to his feet and sprinted off down the alley. He wanted to run towards the tavern where Amyus Crowe was, but the men were between him and the tavern door. Instead he found himself running further and further away from Crowe, from Matty, and from anything he knew.

Footsteps thudded behind him, echoing off the walls of the buildings as he ran past them. His breath rasped in his throat and his heart pounded like a living thing trapped inside his rib cage and fighting to get out. Twice he felt fingers touch the back of his neck and scrabble for a grip on his collar, and twice he had to tear himself loose with a frantic burst of energy. His pursuers were growling beneath their breath as they ran, but apart from that, the thud of their boots, and the sound of his heart, the chase was conducted in complete silence.

He could see as he got halfway down that the alley finished in a brick wall. Sherlock's eyes widened. He was trapped! He turned, desperately trying to work out if he had enough time to run back and find another way, but the men were closing in on him. There were five of them, he noted in a kind of terrified calm, and they were all holding knives or heavy sticks. He wasn't going to get out of this alive.

A voice suddenly sounded very clearly in his head, and he couldn't tell whether it was his brother's voice or Amyus Crowe's voice or his own, but it said: "Alleys and roads lead from one place to another. An alley that ends in a brick wall is illogical. It has no purpose, and therefore should never have been built."

Sherlock swung back and let his gaze scan the brickwork of the alley. No doors, no windows, nothing but a patch of shadow in one corner where the lacklustre sunlight could not penetrate.

And if there was a way out, that was where it would be.

He ran into the shadows. If there had been nothing there then he would have run straight into the brickwork, knocking himself out, but instead there was a slender gap. A means of escape.

The narrow walkway ran between two buildings. He raced along it, hearing shouts of frustration from behind him as the men tried to find the dark way out. Single file they slipped into the walkway after him, the grunts of their breath echoing from the steep brick walls.

Zigzagging through the darkness, Sherlock stumbled out into a wide road lined with doors. He ran on, sensing boots hitting cobbles behind him, and skidded left into another alley, gaining himself a few yards more. A dog sprang out of a gap in the wall as he passed, but he was gone before its teeth closed on empty air. Instead, it turned on the men chasing him. Sherlock heard furious barking and the sound of cursing as the men tried to get away from it. He winced at the noise of a boot thudding into something soft. The dog whimpered and scrabbled away.

Scooting round another corner, he ran full tilt into a man and woman walking along the side of the Thames, sending the man sprawling and himself spinning backwards.

"You little beggar!" the man shouted, heaving himself back to his feet. "I'll teach you what for!" He started pushing the sleeves of his jacket up, revealing muscle-swollen forearms covered with blue tattoos of anchors and mermaids.

"Don't touch him, Bill. He didn't mean it!" The woman clutched at her companion's arm. Her skin was white with badly applied makeup, her lips a crimson slash, her eyes shaded with black powder. The effect was to make her face look like a skull. "He's only a kid."

"I thought he was a thief," the man growled again, but less aggressively this time.

"There's men after me," Sherlock said through his heavy panting. "I need help."

"You know what they do to boys round here," the

woman said. "I wouldn't wish that on my worst enemy. Bill, do something. Help the lad."

"Get behind me," Bill said. Sleeves pushed up, he was obviously itching for a fight and not too concerned who it was with. Sherlock slipped behind the man's massive bulk as his pursuers came around the corner.

"Stop right there," Bill said, his voice low and full of the promise of violence. "Let the kid be."

"Not a chance," said Denny, who was at the forefront of the five men. He brought his hand up, and he was holding a knife. Light trickled along the edge of the blade like a glowing liquid. "He's ours."

Bill reached out to take the knife, but Denny tossed it from his right hand to his left and punched it forward, into Bill's chest. The man fell to his knees, coughing blood, a disbelieving look on his face as if he couldn't accept that these moments, here in this alley, would be his last.

Denny smiled at Sherlock as Bill fell forward onto the cobbled surface of the road. "With you," he promised, "it won't be so quick."

THIRTEEN

Sherlock's whole body seemed to freeze in horror and disbelief, then a white heat of rage passed through him. Stepping forward, he punched his fist hard into Denny's groin. The thug folded up, choking. As he collapsed, Sherlock stepped back and kicked him in the jaw. Something cracked. The man screamed through a mouth that suddenly seemed to have locked in place and was twisted to one side.

The woman—Bill's companion—screamed as well, a high, piercing shriek that cut the air like a knife.

The other four men looked at each other in disbelief, then moved forward and reached out their grimy hands for Sherlock. Every detail was etched into Sherlock's mind: the dirt beneath their nails, the hairs on the backs of their hands, the blood pooling on the ground, the shriek of the woman and the scream of Denny both melding into one continuous whistle of pain. The world seemed to slow to a halt, freeze, and then shatter into pieces around him. He turned to the woman, his mouth dry. "I'm so sorry," he said.

Then he was running again. Two of the men followed, leaving Denny behind, collapsed on the cobbles beside Bill. The woman just stood there, looking down at them both, her scream gradually fading into choking sobs.

Turning a corner, Sherlock saw a massive domed building ahead of him. It looked entirely out of place in the middle of a cleared area of ground that had been planted with bushes and trees. Several roads—wide roads, not alleys—led away from it, and there was a constant bustle of people and horses swarming around outside. Beyond it Sherlock could see a stone wall and, further away, the churning grey surface of the Thames.

Sherlock ran towards it. Where there were people, there was likely to be safety.

Sprinting, he swerved past well-dressed men and women and ducked beneath the shafts of a carriage, heading all the time for the building. As it grew closer he could see that it was decorated with statues and tiled mosaics. A large entrance loomed up ahead of him, and he diverted his course slightly to head straight for it. Behind him, curses and shouts indicated that his pursuers hadn't given up.

The entrance led into a circular hall, lit by the sun shining through a myriad of coloured glass windows in the domed ceiling. The light gave a clownish, harlequin air to the place. In the centre of the building was a hole ringed by a balcony. People were lined up along the balcony, gazing down at something. Over to one side, a wide stairway spiralled round the edge of the pit, into the depths of the earth.

Sherlock dashed across, pushing through the throng of people, and reached the top of the stairway. Turning, he glimpsed the two men shoving their way through the crowd. One of them was a bald man with deformed ears and nose, leading that small part of Sherlock's brain that wasn't frantically trying to work out ways of escape to think that he might have been a boxer. The other was painfully thin, with sharp cheekbones and a pointed chin. They were obviously set on catching him, no matter what. Perhaps before he had broken Denny's jaw they might have given up, but they were driven by a purpose now. One of them had been humiliated, and so Sherlock would have to pay.

He turned and started down the staircase.

The stairs spiralled around the sides of a tremendous shaft, levelling out every now and then on a balcony but then continuing down into the abyss. A smell rose up out of the shaft: a stench that combined damp, rot, and mould into a single fetid odour that made his nose tingle and his eyes water. Sherlock's steps fell into a repetitive routine as he pounded round the sides of the cylindrical shaft. He had no idea what was at the bottom, but a single glance across the shaft told him what would await him at the top. Two of Baron Maupertuis's men were racing down the steps towards him.

He sped up. Whatever was at the bottom of the shaft couldn't be as bad as the certain and probably slow death that was chasing him.

He seemed to have spent much of the past few days running or fighting, and even as his feet clattered against the stone steps and his hand burned as it scraped against the banister there was a part of his mind that wondered frantically what exactly Baron Maupertuis thought he knew that was so important he had to die for it. What exactly was the Baron planning to do, and why was Sherlock an obstacle to his plans?

He was at the bottom before he realized, feet stumbling on the level surface. He was in a gas-lit hall. Two arched tunnels led away from the hall, both heading in the same direction. The arches were fully four or five times the height of a grown man, and made of brick, but the brickwork was wet everywhere he looked. Judging by the direction taken by the tunnels, he knew why. They went straight out under the Thames, and presumably ended at a similar shaft on the north side.

If he could make it to the other side, he might just escape with his life.

He stumbled on into the left-hand tunnel. There were people ambling along as if walking beneath the surface of a river was nothing special. There were even horses down there, being led calmly along. They obviously had no idea about the uncountable tons of water just a few feet above their heads, kept at bay by crumbling brick-work and plaster.

There were times when being too logical was a curse. This was one of those times. Sherlock knew the kind of pressure that was being exerted on the tunnel walls. One slight crack and the water would pour in, drowning them all.

But he kept on running. He had no choice.

Or did he? As he hurried on, he noticed that the two tunnels ran in parallel, and were linked by smaller side tunnels every ten yards or so. In each of the side tunnels enterprising Londoners had set up stalls selling food, drink, clothes, and all kinds of bric-a-brac. If he could just worm his way through one of the side tunnels, he could go back down the other main tunnel to the shaft, return to the warehouse, and find Amyus Crowe.

He veered right, towards the side of the main bore, and nipped into the first side tunnel he came to. A man turned towards him, illuminated by an oil lamp that hung from a nail on his wooden stall. His skin was grey-white and moist, like something that had lived underground for too long. He was wrapped in an old blanket that had become stiff with dirt over time, like some bizarre armour. His eyes seemed to be all black pupils, and he peered at Sherlock for a moment.

"You want a clock?" he said hopefully. "Good time-piece. Always right. Always correct. Grandfather clock, grandmother clock—whatever you want, I got."

"No thanks," Sherlock said, pushing past the stall. It occurred to him that time was meaningless beneath the Thames. No sun, no moon, no day and night. Time just passed. Why would you need a clock?

"What about a nice pocket watch? Never need to ask the time if you got a watch. Young gent like you, impress the ladies with a hunter on a chain. Real silver. Etched as well. You could keep a picture of your sweetheart inside."

Real silver, etched, and certainly stolen property. "Thanks," Sherlock said breathlessly, "but my father has money. He'll be coming through in a minute. Tell him I want a clock, and don't let him go without buying one."

The stallholder smiled, reminding Sherlock of some predatory crustacean lurking beneath a stone, waiting for its unsuspecting prey to pass by.

Sherlock peered round the edge of the side tunnel, back towards the shaft he had entered through, and cursed. His pursuers must have split up. One of them had followed him down the left-hand tunnel, but the other had headed down the right-hand one. He was pushing his way through the crowd, glancing suspiciously at every male who was younger than twenty, just in case. They obviously knew the area better than he did.

He decided to wait for this man to go past the side tunnel entrance, then he would double back. But his plan was dashed straightaway by a sudden commotion behind him. Turning, he saw the stallholder trying to thrust a small carriage clock into the hands of the thug who had followed Sherlock into the left-hand tunnel—the bald man with ears like cauliflowers and a squashed nose. The thug pushed him away with a curse, but the stallholder scuttled back, looking more and more beneath his dirt-encrusted blanket like some hard-shelled creature that lived at the bottom of the sea. He thrust the clock back at the thug, screeching, "You buy for your son! You buy for your son!" The ex-boxer pushed him away again, harder, and this time he stumbled against the oil lamp and knocked it against the wall. The glass smashed and the oil spilt over the stallholder's blanket. The wick, still wet, fell onto the blanket as well, setting it alight.

The flames took hold quickly as the stallholder stood there. Then, thrashing his arms around, he scuttled out into the left-hand main tunnel. People backed away in horror. The stallholder bumped into a passerby, and the fire jumped onto the man's frock coat. The man staggered to one side, brushing at the flames, but succeeding only in setting alight the billowing crinoline skirt of a woman next to him. A horse, being led down the tunnel, bolted at the sight of the flames, dragging its owner along behind it.

Within a few moments the tunnel was seething with flame. Clothes caught light quickly, cloth coverings on stalls followed, and even the wood of the stalls themselves caught fire, despite being damp. Smoke and steam filled the tunnel in a choking mist. Horrified, Sherlock backed away from the smoke and the fire into the right-hand main tunnel, which was mercifully flame-free.

But it still had one of his pursuers in it.

A hairy hand clamped on his shoulder.

"Got you, scum," the man spat. The underarms of his jacket were so blackened with old sweat patches that they had become waxy and stiff. The smell of the man's clothes was indescribable.

Sherlock struggled in his grip, but it was useless. The man's fingers dug hard into his shoulder.

"Denny'll want a word wiv you," the man whispered, bringing his face close to Sherlock's. His breath smelt like something had died inside his mouth. "An' I don't think you're gonna like what he has to say."

Sherlock was just about to reply when he noticed that the floor of the side tunnel was heaving underneath the smoke, undulating as if it were alive. And then he realized it *was* alive. Alive with rats. Frightened out of their holes and burrows by the fire, they had all headed in the same direction—to safety. A living carpet of ragged brown and black fur swept along the floor of the tunnel. People and horses backed away in horror from the mass of hair and teeth and tails. A small child being dragged away by its parents lost its footing and fell. The rats swarmed over it, covering its face.

The man holding Sherlock's shoulder relaxed his grip as the rats swirled about his ankles, biting at him with their tiny teeth. Cursing, he swatted at them with one of his spadelike hands. Sherlock pulled loose from his grip and dived into the mass of living creatures, grasping for the child who had vanished beneath the seething tide. Tiny claws pattered over his arms, his back, his legs, and his scalp. He could smell a rank, dry odour, like old urine. His fingers closed over a small arm, and he pulled hard. A little girl emerged from the flood of rats, eyes wide and mouth already opening to scream. "You're safe," Sherlock said, thrusting her back into the arms of her parents, who were batting and kicking to keep the rats at bay. They snatched the girl from him and hugged her tight.

And then the tidal wave of rats was gone, apart from a few weak and lame stragglers. Sherlock could see them rushing off in both directions, away from the smoke that continued to pour from the side tunnel. The thug who had grabbed hold of Sherlock was still brushing desperately at his clothing, beneath which Sherlock could see moving lumps where rats had run for safety and then become trapped. Sherlock turned and was about to run back towards the south side of the river when he remembered the other two ruffians. They would undoubtedly still be waiting at the top of the shaft. No, his best bet was to head the other way. He ran down the tunnel, towards the north side of the river. There were bridges across the river, and boatmen. He could find his way back.

Sherlock headed along the tunnel, moving further and further away from the fire. Men in uniform with buckets of water ran past him, a ragtag fire brigade charged with the safety of the tunnel. He ignored them and moved on.

Eventually he got to the north side of the Thames.

The shaft there, with its spiralling stairway, was the mirror image of the one on the south side. He trudged up the stone steps, energy almost spent. He had to stop at each balcony level to catch his breath.

Emerging from the darkness into the afternoon light was like emerging from Hell into Paradise. The air smelt sweet, and the breeze was cool against his skin. He stopped for a moment, eyes closed, to appreciate the feelings. So simple, and yet so perfect.

The area around the north side of the tunnel was less disreputable than the south side. Wharves were occupied by ships of all sizes, with goods being run up and down gangplanks by burly stevedores. Sherlock walked along the side of the Thames, past the ships, looking for a bridge that he could use to cross back to the other side. He knew there were bridges over the Thames; he just wasn't sure where they were in relation to Rotherhithe and the tunnel. But logically, if he walked for long enough he would find one. Assuming he was walking in the right direction of course—towards the centre of the city rather than away from it—but he knew that if the tunnel was in East London, which it was, and if he had traversed it south to north, which he had, then if he turned left out of the tunnel entrance he would be heading in the right direction. The Sarbonnier Hotel, where Amyus Crowe had booked their rooms, was just about on the Thames, and on the north side as well, so if he walked far enough then he would probably find it, but what he really wanted was to cross back over and find Amyus Crowe and Matty Arnatt.

After half an hour or so he did find a bridge: a massive affair, with twin towers of grey stone linked by a covered roadway which was lined with shops and stalls. He crossed it wearily, ignoring the cries of the various vendors who tried to sell him everything from a whole ox to a loaded pistol. London appeared to him to be a place of almost infinite possibilities, if you were prepared to pay for them.

At the south side of the towered bridge he turned left again, walking along roads, streets, alleys, and in some cases the tops of thick walls in order to keep heading towards the warehouse at Rotherhithe where he had lost Amyus Crowe and Matty. The masts of ships projected high into the air along the side of the river, forming a forest of slender wood. The smell of the Thames was an ever-present odour of human excrement. If Mycroft worked every day in this place then he deserved some kind of medal just for survival.

A mile or so downstream from the towered bridge, Sherlock came across a ship that was being loaded by a gang of stevedores. They were sweating and cursing, trying to manoeuvre bulky boxes up gangplanks without dropping them into the river. Something about the size and the shape of the boxes intrigued him, and he moved closer, keeping in the lee of a nearby building.

A burly man in a navy blue jacket stood to one side,

consulting a sheaf of papers that were pinned to a board. Every now and then he made an annotation with a pencil, licking it first.

The boxes were identical to the ones that Sherlock had seen in the gardens of the manor house in which he had been kept captive—the beehives with jagged, slatted sides. And nearby were piles and piles of the wooden trays that he had seen slotted underneath the hives. Now they had been wrapped in waxed paper, but their shape was unmistakable.

He had inadvertently stumbled across Baron Maupertuis's operation. *This* was why Denny and his gang had been here!

Sherlock moved closer, watching. Some of the beehives were being loaded onto a pallet that was pulled up on ropes by sweating stevedores and then dropped into the hold of the ship. Heaven alone knew how the bees were being kept from attacking the men, as they had done to the two unfortunates in Farnham. Perhaps the Baron had some method of quietening them down.

As Sherlock watched, a rope holding one of the corners of a pallet that was being swung towards the ship snapped. The pallet dropped sideways, and four beehives slid off. They fell, turning slowly, and smashed into wooden splinters on the stones below.

Men ran in from the side carrying tin buckets with nozzles attached. Something inside the buckets was producing smoke, and the smoke seemed to be lulling the bees into a soporific state. A few escaped, but most of them stayed near the smashed hives, weaving around like drunks. Tarpaulins were thrown across the remains of the hives, and everything was slid across the cobbles and dropped into the foaming torrent of the Thames. Sherlock supposed that it was almost impossible to rebuild a hive after it had been smashed.

"Sherlock?"

A voice called his name softly. He glanced around from his place of concealment. It didn't sound like Amyus Crowe. Or Matty Arnatt.

"*Sherlock?*" The voice was more urgent now. He scanned the area and suddenly became aware of another figure, hidden like him behind a pile of crates. A female figure.

"Virginia?"

She was wearing her riding breeches and a jacket over a plain white linen blouse. She glanced across at him, and her eyes were wide. "What are you doing *here*?" she hissed.

Sherlock scooted over to join her. "It would take too long to explain," he said.

She looked him up and down. "What have you been doing?"

He considered for a moment. "Swimming in rats," he said eventually. "Amongst other things. What's your story?"

She looked away, unexpectedly embarrassed. "I wasn't

going to be left behind while you guys had all the fun," she whispered, "so I got changed into my riding breeches and followed you."

"We went down the river. In a *boat*. How did you follow us?"

She stared strangely at him. "In another boat, of course. I just told the boatman to follow you. He got a bit funny about it, but I had some money that my father had given me, and that seemed to calm him down. While you were watching the warehouse, I was watching you. Then I saw some of the men come this way, and you all seemed to be staying put, so I followed them here."

"I saw nothing of you," Sherlock said lamely.

"Dad taught me all his tracking skills," she said proudly. "If I'm following you, then 'nothing' is exactly what you can expect to see." She paused and reached out to touch his arm briefly.

"What you did was incredibly dangerous," Sherlock said, "but I'm pleased to see you."

She shrugged. "It was better than waiting in the hotel for you all to come back."

"But why follow me? Why not find your dad and tell him what had happened?"

"I was following you," she said simply, "not him. I lost track of where he went."

"But a girl . . . alone . . . in the East End of London . . ." He trailed off, not sure how he was going to finish the sentence. "There are some very bad people around here . . ." he started eventually, and then went on to explain exactly what had happened that afternoon, including the stabbing and the fire in the tunnels. It was a relief to talk about it, but at the same time Sherlock knew that his life had been in mortal danger, and that he still didn't fully understand why.

"They can't be allowed to get away with it," Virginia said when he had finished. "You're just a kid. They could have killed you."

"You're just a kid too," Sherlock protested lamely.

Virginia smiled. "I didn't mean it like that," she said. "I meant we shouldn't be mixed up in something like this."

"But we are," Sherlock pointed out. "And whatever's going on, we have to stop it."

"Well, I'm prepared. I'm in disguise as a boy. I found a hat," Virginia said proudly, pulling it out from beneath where she crouched. It was a peaked cloth cap. She smoothed her hair up behind her head with one hand and slipped the cap on with the other. With her hair hidden and her coat buttoned up, Sherlock could see how she might have been mistaken for a boy. And she was wearing her riding breeches, of course. Girls wore dresses, not breeches. Nobody who didn't know her would have any reason to suspect her.

"Since we're both here," he said, "we ought to take the opportunity to work out where this boat is going." He looked around for the man he had seen earlier—the man with the sheaf of papers. "I think that man over there is the dockmaster, or wharfmaster, or something. We can ask him."

"Just like that?"

"Your father gave me some good tips on how to ask questions."

Looking around and choosing a moment when no-body was facing their way, Sherlock led Virginia out of hiding and across the quay to a point where they could sit on the stone wall overlooking the Thames. He felt the back of his neck prickling, telling him he was being watched, but he suppressed the feeling. Denny was probably with a doctor or a surgeon by now, assuming his jaw really was broken, and the chances were that the other men hadn't got a good enough look at him to tell him apart from any other kid—especially now, when he was covered in dirt, smoke, rat hair, and possibly other things that he didn't want to consider. They sat there on the wall for a good half hour, making desultory conversation and generally becoming part of the landscape. The dock-master, or wharfmaster, or whatever he was, eventually finished his business with the ship and started to walk in their direction. As he came past them, Sherlock looked up and said: "Hey, boss. Any chance of some work on the dock?"

The man glanced scornfully at Sherlock's skinny frame. "Come back in five years, son," he said in a not unkindly tone. "Get some muscle on those bones."

"But I gotta get out of London," Sherlock continued in

a pleading tone of voice. "I can work hard, honest I can." He pointed at the nearby boat. "What about them—they look like they're shorthanded."

"They are," the man said. "They're three men down this afternoon. But I can't see you filling in for any of them, and besides, that boat's not going to take you far out of London."

"Why not?" Sherlock asked.

"It's just going to France and back. Quick turnaround, no stopping off for the crew." He laughed. "You want to get away for a while, go join the Navy. Or hang around here long enough and they'll come and take you."

He moved off, still laughing.

"France," Sherlock said, intrigued. "Interesting."

"I hear you want to join our crew," a voice called from the bows of the boat. Sherlock grimaced and looked away, but the voice continued: "Why don't you and the girl come aboard? Yeah, we know it's a girl. We've been watching you since you both turned up. What, you thought you were invisible?"

Sherlock glanced along the dock to where the dockmaster had stopped and was looking back at them. The expression on his face was sympathetic but stern. He wasn't going to be any help.

Sherlock took Virginia's hand and pulled her upright. "Time to go," he said, but when he turned he found that a loose semicircle of sailors and dockers had formed around them, materializing out of nowhere. Dragging Virginia with him he tried to run, but heavy hands caught him and pulled him away from her. He fought against them, but the hands held him firmly. He saw Virginia struggling as well, but then a hand holding a cloth clamped itself over his face. The cloth smelt medicinal, bitter and heavy. He nearly choked. And then suddenly he found himself falling into a bottomless pit that was exactly the colour of Virginia's eyes, and for a while he slept, and dreamed of terrible things.

FOURTEEN

In his dreams Sherlock was wrestling with a huge serpent. Its body was as thick as a beer barrel, all muscle and ribs for as far as he could see, and its head was a flat triangle edged with sawlike teeth. They were fighting in water, but in his dream the water was as thick and as dark as treacle. The snake slowly coiled itself around him and squeezed, attempting to snap his ribs, but the water hampered its movements and Sherlock was able to prise its coils apart by pushing hard with his arms and legs. But then, as he tried to get away, his swimming was grotesquely slowed by the water and the serpent could once again slip its body around him and slowly tighten its grip. And so it went on, with him eternally struggling to escape and the serpent eternally struggling to hold on to him.

When he finally awoke, he had the feeling that a long time had passed. His mouth and throat were dry, and when he touched his tongue to the top of his mouth it stuck there. He was also very hungry.

After a while, he felt strong enough to sit up without being sick. And what he saw temporarily drove all thoughts of thirst, hunger, and sickness from his mind.

He was lying in a four-poster bed with an embroidered

canopy. The pillows were soft, filled with feathers, and the room beyond was panelled in oak. The floorboards were varnished and covered with exquisitely detailed rugs.

It was the same room in which he had woken up after being knocked out in the boxing match at the fair—the one just outside Farnham.

But how could that be? Baron Maupertuis had abandoned that manor house, leaving it empty. Surely he couldn't have returned so quickly? Why would he?

Sherlock rolled off the bed and stood upright. He ran a hand across his face and was surprised when it encountered something dry around his nose and mouth. He rubbed at the stuff, pulling it off his skin, then looked at his fingers. They were covered with strands of something black. He rubbed his fingers together and noticed that the strands were slightly sticky.

He remembered the cloth that had been clamped across his mouth. Some kind of chemical? A drug to make him sleep? It seemed likely.

And Virginia! A sudden flush of anger drove the last remnants of sleep and nausea from his blood. What had happened to Virginia? If anyone had harmed her, he would—

He would what? Kill them? He wasn't exactly in the best position to do that at the moment.

He had to gather information. Find out what was going on, and why. Only then could he do something about it.

Sherlock stepped across to the curtains and pulled them back, expecting to see the dry red earth and the hundreds of beehives that had been outside the last time he was in the room, but what he saw sent him reeling backwards in surprise.

A short distance from the house a beach of grey sand gave way to rolling spume-topped waves that extended all the way to a ruler-straight horizon. The sky was bright blue. Somewhere in the distance Sherlock could see sails.

He closed his eyes for a moment and thought. Was he hallucinating? It was possible, he supposed, but the dream about the snake and the treacle-like water had been tainted with a bizarre, illogical sensation which, looking back, had meant that he somehow knew that he was dreaming, whereas *this* was sharp-edged and rational.

Was the picture outside the window just that—a perfectly executed painting that gave the impression of beach and sea and blue sky when it was just pigments on canvas or board? He opened his eyes again and looked. Far away, circling above the peaks of the waves, were small white "w" shapes, moving as he watched—seabirds riding the updraughts. That couldn't be faked in a painting. Whatever was out there was real.

And as there was no ocean anywhere near Farnham, the logical conclusion was that he wasn't near Farnham anymore, and probably wasn't even in England. The wharfmaster had said that the boat was bound for France.

This must be France then. And the room? Something as prosaic as the fact that Baron Maupertuis was a creature of habit and liked to have his surroundings as familiar as possible, wherever he was. Assuming that the manor house outside Farnham wasn't his ancestral home, he had probably had it remodelled and redesigned to look like wherever it was that he called home. Which might well be this French . . . *château*? Was that what they called it?

Feeling obscurely pleased with himself for working out something that, he suspected, had been intended to confuse and destabilize him, he didn't even turn when the lock clicked on the bedroom door and it swung inward. He already knew what he would see there—two footmen in black breeches, black stockings, black waistcoats, and short black jackets wearing black velvet masks with eyeholes cut in them. Just like last time. He counted to ten in his mind, then turned. He was partly right—the two footmen standing just within the doorway were both dressed the way he remembered—but a third man stood in the centre of the doorway. In fact, he almost filled the doorway, he was so large. His arms were as thick as an ordinary man's legs while his legs were like tree trunks. His hands were the size and shape of shovel blades, but it was his head that commanded attention above everything else. He was bald, but his scalp was so covered with winding brown scars that it looked, at first glance, as if he had a full head of hair. He wore a long brown leather coat over a baggy grey suit, and the cut of the coat, together with its sheer bulk, made him look even larger.

"The Baron wants to see you," he said in a voice like the grinding of two millstones.

"What if I don't want to see the Baron?" Sherlock said in a level voice. The two footmen exchanged glances, but the scarred man just shook his head slightly. "What the Baron wants, the Baron gets. No other opinions count but his."

"What if I refuse to go with you?"

"Then we pick you up and carry you."

Sherlock knew he was being childish, but he wanted to establish in their minds that he wasn't just a passive prisoner—that he had opinions of his own. "What if I hold on to the doorframe and refuse to let go?"

"Then we break your fingers and take you anyway." The man smiled, but there was no mirth in the expression. It was just a baring of teeth, like a tiger preparing to strike. "All the Baron needs is enough of you to answer questions. That means your head, so your brain can think and your mouth can move, and your chest, so your lungs can breathe and keep you alive. Everything else is optional. Your choice."

Sherlock held on for a moment, just to prove that he knew he had a choice and was exercising it, and then moved towards the doorway. The scarred man didn't move until Sherlock was about to bump into his chest, then he turned to one side, just enough so that Sherlock could pass through the doorway.

"My name is Mr. Surd," he said as he and the footmen followed Sherlock down the hall. "I am the Baron's man-servant and factotum. Whatever he wants done, I do. If he wants a glass of Madeira, it's my job to pour it. If he wants your head on a plate, it's my job to cut it off and deliver it. Not a pleasure, not an onerous task. Just a job. Do you understand me?"

"I understand," said Sherlock. "It was you holding the whip last time I met the Baron, wasn't it? In the shadows."

"Just a job," the scarred man repeated. "But I do take pleasure in a job well done."

The upper hall was just as he remembered it in the house at Farnham, as were the stairs leading down to the main hall. Sherlock had to stop himself from looking for hoofprints from when he and Matty had made their es-cape. It wasn't this house. It was another house that just happened to look like this one.

Virginia was standing outside the room in which, Sherlock remembered, Baron Maupertuis would be wait-ing for them. Two masked footmen stood beside her, next to a large teak cabinet.

"Are you all right?" he asked.

"Strange dreams," she said. "I was riding Sandia, but he was wild and I couldn't control him. We just rode on and on through this landscape that kept melting away whenever I looked at it." She shook herself to get rid of the memory. "What about you?"

"Snakes," he said succinctly.

"What was that stuff they drugged us with? My head's still muzzy."

"I think it was laudanum—morphine dissolved in alcohol. My mother and father used to give it to my sister. I recognize the smell. It's made out of poppies."

"Poppies?" She laughed. "I never liked poppies. They're a very macabre flower."

Mr. Surd pushed past them and pulled open the door into the room where the Baron waited. He gestured for them to go in.

The room was in darkness, as before. Two chairs were set at one end of a massive table whose other end was shrouded in shadow. Heavy black drapes hung at the windows, preventing sunlight from entering the room, and the few areas of exposed wall that Sherlock could see were covered with swords and shields. Against one wall, Sherlock noticed a full suit of armour holding a sword that had been arranged as if there was a knight inside.

Mr. Surd indicated that they should sit. Sherlock considered refusing, but then saw something in Mr. Surd's eyes that suggested the manservant expected him to refuse, and even wanted him to, just so he could do something painful and permanent to ensure that Sherlock complied. So he sat down, with Virginia beside him. Mr. Surd and the four footmen walked off into the darkness at the other end of the room.

The room was quiet for a while, apart from the faint creaking of ropes and wood under stress that Sherlock had heard last time.

Then a whispery voice, like dry leaves rustling in the wind: "You persist in interfering in my plans, and yet you are just a child. I was forced to abandon one of my houses because of you."

"You seem to like to have your houses designed and decorated identically," Sherlock said. "Why? Do you prefer things to be the same?"

There was silence for a while, and Sherlock expected any moment to feel the tip of a whip striking from the darkness, flaying his flesh open, but instead the voice replied.

"Once I find something I like," it said, "I see no reason to suffer anything else. The layout and furnishings of a house, a system of government . . . once I discover something that works, I want it replicated so that things are the same wherever I go. I find it . . . comforting."

"And that's why you have your footmen dressed in black masks—because that way you can believe them to be the same footmen, wherever you happen to be."

"Very perspicacious."

"And we're in, what, France at the moment?"

"You recognized the landscape? Yes, this house is in France. You were both kept asleep on the boat that brought you here, and then on the carriage that rushed you to this place."

"But what about Mr. Surd?" Sherlock asked. "There's only one of him."

"Mr. Surd is irreplaceable. Where I go, he goes."

"You *are* Baron Maupertuis, aren't you?"

"Again, you surprise me. I did not believe that my name was widely known."

"I . . . pieced it together from evidence."

"Very clever. Very clever indeed. I compliment you on your deductive skills. And what else did you piece together?"

Virginia placed a warning hand over his, but Sherlock felt a blossoming pride at the investigations he had made, the facts that he had discovered, the plot that he was beginning to put together. And, he told himself, it was important that Maupertuis know that his plans were no longer secret. "I know you've been keeping bees, and I know they are a foreign species that's more aggressive than any European bee. That means you're not keeping them to make honey, but because of their stings. You want them to hurt or kill people." His brain was racing now, moving the facts around to form patterns that he had only barely suspected before. Amyus Crowe wanted to teach him, train him, but Baron Maupertuis was taking him seriously. The Baron listened to Sherlock's deductions as though they actually meant something, rather than just being theoretical answers to invented

problems, like rabbits and foxes. "You've also been running a factory to produce clothes—Army uniforms, I
think." He paused for a second. There was something
just beyond his reach, a momentous logical destination
to which he had all the steps but the last, which required
an intuitive leap. "Your man—Wint, I think his name
was—stole some of the clothes and stored them in his
house. He was attacked by bees. Another man who worked
on my uncle's estate as a gardener had previously been
making clothes in Farnham—for you, I assume. He was
killed by bees as well. Had he kept some of the clothes
for his own use? Stolen them from you?" The mental fog
that shrouded the final logical destination from him was
clearing now, and he continued triumphantly: "So there's
something about the clothes that causes the bees to attack
them. In their boxes or crates they're safe, but when people
wear them . . . the bees are attracted to them, and sting
whoever's wearing them."

Virginia's hand was clamped hard over his now, but
Sherlock ignored her.

"Those men who were at the warehouse in Rotherhithe—they were talking about shipping the boxes out
to Ripon, Colchester, and Aldershot. Those are all Army
bases. So if the clothes are all being shipped to Army
bases then they're probably uniforms. What did you
do—get some kind of government contract to supply
uniforms to the British Army? The soldiers wear their
new uniforms, probably as they prepare to ship out to

India, and then . . ." Sherlock's thoughts had been racing ahead of him, but suddenly the two snapped back into synchronization. His father. Aldershot. India. Uniforms. "And then you release the bees, and they attack every single private, subaltern, and officer in the British Army," he whispered, appalled at the place to which logic had taken him.

"Thousands of deaths, all occurring mysteriously and unavoidably," the Baron whispered from the darkness at the end of the table. "A demoralizing blow directed at the heart of the British Empire, and delivered by the humble bee—provider of honey for a thousand Sunday afternoon tea parties. The irony is . . . appealing."

"But why?" Sherlock's thoughts were filled with visions of his father, face swollen and covered with boils, falling and choking as the bees stung him again and again.

"Why?" The Baron's voice wasn't any louder, but it was suddenly laden with a viciousness that had been absent before. "*Why?* Because your pathetic little country has delusions of grandeur that have led it to conquer half the world. It would be hard to find a country smaller than England. You're barely a pinprick on the map. On any globe of the world the cartographers cannot write the word 'England' within the boundaries of the island, it's so small. And yet you have the arrogance, the temerity, the sheer self-delusion to believe that the world was set out for your benevolent rule. And the world has just rolled over and let you do it! Astounding. But there are men in the world, military men, who will not let your rampant and predatory instincts go any further. The boundaries of the British Empire have to be pushed back, if only so that other countries can get some breathing space, some room to live. I . . . represent . . . a group of these men. German, French, American, Russian—they have come together to curb your territorial ambitions. You will not rest until the red of the British Empire has spilt across the map; we will not rest until it has been erased apart from your own puny island." He paused. "And possibly British Honduras, in South America. You can keep British Honduras."

"So you plan to destroy the British Army at a single stroke."

"Not so much a single stroke as a progressive disease, striking at soldiers but nobody else. The bees, as you are aware, are unusually aggressive and territorial. They have been bred for aggression—and my, they breed quickly. The contaminant that we have soaked the uniforms in will be absorbed into the soldiers' bodies, and will be sweated out through their skin. The bees, if they smell it, will immediately attack. Once the bees are released from their new homes they will make their way across Britain over the course of several months, stinging all the soldiers to death as they go. We will breed more in secret locations throughout Europe for the next stage of the attack. The terror, the fear, the sheer panic will be our most effective allies. A mysterious plague afflicting soldiers. And

Britain will be relegated to the position it deserves: as a third-rate nation."

"But what about the two men who died—your man and my uncle's gardener? They weren't part of your plot, were they?"

A rustle and a creaking noise from the darkness, as if Baron Maupertuis was shrugging. Or being made to shrug. "I knew that some of the workers were stealing pieces of the uniforms, but I let it go. That was my mistake. One of the hives was knocked over by a horse, and the bees escaped. They became feral, wild, and when they smelt the contaminant on the stolen uniforms they attacked. Mr. Surd had to recover the queen and lure the surviving bees back. A very brave mission."

"Just a job, sir," Mr. Surd said from the end of the room.

Even though he had worked most of it out already, the sheer effrontery of the plot took Sherlock's breath away. And appalling as it was, he couldn't see any obvious flaws. If the bees were as aggressive as Maupertuis said, and if the uniforms were distributed as efficiently as he intended, then it would work. It *would* work.

"My brother will stop you," Sherlock said calmly. It was his last hope.

"Your brother?"

"My brother."

Sherlock heard a whispering from the darkness. It sounded like the gravelly tones of Mr. Surd again.

"Ah," Maupertuis said in his leaf-thin voice. "Your name is Sherlock Holmes. Your brother must therefore be Mycroft Holmes. A clever man. We had already marked him down as someone of interest to our group. It seems you take after him."

"I've already sent him a telegram telling him what's going on," Sherlock said, as calmly as he could manage.

"No," the Baron corrected, "you haven't. If you had, there would be no need for you to have been investigating my boat. Mycroft Holmes would have sent his own agents in to do the work."

His own agents? Sherlock had a sudden, sobering realization of the extent of his brother's powers.

More whispering from the end of the room.

"We may have to deal with your brother regardless," Baron Maupertuis whispered. "If your intelligence is an indication of his then he may well be able to work out our plans and try to stop them. You and he will die within the same week, possibly even on the same day. At the same hour, if I can arrange it, for I am a man who appreciates neatness. And it will save your parents the cost of arranging two funerals."

The full cost of Sherlock's arrogance suddenly descended upon him. By proudly working out the whole terrible plot and demonstrating his cleverness to Baron Maupertuis and then, worse, boasting about his influential brother, Sherlock had condemned them both to death.

"I believe you have told me everything you know," Maupertuis continued, "and I am surprised at the amount you have determined. We obviously need to be even more secretive in future. Thank you for that, at least."

"Why London?" Sherlock asked quickly, sensing that things were drawing to a close and that his—and Virginia's—lives would shortly be terminated. "Why did you move the hives to London before shipping them here rather than, say, Portsmouth or Southampton?"

"Your escape forced us to move earlier than planned," Maupertuis whispered. "There was no berth available in Portsmouth or Southampton, and the ship had been waiting in London for our instruction to move. It was inefficient, taking the hives to London, but it was unavoidable. And with that, your usefulness to me has ceased—yours, and that of the girl who sits beside you. I had intended to threaten her life in order to force you to talk, but no force had to be applied. If anything, shutting you up was the problem."

Sherlock turned to Virginia, feeling his face flush with mortification, but she was smiling at him. "You stopped me being tortured," she whispered. "Thank you."

"You're welcome," Sherlock said automatically, not entirely sure whether he should actually take credit for it.

"Mr. Surd," Baron Maupertuis's voice said from out of the dark. Although he whispered, his voice carried to every corner of the room. It was a voice used to command. "We need to accelerate our plans. Give the order. Release the bees from the fort. By the time they find their way to the mainland and across the country, the uniforms will have been distributed. And then confusion will reign!"

FIFTEEN

The Baron's words echoed chillingly around the dining room. Out in the darkness there was a rustle of activity as a servant left with his orders. Sherlock glanced at Virginia. Her face was pale, but her mouth was set in a determined line. He reached across to squeeze her hand. She gave him a slight smile.

Her spirit gave Sherlock the courage to carry on.

"It's a grandiose plan," he said towards the darkness, "but it just won't work."

There was silence for a moment, broken only by the strange creaking noise that Sherlock remembered from the house in Farnham, like the sound of sea-dampened ship's rigging being strained by the wind and by the pitching and tossing of the ship's hull.

"You seem very sure of yourself," the Baron's voice came back. "For a child."

"Think about it. Just because two men have died as a result of your schemes, that doesn't make your plan foolproof. All kinds of things could wash the chemical from the uniforms, for instance. Remember, it rains in England. It rains a lot. Some of the soldiers will have their uniforms laundered before the bees can get to them—especially the officers." He was getting into his stride now, his mind sparking with ideas as to why

Maupertuis's colossal scheme was doomed to failure. "Some soldiers might prefer their old uniforms, and keep them, or get their regimental tailor to make them new ones rather than using the ones you've sent out. I don't know about France and Germany and Russia, but people in England don't like being told what to do and what to wear. They find ways around orders like that."

"What about the bees themselves?" Virginia added unexpectedly. "How many of them will actually get to the mainland? How many bees do you need to cover all those areas where the Army are based? Have you got enough? And what happens if there's a cold spell and the bees die off, or if there's something in England that eats the bees, or if they just settle down, build a hive, and become part of the natural order there? The chances are they'll end up interbreeding with the local bees, the British bees, and lose all traces of the aggression that your plan depends on."

"All of these factors have been accounted for," the Baron replied in his dry-as-dust voice, but to Sherlock he sounded unsure of himself for the first time. "And even if some uniforms are laundered, and some bees die, what of it? Many of the attacks will be successful nevertheless. Widespread death will occur. The British Army will be paralysed by fear. *Paralysed.*"

"You just don't understand the way the English think, do you?" Sherlock scoffed. His mind ranged back over his lessons at school, over what he had read in the newspapers, curled up in a chair in his father's study, or heard from his brother Mycroft. "Have you ever heard of the Charge of the Light Brigade?"

The sound of creaking in the darkness stopped abruptly. Sherlock had the sudden sense that many ears were listening intently to what he said.

"Oh yes," the Baron hissed. "I have heard of the Charge of the Light Brigade."

"In 1854," Sherlock continued, regardless, "during the Crimean War, the soldiers of the 4th and 13th Light Dragoons, the 17th Lancers, and the 8th and 11th Hussars were ordered to charge the Russian lines during the Battle of Balaclava. They were charging down a valley that had Russian cannons on each side and in front of them, and they just kept on going. They followed orders, without panicking and without mutinying. I'm not saying that mindless obedience to orders is a good thing, but discipline is built into the British soldier like a rod of iron right down his back. I know that—my father is an officer. Officers don't panic. Not ever. No, even if there are deaths it'll be treated just like an outbreak of smallpox or cholera. Don't you understand? *They will ignore it.* That's what the British *do.* That's why the British Empire is so widespread and so strong. *We just ignore the things we don't like.*"

"You speak well," the Baron said, "but I do not believe you. Obviously you want to believe that your Empire is built on rock-solid foundations, but you are wrong. The foundations are rotten, and the edifice will crumble if it is pushed hard enough. You want to believe that tomorrow will be the same as yesterday, but it will not. The world will change, and the balance of power will tip in favour of my associates in the Paradol Chamber."

The Paradol Chamber? What was that? As Maupertuis was talking, Sherlock memorized what might have been an important slip of the tongue that Mycroft would want to know about.

Assuming that Sherlock ever got the chance to see his brother again.

"You want to believe that your brother will continue to be an important man in the British government," Maupertuis continued, "but he will not. He, like the rest of his colleagues, will be swept away by the tide of history. When this bumptious little country of yours is a mere province of a European superpower that can rival America in its size and power, then Mycroft Holmes and his ilk will be surplus to requirements. Their kind will not be needed in the new world order. They will find themselves at the mercy of the guillotine or the garrotte. They will not survive."

Maupertuis's voice had descended to a low hiss by now, so carried away was he with this venomous diatribe directed against a country and a people that he so obviously hated. Why did he hate Great Britain so much? Sherlock found himself wondering what might work best—a reasoned argument, or provoking the Baron into a more emotional state. Either way, the outcome was uncertain. The chances were that the two of them were going to die.

"He is mad," Virginia said quietly but firmly to Sherlock. "Stark, staring mad. His plan is obviously nuts, and the outcome he wants is impossible. Like it or not, Britain is a world power. He can't reverse that."

"I am surprised," the Baron hissed, "that you are defending this country so strongly, girl."

Virginia looked up as he spoke, surprised at her sudden inclusion in the Baron's thoughts. "Why surprised?" she asked. "I don't like to see innocent people killed. Is that unusual?"

"Your country was beholden to this one for over two hundred years," the Baron pointed out. "Everything in America was ruled from London. You were just another county, like Hampshire or Dorset, only larger and further away. You had to rebel against British control and throw off the yoke of Westminster."

"And we did it in a clean fight," she pointed out. "Not by tricks and schemes and secret plans. If we've got to have wars then that's the way they should be—fair and open and clean. There should be rules for war, like there are for boxing."

"Naïve," the Baron murmured. "So naïve. And so pointless. You and the boy will die before you ever find out that your precious world order will be overturned."

"You like operating in the shadows, don't you?"

Virginia continued, and there was a hard-edged tone in her voice that made Sherlock glance at her, wondering what she was up to.

"The successful fighter strikes from the shadows and then hides in them again, so that the bigger, stronger foe does not know where to retaliate," the Baron whispered. "That is the warfare of the future. That is how a smaller foe can overcome a much larger one. By stealth."

"You prefer the shadows? Then let's see how you like the sunlight," she cried, and leaped to her feet. Sherlock sensed a flurry of activity at the shadowed end of the room as Mr. Surd prepared to strike out with his metal-tipped whip, but Virginia darted to one side and the whip sliced into the back of the chair she had just vacated. She grabbed the black velvet curtains that lined the room and pulled on them, hard. Sherlock heard a ripping sound as the velvet tore loose from the curtain rail, and then, with a sound like a distant rainstorm, a whole sheet of material fell to the ground in a slow avalanche of soft cloth, letting bright sunlight spill into the room.

Black-clad and masked figures around the room shielded their eyes, but Sherlock's gaze was drawn to the figure of the Baron, sitting in an oversized chair at the other end of the table. It was, indeed, the same pink-eyed, white-haired man that he had seen in the carriage back in Farnham. The Baron squinted into the light, shielding his face with one hand while the other hand came up with a pair of glasses with darkened lenses that he slipped over his sensitive eyes. His arms were thin and twisted, like the branches of an old oak tree, and his head lolled on his shoulders. He was wearing what seemed to be a military uniform: black, with ornate gold braid decorating the chest and the cuffs. There was something around his forehead, a wooden frame of some kind. His head suddenly straightened up and his eyes glared at Sherlock from behind the dark lenses so intensely that Sherlock could almost feel their heat. He noticed that there were cords leading upward from the frame, and that those cords had pulled taut at the exact moment that Maupertuis's head had straightened up.

Mr. Surd was standing beside the Baron, the scars on his head livid in the light from the window, like a nest of worms across a naked skull. He stared at Sherlock and Virginia with the promise of death in his eyes, brandishing his whip.

"No!" the Baron hissed. "They are *mine!*"

Sherlock's gaze was drawn inexorably back to the twisted body of Baron Maupertuis. There were more ropes attached to smaller wooden frames on the Baron's wrists and elbows, and a larger wooden frame encasing his chest. Thicker ropes led up from the chest-frame, and as Sherlock's gaze tracked them upward, towards the ceiling of the room, he realized that all the ropes were attached to a massive wooden beam like a gibbet that hung suspended above the Baron. The end of the beam closest to Sherlock joined a smaller crossbeam covered with metal hooks and metal wheels on tiny axles. The ropes passed through these hooks and wheels, and Sherlock traced them back to where masked, black-clad servants held the ends. There must have been twenty, perhaps thirty ropes, all connected to parts of the Baron's body. And as Sherlock watched, incredulous, some of the servants pulled on their ropes, exerting all their strength, while others either let theirs go loose or just took up the slack without actually pulling. And as they did so, the Baron jerked upright.

He was a puppet: a human puppet, entirely operated by others.

"Grotesque, yes?" the Baron hissed. His mouth and his eyes appeared to be the only parts of his body that he could move by himself. His right hand came up and gestured at his body, but the movement was caused by a series of ropes attached to his wrist, his elbow, and his shoulder, and smaller cords fixed to rings on his knuckles, all moving not because the Baron wanted them to but because his black-clad servants were anticipating what he would do if he could. "This is the legacy I was left with by the British Empire. You mentioned the Charge of the Light Brigade, boy. A tedious, pointless engagement based on misunderstood orders in a war that should never have been fought. I was there, on that overcast day, with the Earl of Lucan. I was his liaison with the French cavalry, who were on his left flank. I saw the orders when they arrived from Lord Raglan. I knew that they were badly phrased, and that Lucan had misunderstood them."

"What happened?" Sherlock asked.

"My horse was caught up in the charge, and spooked by the cannon fire. I was thrown from the saddle, and I tumbled to the ground in front of hundreds of British horses. They galloped right over me. I doubt they even saw me. I felt my bones break as the hoofs came down on me. My legs, my arms, my ribs, my hips, and my skull. Every major bone in my body was fractured, and most of the minor ones. Inside, I was like a jigsaw puzzle."

"You should have died," Virginia breathed, and Sherlock wasn't sure whether she spoke the words with pity or regret.

"I was found by my compatriots after the British were torn to pieces by the Russian cannon," Maupertuis continued. "They carried me from the battlefield. They tended my wounds. They put me back together as best they could, and helped my bones to heal, but my neck was broken and although my heart still beat I could not move my legs. They didn't dare carry me too far, so I lay there in a tent in the stinking heat and the frozen cold of the Crimea for a year. A whole *year*. And for every second, every minute, every hour, every day, every week, and every month that I was there, I cursed the British and their stupidity in just following orders no matter how stupid those orders were."

"You chose to be there," Sherlock pointed out. "You

were wearing uniform. And you lived when hundreds of good men died."

"And every day I wish I had died with them. But I live, and I have a purpose: to bring the British Empire to its knees. Starting with you, child."

As he spat the words, Maupertuis seemed to float up in the air and land lightly on the table. The ropes above him tautened, pulled on by his black-clad puppeteers. A creaking noise filled the room as the ropes and the wood took the strain of the Baron's weight. Somehow the servants had divined what he wanted them to do. Sherlock assumed they had been working with him for so long that they knew instinctively the way his thoughts were going and could translate them into instantaneous action. As Maupertuis's feet touched the table, Sherlock sprang up from his chair. Beside him, Virginia did the same.

"Baron!" Mr. Surd called. "You don't need to do this yourself. Let me kill the children for you!"

"No," the Baron hissed. "I am not a cripple! I will erase these interfering brats myself! All those months, all that time spent paralysed and designing this harness—it will not be wasted. *I will kill them myself!* Do you understand?"

"At least let me kill the girl," Surd insisted. "At least let me do that for you."

"Very well," the Baron conceded. "Then I will deal with the boy."

Seemingly weightless, Maupertuis drifted towards

Sherlock, his feet moving but barely touching the surface of the table. He extended his hand towards the boy, and for a moment Sherlock thought that the Baron was inviting him up to the table, but instead cords and wires suddenly pulled taut inside the sleeve of the Baron's uniform and a shining blade slid out of a scabbard hidden along his forearm. His twiglike fingers closed around a padded hilt, not so much controlling the blade as giving it some guidance.

Sherlock backed away towards the suit of armour that stood beside the door. He grabbed the sword from its mailed grip, knocking the armour to the floor.

Sherlock was barely aware that Mr. Surd was walking out of the darkness, his metal-tipped whip dangling menacingly from his hand, but then the Baron sprang off the table towards him, swinging his sabre. The scaffold-like structure that held him was on wheels, and there were more servants behind it, pushing and pulling it along and swinging it around. Maupertuis could go anywhere in the room within seconds, faster than Sherlock could move.

The Baron swung his sabre. Sherlock parried clumsily, feeling the impact tear at the muscles in his shoulder. Sparks flew from the point where the blades clashed. The Baron leaped into the air, cleaving his blade down towards Sherlock's head. Sherlock rolled to his left and the Baron's blade tore through the back of the chair where Sherlock had been sitting only moments before, splintering the wood and sending bits of the chair in all directions.

Sherlock glanced desperately to his right. Virginia was backing away from Mr. Surd, who was uncoiling his whip. He sent it lashing out at her, like a striking snake. She flinched away, too late. A gash opened up on her cheek. Blood sprayed in a flower shape across her skin.

Sherlock desperately wanted to rush to help, but the Baron landed lightly on the floor in front of him. Springing to his feet, Sherlock slashed his blade sideways, trying to cut one of the ropes and cords that held the Baron up, but the black-clad servants pulled their master backwards, out of Sherlock's reach. The Baron's white, skull-like face split open in a grimacing smile. His pink, ratlike eyes seemed to glow with triumph. He sprang, his right foot sliding on the carpet and his right arm, holding the sabre, extending forward in a perfect thrust while his left foot braced his body. Sherlock could hear grunts from the servants in the shadows as they threw their weight into the mechanism holding the Baron up. The blade hurtled towards Sherlock's throat. He tried to parry, but his feet tangled in the folds of the carpet and he sprawled backwards, head thudding against the ground.

"I was the greatest fencing master in the whole of France!" Maupertuis gloated. "And I still am!"

Virginia cried out, and Sherlock glanced involuntarily in her direction. Surd had her pinned by the wall. Another cut had been opened up across her forehead.

The redness of the blood was dulled by the copper of her hair, glinting in the sunlight that spilt through the undraped window. Sherlock tried to move towards her but the Baron's sabre came flashing out of nowhere, slashing through Sherlock's shirt collar and carving a line of fire across his chest. Pushing himself to his feet he backed rapidly away, his blade weaving in front of him in a desperate attempt to block the Baron's thrusts.

With a heaving of wooden machinery and a creaking of ropes, the Baron's body levitated and flew forward in a way that no merely human swordsman could match. He swung his sabre horizontally, like a scythe. Despite his claims to be a master swordsman all thoughts of swordsmanship appeared to have vanished from his mind. He was just hacking mindlessly at Sherlock now, and Sherlock's arms were tiring from the effort of blocking the blows. His muscles burned and his tendons felt as tight as violin strings.

Something flew through the air past Sherlock's head, and he turned to look. It was a metal gauntlet, part of the suit of armour he had knocked over earlier. Virginia had scooped it up off the floor and thrown it at Mr. Surd, who was shielding his face. Virginia picked up a metalled boot and flung it. The metal toe caught Mr. Surd above the eye, and he swore.

Sherlock moved backwards as Maupertuis strode forward, the ropes above the broken man creaking under the strain. How did the black-clad puppeteers manage to coordinate their movements so well? Maupertuis walked as well as anyone without those terrible injuries. There was even a swagger in his step.

The Baron raised his sword up past his left ear and slashed diagonally downward at Sherlock's head. Sherlock blocked the blow. Sparks from the point where the two swords clashed flew away like tiny glowing insects, stinging Sherlock's neck and shoulders.

It was hopeless. Maupertuis was a master swordsman, even handicapped as he was by having his every move performed by anonymous servants. Either those servants were themselves master swordsmen—which Sherlock could almost believe—or they and the Baron had trained together for so long that they instinctively operated as a single organism, without the need for communication or thought. How many thousands of hours had Maupertuis spent drilling them until they worked almost as extensions of his will?

Sherlock edged backwards, but his elbow and shoulder banged against something hard. The wall! He had retreated as far as he possibly could.

Maupertuis's elbow jerked back and his sword flashed forward like lightning. Desperately, Sherlock slid sideways, and the blade sliced through the collar of his jacket and further, grinding into the gap between two blocks of stone. Sherlock tried to pull away, but he was pinioned, stuck like a butterfly on a board.

He braced himself, waiting for Maupertuis to withdraw the blade ready for a final strike so that he could slide down and escape, but instead Maupertuis brought his left hand up. Wires and cords writhed like tendons, and something slid out of the Baron's left sleeve. For a moment Sherlock thought it was a knife, but there was something strange about the tip. It looked more like a metal disc with a serrated edge.

Something whirred in the darkness behind Maupertuis and the wheel began to spin, scattering glittering shards of light in all directions. Sherlock could feel the air brushing past his face as the Baron brought the sawtoothed wheel closer and closer to his right eye.

Despair washed over him. Sherlock was no match for the Baron. He couldn't last against this kind of punishment for more than a few moments.

But he had to save Virginia.

The thought spurred him to a final effort. He twisted, pulling his arm out of the jacket sleeve and falling to the flagstones as the whirring disc hit the wall, gouging a shallow rut and scattering sparks and fragments of stone. The Baron cursed and tried to pull his sword from between the stones.

If Sherlock couldn't beat Maupertuis with his skill as a swordsman, he would beat him with the power of his brain. All he had to do was work out a single vulnerability, something he could exploit. And it had to be something to do with the way Maupertuis was moving, or being moved. That was his weakness. Sherlock tried again to strike out at the ropes and cords that held Maupertuis up but the Baron's servants were alert to that, and parried Sherlock's blade effortlessly with the spinning saw in his left hand while his right arm jerked the blade free.

Backing away, Sherlock nearly stumbled over the remains of the chair where he had been sitting, which had been smashed apart by the Baron's sword. The wood clattered as he kicked it, and a fragmentary plan materialized in his mind. Without waiting to think it through, Sherlock bent down and picked up the largest chunk of the chair with his left hand—a piece that incorporated most of an arm, part of the seat, and a carved leg. As the Baron slashed down at Sherlock's unprotected forehead, Sherlock raised the piece of chair. The Baron's blade embedded itself deeply in the wood. Before the Baron could pull it out, Sherlock pushed backwards, raising the sword above the Baron's head. The back of Sherlock's hand rasped against one of the ropes holding Maupertuis up. He twisted the wood, bending the sword nearly out of the Baron's grip, and tucked it behind several other ropes, then let it twist back again. Caught between the ropes, the chunk of the wooden chair hung in the air, suspended. Sherlock let go, then grabbed first one, then another of the remaining ropes and cords and, using all his strength, tangled them up behind the wood.

"What are you *doing*?" the Baron screamed, but it was

too late. The ropes holding him up were now a cat's cradle, pinned in place by the wooden chair leg and arm. Maupertuis dangled helplessly. The servants in the darkness at the end of the room exerted all their strength, but to no avail. They couldn't dislodge the remains of the chair from the ropes.

Stepping back, Sherlock swept his sword through the ropes, severing five or six of them. Tension suddenly released, they *twanged* away into the corners of the room. The Baron's arms dropped, and his head lolled to one side.

"You will pay for this," he hissed.

"Send me an invoice," Sherlock said calmly. He turned to where Virginia was standing, ready to leap to her aid, only to see her bring the sharp-edged iron helmet of the suit of armour heavily down onto Mr. Surd's head. He dropped to the floor, unconscious and bleeding.

"I was coming to help," Sherlock said.

"Strange," Virginia replied. "So was I."

SIXTEEN

"Thank heavens for Baron Maupertuis," Sherlock said in a heartfelt whisper as he slammed the door of the dining room shut behind them. There was no lock on the door, so he threw his weight behind a teak cabinet that stood beside it. Its legs squealed on the tiles as it shifted.

"Why?" Virginia snapped, adding her weight to his. The cabinet slid across the door, preventing it from opening. "What's he ever done for us?"

Baron Maupertuis's servants must have reached the door out of the dining room, because it suddenly opened a crack and thudded against the cabinet. They rattled it a few times, but the cabinet didn't move.

"He likes everywhere he lives to look the same. That's how I know where the stables will be. Come on!" He led the way through the back of the house to an outside door, and when he was certain that none of Maupertuis's servants were outside he and Virginia hurried around the side of the château and found the stables. Judging by the position of the sun, it was mid-morning. They'd been kept drugged for at least a night, possibly more.

Ever practical, Virginia immediately began to saddle two horses. "What are we going to do, Sherlock? We're in a foreign country! We don't even speak the language!"

"Actually"—he blushed—"I do."

"Do what?"

"Speak the language. A little, anyway."

She turned and gave him a funny look. "How come?"

"My family is descended from a French line on my mother's side. She used to insist that we learn the language. It was our family heritage, she said."

Virginia reached out to touch his arm. "You don't talk about her," she said. "You talk about your father and your brother, but not her."

"No," Sherlock said, feeling his throat close up. He turned away so she wouldn't look him in the eye. "I don't."

Virginia tightened the final straps on the horses. "So, given that you *do* speak the language, where do we go? Do we ask for help?"

"We head for a port," Sherlock said. "Maupertuis gave the instruction to release the bees. If we don't stop them, they'll kill people. Maybe not as many as Maupertuis expects, but some British soldiers will still die. We have to stop them being released."

"But—"

"One thing at a time," he said. "Let's get to the coast. From there we can send a telegram to my brother, or something. Anything."

Virginia nodded. "Mount up then, master swordsman."

He grinned. "You were pretty magnificent in there as well."

She grinned too. "I was, wasn't I?"

Mounting their horses, they rode away from the château just as shouts began to ring out and an alarm bell began to peal. Within moments, Sherlock knew, they would be too far away to catch.

In the nearest village they stopped to ask where they were. They were both hungry, but they had no French money, and all they could do was look longingly at the sausages hanging up in the shop windows and the bread rolls, as long as Sherlock's arm, that were stacked up on trays. A farmer told Sherlock that they were a few miles from Cherbourg. He pointed them to the right road, and they kept going.

Virginia glanced over appraisingly at him, at one point. "Not bad," she said. "You ride like it's a bicycle, not a living creature, but still—not bad."

They stopped again, half an hour later, on the edges of a pear orchard, and filled their pockets with pears which they ate as they rode on, the juice trickling down their chins. The countryside flashed by, familiar and yet different from what Sherlock was used to in England. His head pounded like the thundering of his horse's hoofs. He needed to work out what they were going to do when they reached Cherbourg.

By the time they got there, he had no clearer an idea.

The town was built on the side of a hill that led down towards the glittering blue waters of a harbour. The hoofs of the horses clattered on the cobblestones, and they were forced to slow down to an amble so they could get through the crowds that were thronging around the various stalls and shops lining the winding streets. It was a scene that could have been anywhere along the south coast of England, apart from the style of the clothes and the preponderance of cheeses on the stalls.

Sherlock and Virginia dismounted and, reluctantly, left their horses tethered to a fence. Someone would look after them. He tested his language skills to the limit by asking whether there was a telegraph office around, and was devastated to find that the nearest one was in Paris. How were they going to get word to Mycroft now?

They had to find a ship and get back to England. That was their only hope.

They found the harbourmaster's office, and asked about ships or boats sailing to England. There were several, the harbourmaster told them. He laboriously went through the names. Four were local boats that took goods for market—cheeses, meats, onions—back and forth. He could put in a good word for them with their captains.

The fifth was a British fishing boat that had docked unexpectedly that morning.

It was named *Mrs. Eglantine.*

Hearing the name was like having a bucket of cold water thrown into his face. For a frozen moment Sherlock was convinced that Mrs. Eglantine—his uncle and aunt's housekeeper—was the mastermind behind this whole thing, but then better sense prevailed. Someone was using the name like a flag, to attract his attention. And they had.

The *Mrs. Eglantine* was a small boat, tucked into a pier on the edge of the dock. Fishing nets were strung around it like cobwebs. Amyus Crowe and Matty Arnatt were waiting for them beside its gangplank.

Virginia rushed into her father's arms. He swung her up into the air and hugged her close. Sherlock pounded Matty on the back.

"How did you know where to find us?" he asked. "How did you even know which *country* to look in?"

"You got to remember, I'm a tracker by trade," Crowe said. "When you didn't return to the hotel, and when we realized that Ginny was missin', we tried to retrace your steps. I heard about the fire in the Rotherhithe Tunnel, an' a little bit of questionin' established that a boy fittin' your description was seen running away. Meanwhile, Matty here traced the boat that took Ginny to the docks. By the time we got there, Maupertuis's ship had sailed, but we found a dockmaster who remembered seein' both of you taken on board. *Dragged* on board, he said. The ship set sail, but he remembered hearin' the sailors saying as to how it was a short trip across the English Channel to Cherbourg. So we hired ourselves a fishin' boat and headed on over to look for you. We arrived here only shortly after Maupertuis's ship did. Either they were slow, or they stopped somewhere along the way. Not sure which." His voice was as solid and thoughtful as ever, and his words gave nothing away about his mental state, but Sherlock thought that he looked older somehow, more tired. He kept his arm around Virginia's shoulders, pulling her close. She didn't seem to want to pull away. "I found out that the Baron had a place nearby, an' I was just about to hire some local men to form a posse when you showed up. A useful confluence of paths, I would say."

"It makes sense," Sherlock said. "We were heading for the nearest port to Baron Maupertuis's château. That was obviously where his ship would dock, and you were following his ship. The chances were we would all end up in Cherbourg at some stage." He smiled. "The only amazing thing is that you found a boat named after my uncle's housekeeper. What are the odds of that?"

"She used to be called the *Rosie Lee*," Crowe said, smiling back. "I reckoned as to how a more familiar name might attract your interest, if you were in the area an' lookin' for a way back to England. I was goin' to rename her the *Mycroft Holmes*, but her captain informed me in no uncertain terms that ships an' boats get women's names."

"You *expected* us to escape from the Baron?"

Crowe nodded. "I'd have been disappointed if you hadn't. You're my pupil, an' Ginny's my kin. What kind of teacher would I be if you'd both just sat back an' let yourselves be kept prisoner?" His words were jocular, and there was a smile on his face, but Sherlock could sense a deep undercurrent of unease, perhaps even fear, within

Crowe that their appearance had only just begun to wear away. He reached out with a big hand and grabbed Sherlock's shoulder. "You kept her safe," he said, more quietly. "I thank you for that."

"I know that everything you did to get here was logical," Sherlock said, just as quietly, "and it all worked, but what if it hadn't? What if we'd never escaped, or if we'd gone a different way, or if you'd been at one end of the dock and we were at the other, getting on a different boat? What then?"

"Then things would have turned out differently," Crowe said. "We are where we are because things happened the way they did. Logic can shorten the odds considerably in your favour, but there's always random chance to contend with. We were lucky—this time. Next time—who knows?"

"I don't expect there to be a 'next time,'" Sherlock said. "But we still need to stop the Baron's plans."

"What are they?" Crowe asked, his face creasing in puzzlement. "I've pieced some of it together, but not everythin'."

Quickly, Sherlock and Virginia explained about the bees, the contaminated uniforms, and the plan to kill off a substantial portion of the British Army as it rested in its barracks in England. Crowe was as sceptical as Sherlock about the plan's efficacy, but he agreed that there would be some deaths, and that even one death was too many. The bees had to be stopped.

"But how can the bees find their way across the sea to England, an' then find their way to the barracks?" Crowe asked.

"I've been reading about them in my uncle's library," Sherlock replied. "Bees are amazing creatures. They can distinguish between hundreds of different scents, at concentrations far, far smaller than a human would require, and they can travel for miles in search of the source of those scents. I wouldn't be surprised if it were possible." He paused, remembering. "He talked about a fort. He told his man—Mr. Surd—that the bees had to be released from a fort. Are there any fortifications along this coast, or along the coast of England, that he might be using?"

"It's not that kind of fort," Matty Arnatt interrupted.

"What do you mean?"

"There's forts built out in the English Channel, round Southampton and Portsmouth and the Isle of Wight, like islands," he said. "They was put there in case Napoleon ever invaded. Most of them are deserted now, 'cause the invasion never came."

"How do you know?" Virginia asked.

Matty scowled. "My dad was stationed on one of them when he was in the Navy. He told me all about them."

"So what makes you think Maupertuis is using one of them?" Sherlock asked.

"You said as how he hates the British 'cause of what happened to him. Don't it make sense that he'd use one of the forts that we built to defend ourselves against the French back against us?"

Crowe nodded. "The boy has a point. And although his ship left London a while before Matty an' I could hire ourselves a boat, they only arrived in Cherbourg just before us. They must'a stopped off at one of those forts to leave the beehives behind."

"But there's loads of them," Matty said. "We ain't got time to search them all."

"He wouldn't want the bees to have to fly too far," Sherlock pointed out. "We're looking for the fort nearest the coast. And he'd want them to be close to a fair-sized Army base. We need a map of England and the coast, and we need to draw lines between every offshore fort and every British Army base. We're looking for the shortest line." He glanced between Amyus Crowe and Virginia's amazed faces. "Simple geometry," he said.

"What do we do once we've found the right fort?" Matty asked.

"We could head back to the British coast, send a message to Mycroft Holmes," Crowe rumbled. "He could send a Royal Navy ship out to the fort."

"Too much of a delay," Sherlock said, shaking his head. "We need to go there ourselves. Now."

In the end, they did both. The *Mrs. Eglantine*, formerly and soon to be again the *Rosie Lee*, set out from Cherbourg while Crowe and Sherlock drew lines on maps and identified the most likely fort. When they drew near, several hours later, the sun was heading for the horizon and the English coast was a dark line in the distance.

"This fishing boat'll be spotted straightaway," Crowe pointed out. "Even with the sails down the mast'll be seen, assumin' they're keepin' watch—and if I were them, I would be."

"There's a rowing boat lashed to the side," Sherlock said. "I spotted it when we boarded. Matty and I can row across to the fort. You keep going to England. Raise the alarm."

"How about if I row to the fort and you, Matthew, and Ginny head for the coast?"

"We can't sail," Sherlock pointed out. His heart was thudding fast within his chest at the thought of what he was volunteering for, but he could see no alternative. "And besides, the Admiralty and the War Office will believe you before me."

"Logical," Crowe conceded reluctantly.

"Wherever you land," Sherlock continued, "if you're near Portsmouth Dockyard, Chatham Dockyard, Deal, Sheerness, Great Yarmouth, or Plymouth, there are semaphore stations. If you give them a message they can flash it across-country via the chain of semaphores, all the way to the Admiralty. It's probably quicker than a telegram."

Crowe nodded, smiled, then stuck out his huge, calloused hand and shook Sherlock's hand. "We'll meet again," he said.

"I'm counting on it," Sherlock replied.

Sherlock and Matty slipped into a rowing boat and rowed hard and fast towards the location of the fort. As they had agreed, Crowe and Virginia carried on towards the English coast, where they could send a message alerting the government.

Virginia stood on the side of the *Mrs. Eglantine* as it drew away from the rowing boat, staring at Sherlock. He gazed back, wondering if he would ever see her again.

The sea was grey-green and choppy as the two boys pulled on the oars. The fort was a dark blob on the horizon that never seemed to get any closer, no matter how hard they rowed. Sherlock could taste salt on his lips. He wondered how he had ever managed to get himself tangled up in this strange adventure.

After a while, he looked up to find the fort was just a few hundred feet away: a mass of wet, seaweed-encrusted stone that seemed to erupt from the waters of the English Channel. Somehow, they had managed to close in on it without noticing. It seemed empty, deserted. He scanned the crenellated rim, where only a few decades ago British forces would have been watching the sea for approaching French warships. He could see nobody. Nobody at all.

The rowing boat coasted the last few feet to the black bulk of the fort. It ended up at the base of a set of water-slicked stone steps that led upward.

Quickly, Matty tied the rope to a rusted iron bar that had been cemented into a gap between the stones. The two boys scrambled up the steps. Sherlock nearly lost his footing, and Matty had to grab him to stop him toppling into the water.

"How do we know it's not too late?" Matty asked.

"It's night. Bees are dormant at night. The Baron's servant hasn't had much more time to get here than we have. The bees will be released in the morning."

When they got to the top, they knelt behind a low stone wall that ran around the outer edge of the fort. The gaps between the stones were infested with moss.

Sherlock scanned the top level—he supposed it was technically the deck, although this particular "vessel" wasn't going anywhere—but the flagstones were empty of anything except coils of rope, tufts of sea grass, and the occasional splintered crate.

Across the other side of the fort he saw the sudden flare of a match illuminate a bearded face with a scar running across it. Whoever was in charge of this fort had posted guards. He and Matty needed to be careful.

The guard was moving away from them, and Sherlock spotted him passing an opening in the stone deck that had a wooden rail running around three sides of it. Probably a stairway into the depths of the fort. As the man moved on, Sherlock tugged at Matty's shirt and pulled him over.

He was right. A set of stone steps led down into

darkness. The smell of dankness and decay rose up to greet them.

"Come on," Sherlock hissed. "Let's go."

The two of them scuttled down the steps into the depths of the fort. At first it seemed as black as the depths of Hell in there, but after a few moments Sherlock's eyes adjusted and he could make out oil lanterns fastened to the wall at regular intervals. They were in a short corridor that seemed to open up into a larger, darker room which the orange wash of light from the lamps barely illuminated.

Sherlock and Matty crept along the corridor to where the walls suddenly opened up. The circular space revealed probably occupied most of the level they were on. Stone pillars every few yards supported the roof overhead, but what made Sherlock's breath quicken was the beehives, lined up in a regular pattern across the flagstones. There were hundreds of them. With tens of thousands of bees in each hive, that meant something like a million aggressive bees were located just a few feet away from him. He felt his skin itch in an unconscious response to their nearness, almost as if they were walking across his shoulders and down his spine. Whether or not Maupertuis's grand scheme would work across the whole of Britain, the presence of all these bees in one place was definitely dangerous to anyone in the locality.

"Tell me we're not going to carry them up the stairs and throw them over the edge," Matty whispered.

"We're not going to carry them up the stairs and throw them over the edge," Sherlock confirmed.

"Then what are we going to do?"

"I'm not sure."

"What do you mean, you're not sure?"

"I mean I haven't thought it through yet. It's all been a bit of a rush."

Matty snorted. "You had plenty of time on the fishing boat."

"I was thinking about something else."

"Yeh," Matty said, "I noticed." He was silent for a moment. "We could set fire to them," he pointed out.

Sherlock shook his head. "Look at the spacing. We could set fire to one or two of them, but the flames wouldn't spread and the bees would probably get us."

Matty looked around. "What are they eating?" he asked.

"What do you mean?"

"We're in the English Channel. There's no flowers out here, and I don't think seaweed counts. What are the bees eating?"

Sherlock thought for a moment. "That's a good question. I don't know." He glanced around. "Let's look round, in case we find something. Split up, and meet on the other side. Don't get caught."

Matty headed left and Sherlock headed right. Looking back, Sherlock saw that the gloom had already swallowed Matty up.

The serried ranks of beehives formed an almost hypnotic pattern as he passed by them. He couldn't see any bees—perhaps the darkness was keeping them confined to the hives—but he thought he could hear them: a low, soporific buzz, almost on the edge of his consciousness. He noticed that there were wooden frames set up at various points in the cavernous space. Some of them held wooden trays, others were empty. Sherlock wondered where he had seen trays like that before. Something about them was familiar.

A grotesque figure came into view through the gloom: a man dressed in an all-encompassing canvas suit whose head was covered with a muslin hood held away from his face by bamboo hoops. He was bending over a large box—one of many that Sherlock could now see were lined up along this portion of the curved wall that bounded the space. He straightened up, holding a tray like the ones that had been fitted into the easel-like frames scattered around, and walked towards the hives. A fine haze seemed to rise up from the tray as Sherlock watched him go.

He remembered just as the man in the bee-suit reached a frame and slotted the tray inside. He'd seen beekeepers in the same suits at Baron Maupertuis's manor house just outside Farnham removing similar trays from underneath the hives. And then suddenly everything fell into place—the trays, the haze of powder that rose up from them, the ice that he'd seen the thug Denny unloading from the train in Farnham, and Matty's question about how the bees ate in the absence of flowers. It was all so perfectly logical! Bees collected pollen from flowers, storing it on fine hairs on their legs until they got to the hive, and then used it as food. Put a tray beneath a hive, and create some kind of "gate" that the bees had to go through to get into the hive, and you could brush some of the pollen from their legs and collect it in specially positioned trays. Put the trays on ice and you could store the pollen for when you needed it—for instance, when the bees were being kept somewhere where there were no flowers. Place the trays scattered around, and the bees could collect the pollen from them, not even realizing that this was the second time they had collected the pollen.

As he was remembering Farnham and the station, another memory clamoured for Sherlock's attention: something that Matty had told him. Something about powder. About bakeries. He ransacked the lumber room of his memory, trying to bring the words to mind.

Yes. Powder. Flour. Matty had mentioned a fire that had occurred at a bakery where he once worked. He'd said that a powder like flour was highly inflammable when it was floating in air. If one speck of flour caught fire then it would spread from speck to speck faster than a man could run.

And if it worked for flour, it might just work for pollen.

"Penny for your thoughts," said a voice behind him.

Sherlock turned, knowing what he would see.

Mr. Surd, Baron Maupertuis's faithful retainer, was standing in the shadows. The leather thong of his whip spilt from his hand and curled around his feet.

"Never mind," Surd said, advancing on Sherlock. "If the Baron wants to know what's in your head, I'll just give him your head and he can pull it out himself."

SEVENTEEN

Sherlock stepped to one side. Mr. Surd swung around to track him. The metal tip of the whip scraped along the ground as the man moved.

Surd's face was a mask of polite indifference, but the scars crisscrossing his scalp were red and inflamed with anger.

"Did the Baron give you a hard time?" Sherlock taunted. "Letting us escape like that couldn't have done much for your reputation. I'll wager the Baron discards useless servants like any other man throws away a used match."

Surd's face remained impassive, but his hand flicked and the whip lashed out. Sherlock jerked his head to one side a split second before the metal tip would have sliced his ear off.

"That's a neat circus trick, but there's any number of better tricks out there," Sherlock went on, trying not to let his voice waver and betray him. "Perhaps Maupertuis could hire a knife-thrower next time."

Again the whip flickered out, its tip snapping past Sherlock's left ear with a *crack* that momentarily deafened him. He thought it had missed, but a sudden warm splatter of blood on his neck and a growing icy pain at the side of his head suggested that the metal tip had made contact. He staggered to one side, holding his hand to his ear. The pain wasn't that great, not yet, but he wanted to change their positions and he wasn't quite there yet.

"Every taunt that you throw in my direction is another strip of flesh I'll peel from your face," Surd said calmly. "You'll be begging me to kill you, and I'll just laugh. I'll laugh."

"Laugh while you can," Sherlock said. "Perhaps I can persuade the Baron to employ me in your place. At least I've proved I'm more competent than you."

"I'll keep you alive just long enough for the girl to see what I've made of you," Surd went on as if Sherlock hadn't said anything. "She won't want to look at you. She'll scream at the sight of you. How will that feel, boy? How will it feel?"

"You talk a good fight," Sherlock said. He took another step to one side. Surd moved as well.

The wooden boxes containing the trays of pollen were directly behind Sherlock now. He reached behind with his right hand and let his questing fingers close around the edge of one of the trays. It was cold from the ice beneath it.

"What are you doing, boy?" Surd asked. "You think there's anything there that will save you? You're wrong. Wrong."

"The only thing that will save me is my brain," Sherlock said, bringing the tray around in front of him. Pollen spilt from it, yellow and powdery, making him cough.

Surd struck out with his whip again, aiming for Sherlock's right eye, but Sherlock held the tray up like a shield and the whip curled around it, the metal tip sinking into the wood and sticking. Sherlock tugged hard, pulling the handle of the whip from the grasp of the surprised Surd and throwing it to one side.

Surd bellowed like a bull and rushed forward, arms spread wide. Sherlock grabbed another tray from the box and smashed it over Surd's head. The man reeled back, enveloped in choking yellow powder. If Surd survived, he would have even more scars on his scalp.

Of course, if Surd survived then Sherlock would probably be dead.

He stepped forward and grabbed Surd's ears. Bringing his knee up, he banged Surd's face down onto it. Surd's nose broke with a *crack* just as loud as the one from his whip. He staggered backward, blood waterfalling down his mouth and chin.

Before Surd could attack again, Sherlock grabbed the whip from the floor and pulled the metal tip from the wooden tray, disentangling the leather thong. As Surd, raging like a madman, surged out of the cloud of pollen towards Sherlock, he lashed out with it. He'd never used a whip before, but watching Surd had shown him how to do it. The whip curled out towards the bald thug, the metal tip slicing across his cheek. Surd was flung back by the impact.

Straight into one of the beehives.

It fell, and Surd fell with it, *into* it. The wooden slats burst apart as they hit the stone floor together, covering him in the gooey, waxy interior of the hive.

And bees. Thousands of bees.

They covered his face like a living hood, crawling into his nose and mouth and ears, stinging everywhere they went. He screamed; a thin, whistling sound that got louder and louder. And he rolled, trying to crush the bees but succeeding only in knocking another hive over.

Within moments, Mr. Surd was invisible beneath a blanket of insects that were stinging every square inch of flesh they could find. His screams were muffled by the bees filling his mouth.

Sherlock backed away, horrified. He'd never seen anything like this before. He'd been fighting for his life, but what was happening to Surd was so terrible that he felt sick. He'd killed a man.

"I can't leave you alone for a moment, can I?" Matty said from behind him.

"You think I like getting into fights?" Sherlock said, aware that his voice was trembling on the edge of hysteria. "They just seem to happen to me."

"Well, you seem to acquit yourself all right," Matty conceded.

"I know what to do," Sherlock said, trying to get his voice under control. He indicated the clouds of yellow pollen dissipating through the cavernous space inside the fort. "There's trays of pollen stacked up in those boxes. We need to spread that pollen through this place."

"Why?" Matty asked.

"Remember what you told me about the bakery in Farnham?" Sherlock asked.

Matty's eyes lit up with understanding. "Got you," he said. Then his face clouded over. "But what about us?"

"We have to stop this, and stop it now. We're less important than the hundreds, maybe thousands of people who will die if we don't stop it."

"Even so . . ." Matty said. He suddenly grinned at Sherlock's shocked expression. "Only joking. Let's get on with it."

Together they grabbed as many trays of cold yellow pollen from the iced boxes as they could and ran through the aisles between the hives, letting the powder spill out in expanding clouds behind them. Within ten minutes the air was full of floating motes, and they could hardly see ten feet ahead of them. It was hard to breathe without choking. Sherlock grabbed Matty by the shoulder.

"Let's go," he said.

Blinded by clouds of pollen, they groped their way towards the corridor to the stairs, fighting their way through the yellow clouds, trying not to knock over any of the hives.

Sherlock's foot kicked against something soft, and he almost fell over. Looking down he saw a puffy mass of red-splotched flesh that he just about recognized as

Mr. Surd's face. Surd's eyes were invisible in swollen folds of skin, and his mouth was full of dead bees.

In spite of everything, Sherlock felt a powerful urge to help the dying man, but it was too late. Feeling cold and sick inside, he kept going.

He came up against a stone wall. Left or right? He chose left, and guided Matty after him by grabbing his shirt and pulling.

It seemed like hours but was probably less than a minute before they found the corridor. Sherlock turned and looked back. There was nothing behind him but a roiling wall of yellow powder hanging in the air.

He reached out and took an oil lantern from the stone wall of the corridor. Weighing it in his hand, he thought about the bees, innocent of anything apart from just being themselves.

He had no choice.

He threw the lantern. It arced away into the cloud of pollen and vanished. Moments later he heard the shattering of glass as it hit the flagstones.

Followed by a massive *whump!* as the pollen caught fire.

An unseen fist pushed Sherlock in the chest. He flew backwards, down the corridor. The very air in front of him seemed to be burning, and he felt his eyebrows and the hairs on his eyelids singeing. He hit the ground hard, and rolled. Matty landed on top of him.

They scrambled to their feet and glanced backwards. The corridor behind them opened out onto an inferno of flames. Covering his mouth with his hand, Sherlock led Matty up the stairs to the top of the fort. Air rushed past them, feeding the fire beneath.

Guards were rushing back and forth, bellowing and panicking on the top of the fort. The sky was dark, with just a red line on the horizon showing where the sun had been. They paid no attention to the two boys who ran past them, climbed down the stairs to the sea and then into their rowing boat.

As they rowed away, Sherlock turned back to look. The entire fort was ablaze. Maupertuis's thugs were throwing themselves off the top and into the water. Some of them were on fire, falling like shooting stars through the darkness into the sea.

It was a sight that Sherlock would never forget.

The journey to the English coast was a blur of aching arms, flash-burned skin, and sheer exhaustion. Later, Sherlock would wonder how he and Matty ever made it without capsizing or getting lost and drifting out to sea.

Somehow Amyus Crowe had worked out where they would end up. Perhaps he had calculated it based on tides and wind direction, or perhaps he had just guessed. Sherlock didn't know, and frankly didn't care. He just wanted to be wrapped up in a blanket and helped to a comfortable bed, and for once what he wanted was what actually happened.

He woke the next morning with the gulls crying outside the bedroom window and the sun glinting off the sea and making rippling patterns on the ceiling of his room. He was starving. Throwing off the bedcovers he dressed in clothes that weren't his, but were the right size and had been left on the back of a chair, waiting for him. He walked down stairs that he didn't remember climbing up, to find himself in the parlour of a tavern that obviously rented out its rooms to travellers. And adventurers.

A stretch of open ground led away from the front of the tavern, and then dropped sharply towards the sea. Sherlock had to screw his eyes up against the brightness of the sun. Matty Arnatt was sitting at a table outside, wolfing down a huge breakfast. Amyus Crowe was beside him, smoking a pipe.

"Mornin'," Crowe said amiably. "Hungry?"

"I could eat a horse."

"Best not let Ginny hear you say that." Crowe indicated a seat at the table. "Sit yourself down. Food will be ready soon."

Sherlock sat. His muscles ached and his ears still rang from the explosion, and his eyes were dry and itchy. Somehow, he felt different. Older. He'd seen people die, he'd caused people to die, and he'd been drugged and tortured with a whip. How could he go back to Deepdene School for Boys now?

"Did everything get sorted out?" he asked eventually.

"Your brother got the message we sent, and he went straight into action. I believe there's a Navy ship headed out to the Napoleonic fort, but from what you murmured last night I guess they won't find much but ashes. And even if the British government can persuade the French to check out Maupertuis's château, I think they'll find it empty. He'll have got out, with his servants. But his plot has fallen apart like a house of cards in a strong breeze, thanks to you and Matthew here."

"It would never have worked," Sherlock said, remembering the confrontation between him, Virginia, and the Baron. "Not the way he wanted it to."

"Perhaps. Perhaps not. But I think some people would have died, and you saved them. You can thank yourself for that. And your brother will thank you too, when he arrives."

"Mycroft is coming here?"

"He's already on the train."

A woman in an apron came out of the tavern carrying a plate that seemed to be laden with every possible item that a person could want for breakfast, plus several that Sherlock didn't even recognize. She smiled and put the plate in front of him.

"Tuck in," Crowe said. "You deserve it."

Sherlock paused for a moment. Everything around him seemed simultaneously overly sharp and yet slightly distanced.

"You okay?" Crowe said.

"I'm not sure," Sherlock replied.

"You've been through a lot. You were knocked out, and you were drugged with laudanum, not to mention several fights and a long stretch of rowing. That's all bound to have an effect on your system."

Laudanum. Remembering the strange dreams that he'd had after he had been drugged, while he was being taken to France, Sherlock felt a twinge of—what? Melancholy, perhaps. Wistfulness. Surely not . . . longing? Whatever the feeling was, he pushed it away. He'd heard stories about people becoming dependent on the effects produced by laudanum, and he had no desire to go down that route. None at all.

"How's Virginia?" he asked to break the mood.

"Annoyed that she missed all the fun. And missing her horse, of course. She wants to look around the town, but I said she can't go alone. I guess she'll be glad you're awake."

Sherlock gazed out at the sea. "I can't believe it's all over," he said.

"It's not," Crowe said. "It's part of your life now, and your life keeps on goin'. You can't separate these events out as a story with a beginnin' and an end. You're a different person because of them, and that means the story will never really finish. But as your tutor, the question I have is, what did you learn from it all?"

Sherlock thought for a minute. "I learned," he said eventually, "that bees are fascinating and sorely neglected creatures. I think I want to know more about them. Perhaps even try to change people's opinions of them." He grimaced. "I probably owe them that, having killed so many." He glanced over at Matty Arnatt. "What about you, Matty? What did you learn?"

Matty looked up from his breakfast. "I learned," he said, "that you need someone to look after you, otherwise your logical ideas are going to get you killed."

"Are you volunteering for the position?" Amyus Crowe asked, eyes crinkling with good humour.

"Dunno," Matty replied. "What's the pay like?"

As Amyus laughed, and as Matty protested that he was serious, Sherlock gazed out at the constant, timeless sea, wondering what would happen next in his life. He felt as if he had been diverted onto a road that he hadn't known existed. What would he find at the end of it?

Something moved to one side of his vision, attracting his attention. He glanced past the tavern, to where the road led away in two directions. A carriage was approaching—a black carriage drawn by two black horses. For a moment he thought that Mycroft had arrived, and he started to get up.

And then with a chill he saw a bone-white face and pink eyes glaring at him through the glass before a gloved hand firmly pulled down the blind as the carriage passed by, and he knew that he was right: things never would be the same again. Baron Maupertuis and the Paradol Chamber were still out there, and they would never rest.

Which meant that he could never rest either.

ACKNOWLEDGEMENTS

I've consulted a number of books in order to get the history of the time and the area about right. In particular, I would like to acknowledge the following works:

London's Lost Route to Basingstoke: The Story of the Basingstoke Canal by P. A. L. Vine, published by Alan Sutton Publishing, 1968 (revised and expanded in 1994). Great material about the local waterways and canals in the Farnham area.

The Tongham Railway by Peter A. Harding, self-published, 1994. Obviously the product of one man's obsession, but immensely useful.

Bygone Farnham by Jean Parratt, published by Phillimore & Co. Ltd, 1985. Useful if only for the exhaustive list of pubs and taverns it contains, which suggests that every second house in Farnham sold beer.

London Under London—A Subterranean Guide by Richard Trench and Ellis Hillman, published by John Murray (the original publisher of the Sherlock Holmes stories in book form), 1984. The classic guide to London's underground rivers and tunnels.

Subterranean City—Beneath the Streets of London by Antony Clayton, published by Historical Publications, 2000. Covers much the same ground (as it were) as Trench and Hillman's book, but benefits from material more recently discovered. Or perhaps "unearthed" would be a better word.

The London of Sherlock Holmes by Michael Harrison, published by David & Charles, 1972. An invaluable and immaculately researched investigation of what London would have looked like to the eyes of Sherlock Holmes.

AFTERWORD

Arthur Conan Doyle wrote fifty-six short stories and four novels about Sherlock Holmes. You can still find them in most bookshops. When he first appeared, Sherlock was around thirty-three years old and was already a detective with an established set of habits and abilities. In his last appearance he was around sixty, and had retired to the Sussex coast to keep bees. Yes, bees.

My intention with the book you are holding, and with the books that will follow, is to find out what Sherlock was like before Arthur Conan Doyle first introduced him to the world. What sort of teenager was he? Where did he go to school, and who were his friends? Where and when did he learn the skills that he displayed later in life—the logical mind, the boxing and sword-fighting, the love of music and of playing the violin? What did he study at university? When (if ever) did he travel abroad? What scared him and whom, if anyone, did he love?

Other people have written about Sherlock Holmes over the years, to the point where he is probably the most recognized fictional character in the world. The number of stories written about Sherlock by other writers far exceeds the number written by Arthur Conan Doyle, and yet it is Doyle's stories that people keep returning to. There is a reason for that, and the reason is that he *understood* Sherlock from the inside out, while the other writers, for the most part, merely tried to copy the outside.

Arthur Conan Doyle gave little away about Sherlock's early years, and most writers since then have avoided that period of time as well. We know little about his parents, or indeed where he lived. We know he was descended on his mother's side from the French artist Vernet and that he had a brother called Mycroft, who appears in a few of the short stories, but that's about it. That has given me the freedom to create a history for Sherlock that is consistent with the few hints that Conan Doyle did let slip, but also leads inevitably to the man that Conan Doyle described. In this endeavour I have been lucky to have had the approval of Jon Lellenberg, the representative of the Sir Arthur Conan Doyle Literary Estate, and the approval of the surviving relatives of Sir Arthur Conan Doyle: Richard Pooley, Richard Doyle, and Cathy Beggs. I have been lucky, too, to have the approval of Andrea Plunkett, owner of several trademarks in Europe. I have also been fortunate in having an agent and an editor—Robert Kirby and Rebecca McNally, respectively—who understood completely what I wanted to do.

Various writers have attempted to produce their own biographies of Sherlock Holmes, tying together what Doyle revealed with actual historical events. These works are inevitably flawed, incomplete, and personal, but I confess that I have a sneaking fondness for William Baring-Gould's *Sherlock Holmes—A Biography of the World's First Consulting*

Detective, and have taken some details (most notably, dates) from that iconic work.

I promise that there will be more adventures of Sherlock Holmes at school and university, but in the meantime you might want to seek out the original stories by Arthur Conan Doyle. The short stories have been collected together in five books—*The Adventures of Sherlock Holmes, The Memoirs of Sherlock Holmes, The Return of Sherlock Holmes, His Last Bow,* and *The Case-Book of Sherlock Holmes.* The novels are *A Study in Scarlet, The Sign of Four, The Hound of the Baskervilles,* and *The Valley of Fear.* If you want to go further, you could do worse than seek out the three more recent Holmes novels by Nicholas Meyer—*The Seven-Per-Cent Solution, The West End Horror,* and *The Canary Trainer*—as well as Michael Hardwick's *The Revenge of the Hound* and Lyndsay Faye's *Dust and Shadow.* You might also like to check out Michael Kurland's stories told from the point of view of Sherlock Holmes's archenemy, Professor James Moriarty, which provide a refreshing alternative look at the Great Detective—*The Infernal Device, Death by Gaslight,* and *The Great Game.* Secondhand bookshops or eBay might be your best bet.

Until next time, when Sherlock tangles with an American assassin and faces the repulsive Red Leech . . .

COMING IN FALL 2011

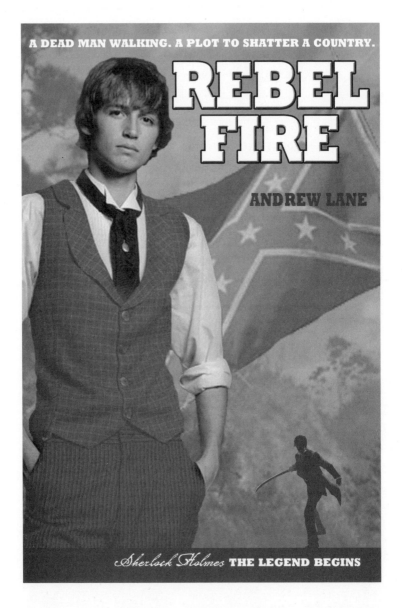

A DEAD MAN WALKING. A PLOT TO SHATTER A COUNTRY.

REBEL FIRE

ANDREW LANE

Sherlock Holmes **THE LEGEND BEGINS**

In his next adventure, Sherlock pursues a kidnapped Matty across the ocean to America, where he uncovers a plot to resuscitate the Confederacy—an outrageous scheme masterminded by a fiend with a terrible fondness for bloodsucking creatures . . .